More Advance Praise for *Daughters of Chaos*

"Jen Fawkes has written a wild adventure. Rooted in historical events, this is a genre-shattering book that is both intellectual and a ripping page-turner. Surprisingly and blessedly strange!"

—Megan Giddings, author of *The Women Could Fly*

"In her elemental inventiveness, Jen Fawkes is descended from the Angela Carter of *Wise Children* and *The Bloody Chamber* but is also up to something exhilaratingly new. *Daughters of Chaos* is joyful and bold, populated so richly with twins and prostitutes and mythical creatures and historical figures that in the great thrill of watching its tapestry unfurl, the enormity and seriousness of the questions Fawkes is asking snuck up on me. This novel is interested in nothing less than the forces of chaos and order and the question of where lies threat and where salvation. Ambitious, vast, expertly crafted—an extraordinary achievement."

—Clare Beams, author of *The Illness Lesson*

"*Daughters of Chaos* lives up to its name! Celebrating the messiness of women's lives and struggles against the backdrop of the Civil War, *Daughters of Chaos* delivers a world that feels both real and surreal, a history that is itself steeped in our primordial stories about who we can and cannot be and who we can and cannot love."

—Gwen E. Kirby, author of *Shit Cassandra Saw*

"*Daughters of Chaos* is a deeply feminist story that weaves together Greek mythology, Civil War history, sisterhood, fire, sex, and love. Fawkes creates a delicious tapestry as she layers found text, journal entries and letters, narrative and playwriting, resulting in a lush and immersive novel. From Ephesus to Nashville and beyond, Fawkes's wide perspective allows her to shine light on women lost to time while embracing surprising parallels that will delight any fan of the classics. Her dramatis personae sing long after you've closed the book."

—Elizabeth Gonzalez James, author of
Mona at Sea and *The Bullet Swallower*

"Jen Fawkes possesses one of the brightest new narrative voices of the last few years. In 2020 and 2021, her strange and shimmering story collections burst into print in immediate succession, one and then two, like a perfectly calibrated fireworks display. Now comes her first novel, which might be the most dazzling book she's written yet. It's a beautiful spinning knife of a story that whirls back through the 1800s, the 1500s, the fourth century BC, and the age of myth to slice out an image of the pain and the power that women have inherited from antiquity—historical fiction of a sort, but informed by both our own moment and the Old Attic Comedies."

—Kevin Brockmeier, author of *The Ghost Variations*

DAUGHTERS
OF CHAOS

DAUGHTERS
OF CHAOS

A NOVEL

JEN FAWKES

THE OVERLOOK PRESS, NEW YORK

ABRAMS The Art of Books
195 Broadway, New York, NY 10007
abramsbooks.com

For Bill, and for Chaos—the architect of everything

There is no beast, no rush of fire, like woman so untamed. She calmly goes her way where even panthers would be shamed.

—Aristophanes, *Lysistrata*

Saturday, May 26, 1877
Monterey, CA

At the very end, Hannah wanted to talk about translation. She avoided the subject of the inky, lemon-sized growth visible beneath the skin of her abdomen, the sweat that soaked our bedding nightly, the agonies that made her shriek and writhe in her sleep.

"Which is more important," she asked at one point, her voice a whisper, "fidelity to the text or the author?"

"The text." I brushed a damp red lock away from her forehead. "Authors don't exist."

Hannah laughed—a silvery sound I hadn't heard in weeks. "Sylvie." She gritted her teeth, strained to sit up, failed. "Sylvie."

"Yes, my sweet?"

"The girls. Marina and Brigitte. Tell them."

I shook my head. "I can't. I'm not their mother, not anymore."

Hannah shut her dark eyes, took a breath, and fought, again, to drag her torso up from the pillows. This time she made it. Illness had ravaged her lovely face, but to my eye, Hannah Holcombe was just as I'd first seen her—singing and shaking a tambourine, red braids coiling from beneath her bonnet to slither over her shoulders, dressed like her black-clad Sisters but clearly her own creature.

"Sylvie," she said.

"Yes?"

"You *do* exist. Marina and Brigitte need you."

I shook my head. "They have the Parkers. I gave them wonderful parents."

I

"Sylvie Swift." Hannah's voice was stronger than it had been in months. She sounded like the young woman who'd marched into my life fifteen years earlier, down a crowded street in Nashville, Tennessee. "We all need our mother," she said, "however changeable she may be."

Two days later, Hannah slipped away. With the help of Jon and Luke, our part-time deckhands, I buried my lover along the stream, beneath the apricot tree. As I positioned the white stone into which Jon had carved her initials—HH—I felt a chasm opening within me. A damp, murky space rife with eternal echoes. I pictured myself leaving the home Hannah and I shared for fourteen years, filling my pockets with stones, and opening the villa's gate. Walking past the red clay roof and breezy balconies of the customhouse—where crates of foreign spices, textiles, and produce tarried, waited to be taxed—and down to the shore, into the salty, wet arms of the sea.

Instead I turned, in the following days, to my neglected translation of *Veronique et Tous Ses Amants*—*Veronica and All Her Lovers*—the latest novel from the French pornographer Jacques Babin. I've translated Babin's two previous books—bitingly funny, and each more erotic than the last—and the familiarity of this work anchored me to the world, prevented me from joining my dearly departed Hannah. Minutes before she died, she asked me to tell her one thing people would never guess about the act of translation. I thought for a time, considered the raw power of deciding what is left unsaid. The fact that good translations are, at once, radical transformations and perfect copies.

"All acts of writing," I finally said, "are acts of translation."

Two months have now passed since that bleak day, and I've finished adapting *Veronique et Tous Ses Amants*. This morning as I followed the stream, headed for the apricot tree, I stumbled upon a startling threesome: grizzly bears, a mother and two cubs. I froze, but the she-bear was already spinning, already rising on hind legs. She was thin, and stood well over six feet, and her fur—a blend of chestnut, henna, and copper—looked ragged. Even so, she opened her jaws wider than seemed possible, exposing lethal, rust-toned teeth, and her roar made the whole scene waver, as though we were all temporary beings—as though at any second, we might disappear.

We held this tableau for a time, until the cubs began butting against their mother's legs and whining. Deciding I wasn't a threat, the she-bear dropped to all fours and lumbered away, trailed by her young. I waited until they were no longer visible, then I waited another quarter hour. By the time I arrived at Hannah's final resting place, I'd made up my mind to begin a new project—one that will be my last.

"I'm going to write it all down, Hannah," I said as I knelt beside her grave, my fingertips piercing the cool earth. "The whole story. Maybe I'll give it to the girls. Maybe I won't, but I plan to write the whole damn thing down."

Sunday May 27, 1877
Monterey, CA

This ten-room villa, built by Spanish missionaries four decades ago, was far too big for me and Hannah. But we took it right after we arrived in California, when I was pregnant with you, Marina, and you, Brigitte, and we thought we needed the space. What we'd brought from Nashville fit easily into one of the villa's spacious, airy chambers, and early on, Hannah and I rattled around the place like dried seeds in a maraca, or gears in a broken clock. Hannah loved to barter, though, nearly as much as she loved to work with her hands, so over the years, our home became stocked, and eventually overrun, with refurbished rockers and step stools, with grandfather clocks and divans, with drop-leaf tables and glass-front hutches, with hundreds of cloth- and leather-bound volumes.

Eventually, the goods we'd brought from Nashville were consumed by the clutter, and locating the records I needed to reconstruct my history took me two whole days. I didn't recall scattering the documents—some jaundiced and crumbling with age—among a battered footlocker, a steamer trunk, and a dusty packing crate, but apparently I had. Or perhaps my dear Hannah had dispersed them. Perhaps she, like me, had sought these reminders only when she was sure she was alone in the villa, hoping to give me—as I'd hoped to give her—the impression that she was looking doggedly forward, toward the future, and never back, into the past.

To support my story, I've gathered newspaper clippings, correspondence, a child's charcoal and pastel drawings. An antique playscript that rightly belongs in a vault at the Smithsonian. A red clothbound book, published in 1828, about the Venetian poet Gaia Valentino. Volumes 3, 6, 8, 9, 11, 14, and 21 of the *Encyclopaedia Britannica* (eighth edition). Now that I've spread this archive of evidence across the worktable Luke and Jon set up for me on the veranda, I am cowed by the enormity of my task. I consider quitting before I start. Then I picture the two of you: Marina and Brigitte, Brigitte and Marina.

"My daughters," I whisper. "Daughters of Chaos."

I make myself a cup of hibiscus tea, settle into my chair, and go to work.

Encyclopaedia Britannica
Eighth Edition (1860)
Volume 6, Burning glasses–Climate, p. 415

CHAOS, that state of confusion in which matter is supposed to have existed before it was reduced to order by God. The term is taken from the Greek mythology, according to which Chaos was the vacant and infinite space which existed before the creation of the world, and out of which the gods, men, and all things arose. (Hesiod, *Theog.* 116; Ovid, *Met.* i. 5.) See CREATION and GEOLOGY.

Encyclopaedia Britannica
Eighth Edition (1860)
Volume 11, GRA–HUM, p. 536

HISTORY may be considered either as a department of human knowledge and intellectual exercise, or as a form of literary composition. In the observations that follow, we shall consider it under both these aspects.

Yesterday I made the hour-long trek to the ranch where you, Marina, and you, Brigitte, have grown up. I parked my buggy a mile from the only home you know and navigated rutted lanes and waist-high grass on foot, to a gap in the hedge that commands a clear view of the riding pasture. As usual, I brought my Belgian Porro prism binoculars— a birthday gift from my dear Hannah, one given me for this purpose— in order to watch you up close, as well as from a distance.

Your adoptive uncle gifted you each a roan stallion six months ago, on the day you turned fourteen, and yesterday I stood for an hour, watching the two of you—identical in every way—riding in tandem. Strong legs directing horses, ash-blonde hair flying like riotous banners. With each passing day you look more like my mother, Brigitte, and my sister Marina—the women for whom I named you three minutes after you rushed, one by one, from my body—and nothing gives me a deeper thrill than hearing you speak.

"Marina!"

"Brigitte!"

"Race you to the lane and back?"

"You're on!"

Your names are the single request I made of your adoptive mother. I agreed, in every other respect, to divest myself of parental rights. You believe that you were conceived on this sprawling ranch; your actual point of origin, however, was 2,200 miles from this bucolic spot, in a filthy, war-torn, occupied Southern city, and out of wedlock to boot.

The same cannot be said of me and my twin, who *were* born in a bucolic spot—the marriage bed of Horatio and Brigitte Swift, near a freshwater stream, in the town of Whitley Courthouse, Kentucky. I came first, and backward, clinging to my brother's hands. Once the fluid had been scooped from our mouths, sponged from our fire-new skin, and we'd been settled into a laundry basket, I kept hold of your uncle Silas. He lay quietly, but even after I drifted into slumber, Papa said, some part of me remained in motion.

The fifty-six hours of labor we'd demanded left our mother—a promising actress our father met in Nashville, Tennessee, where she played Bianca in a production of *The Taming of the Shrew*—without the strength to stand, or indeed to live, and before we were six hours old, Brigitte Swift was a ghost. Horatio sat beside the empty vessel of his beloved for two days, motionless, while his mother, Ellen, and our ten-year-old sister Marina fed Silas and me goat's milk, changed us, and rocked us to sleep.

"I'll never understand what your father was thinking," Grandmother Swift sighed to Marina at one point, "marrying a feeble gal like that."

"Feeble?" Marina said. "What do you mean?"

"My dear child," Ellen said, "one look at Brigitte Blanchard told me she didn't have the strength to bring life into this hard world."

When Marina repeated this to our father, Papa slammed into the kitchen, where his mother stood pounding out pork chops, wearing an apron over a green silk dress, wisps of gray hair escaping her high-set chignon, half-moon glasses perched on her nose. Papa approached Grandmother Swift, and when she next lifted her meat mallet, he seized her wrist, halting a downward strike.

"Son?" she said. "What's wrong?"

"All these years," he said, "I thought it was about me."

"What?"

"The way you treated Brigitte," he said. "I thought you were afraid of losing me, but now I see that you were simply afraid of my wife."

"Don't be absurd."

Papa shook his head. "She told me everything. The day before we were wed."

"Horatio, please," Ellen said, trying to free her wrist, "I have work to do."

"Until I met her," Papa said, "I knew nothing. I *felt* nothing, but you tried to buy her off. To send her away."

"You're hurting me."

Releasing her roughly, Papa turned aside. The rear door stood ajar, and he crossed to it and gazed out. "She wanted me to know," he said, "to have every opportunity to leave. You called her a witch, a succubus, she said, accused her of entrapping me. You offered her three thousand dollars to disappear."

"We knew nothing about her!" Hands open and pleading, Grandmother Swift stared a hole through the shoulder blades of her only living son. "Where she came from, who her people were, what she believed. She was an actress, for God's sake! You were too blinded by love to see it, Horatio, but your wife was always playing a part!"

Papa spun to face her. "Not for me," he said. "Brigitte was the strongest woman alive. Stronger than you'll ever be."

"Nonsense!"

"Can't you see," he said, "that strength and power aren't the same thing? Power requires other people. Strength one has when one is alone."

Ellen shook her head. "I don't understand."

"Then I'll speak plainly," Horatio said. "I want you to leave. I don't want to see you again until you can admit that you were mortally afraid of, and wildly unfair to, the woman I loved."

Grandmother Swift untied her apron. "Anything I did, I did for you."

"Go home, Mother."

She blinked rapidly. Her gaze landed on Marina, who sat in the rocker, clutching the basket where Silas and I slept. Ellen turned to Papa and opened her mouth, but he shook his head. She hung her apron on the nail beside the rear door, smoothed down the bodice of her dress. Lifting her chin, our grandmother exited the large outbuilding that housed our kitchen.

But she was the source of Horatio's own stubbornness, and Ellen refused to admit that she was afraid of Brigitte's strength or apologize for her attitude toward our mother. No amount of pleading on the part of her husband would sway her, and the split sparked on the day of Silas's and my birth—not to mention Brigitte's death—became a permanent rift. Since the Swift Lumber Mill, which employed two-thirds of Whitley Courthouse's population, had heretofore supported our family and owned our spacious, well-appointed home, Papa, Marina, Silas, and I moved into a boardinghouse on the banks of the Cumberland River. Three rooms, second floor rear. In lieu of working at the mill founded by his father, Benjamin Swift, in 1796, Horatio took up drinking apple brandy and tinkering. After mending clocks and spinning wheels, china dolls and hand mixers and telescopes, Papa would hawk his refurbished goods in front of the Whitley County courthouse. Silas and I accompanied him on these sales junkets, once we could walk without assistance, helped him arrange his goods on tatty woolen blankets and dream up sales pitches. Silas loved these outings, but I secretly hated selling things with Papa, which made my heart beat so frantically I feared the organ would tear itself from the prison of my chest, travel up my throat, and burst from my mouth.

"You don't have to go to the courthouse," my sister would remind me. "You don't have to do *everything* Silas does."

Marina was correct, but at six and eight and ten, I did not believe her. As we learned to read, Silas and I devised a secret language—a mix of English letters and hieroglyphs of our own invention—that only the two of us could decipher. My brother was the sun to my moon, the white to my black. It seemed that I existed to orbit him, to contrast with him—to make Silas Swift more clearly seen. And whenever Marina said anything different, I would regard her with pity.

"You might understand," I would sigh, "if *you* had a brother."

"But I *do* have a brother. Silas is my brother, too."

"He is not!"

"I'm afraid so, Sylvie."

I was fiercely proprietary about my twin, and though I adored Marina—who at age ten had stepped without hesitation into the thankless role of surrogate mother—I could not quash the scorch of jealousy that flamed up in me at the thought of sharing Silas.

Which is why I never told anyone about the fires. I'm astonished by how sharply I see the distant past from where I now sit on this breezy veranda, sipping tea, arranging my documents. Even as a girl, I knew fire was dangerous, and acting as Silas's accomplice caused me paroxysms of guilt. I would lie awake in our room at night—unable to close my eyes for fear that flames might scorch the undersides of my lids—but it wouldn't have occurred to me to turn in Silas. To pull Marina or Papa aside and tell them my twin was putting people in danger. For though the fires we set terrified me—though they made my stomach turn somersaults—the threat they posed was *ours*. It belonged to Silas and me in a way I still cannot articulate.

From the day we learned to crawl, your aunt Marina used to say, she knew she could find us at the hearth, but years would pass before I grasped this simple fact: Though my brother and I gazed upon the same fire, we each *saw* a different thing. We witnessed our first conflagration at age nine, on the last balmy day of July 1850. Silas and I were sprawled in the grass near the boardinghouse cistern at dusk, listening to bugs drone, watching fireflies spark, when Papa appeared, a wooden bucket in each hand.

"One of the Stanford barns is ablaze!" he gasped as we pumped the cistern, filling his buckets with water drawn from the aquifer. "Let's pray there's not a firebug loose in the county."

We trotted after your grandfather to the Stanford family's tobacco farm, nearly a mile distant, on the far side of Whitley Courthouse's finest sledding hill. A glow ringed the knob like a red circlet, and as we crested the rise, I felt my brother stiffen. Below us, orange tongues licked inky sky, and a cloud of smoke hovered over the flaming barn. I tugged at Silas as the plume rearranged itself, seeming to take the shape of a bear. My brother sprinted down the hill toward the incinerating building, through whose doors a stream of men surged. In and out, in and out. When I reached Silas, I was surprised to see tears wetting his cheeks.

"Silas?" I touched his arm. "What is it?"

"Don't you see?"

"See what?"

He stepped toward the barn. "People," he said breathlessly, "people inside the fire."

"Someone's trapped in the barn?"

"Not trapped," he said. "They want to be there. They're happy to burn."

Silas was drawing perilously close to the inferno, so I darted forward, grasped his shirt, and brought us both down into the parched grass.

"Happy to burn?" I sat up. "What are you talking about?"

"Look closely." He positioned himself behind me, took my head, tilted it toward the blaze. "The fire at home is too small," he said, his exhalations hot on my neck, "but I see them clearly now."

"Who?"

People marching into the blaze, my brother said, so they could start things over. I stared at the waltzing flames with all my might, then I glared at them harder, but no matter how I strained, I saw no people inside the fire. I saw only a conflagration, eating away at an old tobacco barn, and I was filled with resentment.

When faced with open flames in the years that followed, I always searched them for Silas's people. On the night, for instance, when I set ablaze a stately mansion across the street from the Tennessee State Capitol, or each time I contemplated the hearth that warmed the Music Room in the brothel where I lived during the year I spent in Nashville. It wasn't until I had my own otherworldly experience, however, that I saw my resentment of my brother's fire-visions for what it was—jealousy, pure and simple.

I can't say exactly why I longed for proof of the mystical at work in our seemingly explicable world. But I can say that in due time, I would be provided such proof in abundance.

* * *

Three years after the Stanford barn caught fire, not long after our twelfth birthday, your aunt Marina shook me awake early one Sunday. She warned me not to wake Silas, but to dress quietly and meet her in the boardinghouse drawing room. Eager to spend time with my sister—who was always busy organizing Horatio's secondhand goods and paying our bills, mending our clothes and scrubbing the floors—I did as she instructed.

Outside, Marina led me away from the Cumberland River, toward the house in which Silas and I were born. We walked past the place— now occupied by the family of the man who purchased the Swift Lumber Mill after a fever killed our grandparents, first Benjamin, then two days later Ellen. We followed the freshwater stream to the clearing where our mother was buried. Her stone read "Brigitte Blanchard Swift—Beloved Wife and Mother," and my heart broke for her, as it always did, because Brigitte was all alone, without even the company of other dead people.

Once my sister had arranged a clutch of deep pink roses atop the grave—clipped from the bushes in front of Mrs. Marigold's, blooms our landlady tended as though they were her children—Marina sank to the grass and indicated that I should do the same.

"The day our mother died," she said, "she called me to her and took my hand. She was so pale, Sylvie, with scarlet patches in her cheeks and all over her chest. Her sunken eyes were dim, but she squeezed my fingers. She said she had to go soon. She needed to tell me a story, she said, and she made me promise to repeat it to you.

"We come from a long line of actors. In fact, our great-great-grandmother, Euphemia Blanchard, was among the first women to appear on the French stage."

"My stars," I said.

"When Euphemia was fifteen, she married another actor, a man who became increasingly bitter as her career blossomed and his did not. For six years he berated and abused his wife, then one morning when Euphemia failed to show up for rehearsal, her colleagues—afraid her husband had done something unthinkable—marched en masse through the cobbled streets to their rooming house. Euphemia's director knocked on the door and, receiving no answer, pushed his way in.

"Inside, they found no Euphemia, no husband. But the furniture was overturned, as though there'd been a struggle, and the floor was streaked with viscous red fluid. They questioned the elderly couple next door, who reported that in the dead of night, they'd been woken by nightmarish sounds. Banging and smashing, bellowing and shrieking.

"*It sounded like a wild animal had gotten in*, the wife said, her voice atremble, *and was tearing someone apart*.

"*Like a lion, or a bear*, the husband said. *Or maybe a bull.*

"*No, no*, said the wife. *It was much bigger! It sounded like a dragon, or a hydra.*

"The director filed a report with the authorities, but they never located Euphemia or her husband. A year later, our great-great-grandmother reappeared at the theater one afternoon and assured her colleagues that she was as right as rain. After a night of intense quarreling, she said, she'd finally left her husband, then traveled to Spain to recover at the home of some distant relations. Eventually Euphemia remarried—a happy union with her director—and gave birth to seven healthy daughters.

"When she'd finished her story," Marina said, "our mother tugged me down to whisper in my ear. *My Mari*, she said, *you have the strength of one hundred thousand men, as will Sylvie. You will both do great things. Great, horrible, earthshaking things.*"

Thursday, May 31, 1877
Monterey, CA

Silas and I were the same age you are now—fourteen—when we woke one day in September of 1854 to find our older sister missing. One evening Marina fed us, helped us work on penmanship or arithmetic, and pecked our foreheads; the next morning she was gone. Stranger still, your grandfather refused to answer our questions. In the beginning, when we asked what had become of her, Horatio would say, "Marina is no longer a part of this family," which later shifted to, "Marina is dead to me," and finally, "Marina never existed."

But we knew this was untrue, for our known world was filled with the sights and sounds of Marina. She was forever singing; every night after she'd scrubbed our hands and faces and helped us into nightclothes, she serenaded us with a lullaby in a tongue Silas and I did not know. Our sister loved bathing, and she did so early each morning in the freshwater stream, wearing a costume she'd crafted by sewing the hem of one of Papa's undershirts to the waistband of a pair of his old trousers, cut off below the knee.

One winter, Horatio dragged home a cast-off copper bathtub, rusted and full of holes, and spent a week repairing it for Marina. Heating water and running it up from the boardinghouse kitchens took my sister all morning, but once she'd sunk into her cauldron—set up in a corner of the living room—she would remain there for hours, singing to herself, steam rising from the screens that hid her bathtub from view.

In the evenings, your aunt Marina recounted strange, unsettling tales that spilled from her as though printed on an internal scroll—stories about sentient mountains and warmhearted killers. Stories about women who changed themselves into she-bears or lionesses, into clouds of bees or leviathans.

"Don't be silly," Silas said more than once, in exasperated response. "People can't turn into animals or monsters."

"How do you know?" said Marina.

"Because I live in the world. And I have eyes."

"The fact that you've never seen something," my sister said, "doesn't mean it doesn't exist. Have you seen China? Or an elephant? Or the Mississippi River?"

"You know I haven't!"

"Do you believe in them?"

Silas nodded. "Of course."

"Why?"

He scratched his head. "I'm not sure."

Marina seized his hands. "The world holds so much more than we can imagine, Silas. Don't close your mind to the possible in favor of the certain."

Though I couldn't fully grasp what Marina meant when she said such things, my sister's passion and conviction made me admire her to the point of hero worship. Unlike Silas and me, who'd inherited Horatio's unruly dark curls, gray eyes, and angular frame, Marina was a near copy of Brigitte—petite and shapely, with dusky blonde hair that fell like a waterfall to her waist and eyes of amber, a shade that seemed to glow softly at dawn and dusk. I was mesmerized by her beauty, and by the figure that dangled always from a delicate chain about her neck. This golden icon wore a crown that appeared to be made of bricks, and a dozen eggs, or extra breasts, sprouted from her torso. Her arms were open, her hands frozen into an attitude of welcome. I was five the first time I climbed into Marina's lap and asked about the pendant.

"Who's this?"

"A great deity."

"What's a deity?"

"A god."

"You mean there's more than one?"

She nodded. "There are millions."

"My stars," I said. "What's she the god of?"

"She's the ruler," she said, "of wild animals and woodlands and the moon. She brings new life into the world, and she snatches life away. She's also the protector of women and girls."

"Who does she protect girls from?"

"Anyone. Everyone. She even protects us from ourselves."

I considered her words. "How do you know all this?"

"Our mother taught me," she said, "when I was just about your age."

"She did?"

"She did."

As I stroked the tiny golden figure, a shiver stole through me, and I thought I heard this: the faraway sound of dozens of women's voices, raised in harmonious song. "Marina," I said, "what's this god's name?"

My sister smiled. "She's been called many things, by many peoples. Tiamat, Cybele, and Isis. Rhea, Ishtar, and Gaia. Reitia, Diana, and Bona Dea. For the worship of this deity began before recorded time."

"Marina," I asked, "what do *you* call her?"

"Artemis," she said. "I call her Artemis."

* * *

As the days crept into weeks and months, the neat pathways your aunt Marina had dug out and maintained against Horatio's towering supply of secondhand goods vanished, and our boardinghouse rooms became overrun with debris. We were soon buried in limbless dolls and the inner workings of grandfather clocks, in wagon wheels in need of patching and shoes in need of resoling. Silas and I sorted these items into discrete piles, but try as we might, we could not return the place to Marina's previous organization.

Even more alarming than the change Marina's absence brought to our rooms was the change it caused in Papa, who began taking his first apple brandy earlier each day. Eventually he started at first light, and by noon, Silas and I were unable to rouse him. As children, we found each day interminable; how I now long to discuss with my twin the way time shrinks and withers, as one hurtles through adulthood. Though he couldn't walk a straight line, Horatio kept hauling home broken goods, so Silas and I took over the tinkering. My brother was better at the work than I, which may have had to do with our relative ability to sit still. Even as a toddler, Silas could remain immobile for so long I wondered if he was sleeping with eyes open. I, on the other hand, to this day have trouble keeping still.

The goods Silas and I refurbished were passable, and we managed to sell them in front of the Whitley County courthouse, but I suspect those sales were motivated mainly by pity. After Marina's departure, Silas and I rarely bathed or combed our hair, and we soon took on the feral look of street urchins. The proceeds of our labors did not cover the cost of our rooms, let alone our meals, and if not for the envelopes that began arriving monthly—mailed from Nashville, Tennessee—Horatio, Silas, and I would have starved.

"What's this?" I asked Papa the first time I found one of the envelopes, buried beneath a stack of newspapers atop a listing workbench.

Horatio sat on the boardinghouse back porch in a rocker, studying a sketch of our mother in profile. He tore his eyes from the image long enough to take in the fat, still-sealed envelope I dangled before him, addressed to *Horatio Swift and Family, Mrs. Marigold's Boardinghouse, Whitley Courthouse, KY.*

"That's not ours," he finally said.

"It's addressed to us."

"Still."

"Shouldn't I open it?"

"I wouldn't."

"Aren't you curious?"

"No."

"What should I do with it?"

"Burn it?"

I decided, instead, to show the envelope to Silas—who was ready and willing to burn it—but elected first to see what was inside.

"My first thought was Marina," I said as he loosed the flap, "but the handwriting is all wrong." Unlike the rest of us, Marina was left-handed, and her script was large and wild with a hard slant. As my brother extracted a bundle of federal banknotes from the envelope, I shrieked.

"This is more than a hundred dollars," he said.

"Is there a return address?" I asked. "What's the postmark?"

"No return address," he said, his eyes leaping up to meet mine, "but it was mailed from Nashville."

Our parents had met in Nashville, that we knew, but Papa had never mentioned knowing anyone who lived there still. Silas located a cracked magnifying glass, and we combed over the yellow rectangle as though it contained microscopic clues. But no matter how hard we looked, the envelope yielded no leads that might indicate its origin, purpose, or meaning.

"Maybe it's a mistake," I finally said. "Maybe we should report it."

Silas blinked. "To whom?"

I shrugged. Late that night, my brother shook me awake. Scents of sulfur, pitch, and smoke wafted from his hands, his hair. There were streaks of soot on Silas's cheeks.

"It's our legacy," he whispered feverishly.

"What?"

"The money in the envelope."

"You went out?" I sat up. "Why didn't you wake me?"

"I tried," he said, "but you were sleeping like the dead."

I was—and still am—a notoriously light sleeper, and for the first time in our lives, I understood that my brother was lying to me. Silas hadn't wanted me to accompany him, as I'd done many times before, and by extension, there was a chance that we wouldn't always function as a unit, a system—a four-legged, two-headed animal.

"I don't understand, Silas. What happened out there?"

"I saw a creature in the flames tonight," he said, his eyes aglow with an elation I didn't recognize. "She had the face of a woman with long, glistening hair, and the body of a dragon. She looked right at me and called me by name. She said she's an ancient being of great contradictions, and that she is our underwriter."

"Underwriter?"

He nodded with great solemnity. "She said the money belongs to us, Sylvie. That it's a tribute."

I wanted to believe in your uncle Silas's dragon-woman, but as I didn't share his fire-visions, I could not. If the yellow envelope had borne a return address, I would have insisted that we try to return the banknotes, but the fact of the matter was that Horatio, Silas, and I were in desperate financial straits, and there was really no question of our keeping the money.

Unable to return to slumber, I tossed and turned for the rest of the night, muttering four words under my breath: *we have no choice, we have no choice.*

TWO DEAD IN FREE SCHOOL FIRE

WHITLEY COURTHOUSE, KENTUCKY—LATE Saturday night, persons unknown torched the Whitley County Free School, founded by William Richardson of the American Missionary Association. Richardson was a disciple of the abolitionist John G. Fee, who founded the Madison County settlement of Berea.

The Free School opened two years ago and faced stiff opposition from the start. "Kentucky is a pro-slavery state," Mr. Butler Stanford, the county's largest landowner, told this reporter. "Our citizens never asked for, and do not want, any Free Schools."

Richardson lived in two rooms at the back of the school building, and one of the bodies discovered in the ruins has been identified as his. The second body is that of Horatio Swift, well-known local citizen and steadfast supporter of William Richardson, who helped Richardson build his Free School two years ago.

Saturday, June 2, 1877
Monterey, CA

The day after the Whitley County Free School burned to the ground, Deputy Sheriff Yancy Cox showed up at the boardinghouse asking for me and Silas. As a girl, I'd had a savage crush on Yancy, who was two years ahead of us in school, and when I was fifteen, he took me riding in his daddy's wagon. We parked atop a wildflower-carpeted rise, and as the sun lowered itself into the foothills, Yancy tilted his blond head and kissed me. I recall a medley of sensations flaming through me in that moment—the soft, dewy pressure of his lips, the warmth of his fingertips, the tensing of his lanky frame—all mixed with the abrupt, inarguable understanding that I did not love Yancy Cox and never would.

As Silas and I accompanied him the quarter mile to the sheriff's office, Yancy refused to meet my gaze, and I sensed that this had nothing to do with our juvenile kiss, but with what now lay in store for my brother and me. Located across from the courthouse, the office was sandwiched between Cox's Dry Goods and Miller's Mercantile, in a storefront with grimy windows and a swing sign that read SHERIFF. This was the first time I'd ventured through the whitewashed plank door, which stood always ajar, and within, I found a dim office that housed a battered desk. An empty holding cell stood in a far corner, and one brick wall was covered, floor to ceiling, with wanted posters. As the sheriff shook hands with Silas, I studied the faces of the wanted, Papa's voice echoing in my ears: *Outlaws are just lawmen turned inside out.*

Sheriff Jefferson ushered us through one door, then another, and we found ourselves in the county morgue. The long, narrow room featured two cooling boards—cane latticework platforms whose perforations allowed not only bodily fluids to drain from the deceased, but also blocks of ice to be placed beneath them, to slow decomposition—a key feature when one went home to glory in August. Only one of the tables was in use, and the county coroner smiled apologetically as he folded back a blue cloth to reveal a blackened man-shaped figure whose posture—tilt of neck, curve of wrist, bend of knees—signaled Horatio Swift.

"No." Silas's hands flew up as though he could push away the sight. "Please."

Papa's skin and hair were gone, but he'd been born without a right pinkie toe, and the charred remains before us were missing the same appendage. In addition, the gold wedding band Horatio hadn't removed since the day he'd wed Brigitte Blanchard encircled the body's left ring finger. A chill raced over me, and I heard an odd, increasingly loud thumping—a sound I soon realized was my own heartbeat. Deputy Cox pressed a piece of paper—Papa's favorite sketch of our mother in profile—into my hand and said, softly, that he'd found it thirty yards from the smoldering ruins of the Free School, tucked beneath a spicebush, anchored by a smooth, black stone.

"I hate to make you do this," Sheriff Jefferson said as he helped Silas, who seemed on the verge of collapse, into his office and one of the low-backed, armless wooden chairs that stood before the desk. "I know it's just god-awful."

"Who's responsible?" I asked. "Do you have any idea?"

"There are several candidates," he said. "You know how most folks in the county felt about the Free School."

Feeling lightheaded, I lowered myself into the other chair. "But you're investigating?"

"Of course," he said. "Does either of you know why Horatio went to the school at night? Was that unusual?"

"He never went there at night," I said.

"Silas?" said Sheriff Jefferson. "You know what he might have been up to?"

My brother's hands clutched at empty air in his lap. His lips were moving, but no sound emerged.

"Silas?" I nudged him with an elbow. "What's wrong with you?"

He dragged his gaze up to meet mine, and for an instant, I didn't recognize him. *You're not my brother*, flashed through my mind. *You're a man I will never know.*

"Son?" said the sheriff gently. "Do you have something to tell me?"

A foreign sound erupted from Silas—part cry, part roar. He leapt up, his chair clattering to the floorboards, then bolted like a spooked animal through the open door.

"Apologies," I said. "I don't know what's come over him."

The large lawman stood, rounded his desk, settled on the corner before me. He stroked his mustache. "I might," he said. "How old are you two now?"

"Eighteen."

He nodded. "I was sixteen when my daddy died, and I'm still not over it. I read a book once that said our parents are our personal gods—enormous, mythic, eternal. Their loss shakes us in the same way we'd be shook if one Sunday, the preacher told the entire congregation that there wasn't no God. That He was just a collection of stories handed down, generation to generation."

I considered his words. "Do you believe that?"

He shrugged. "I don't know, but thinking about it overtook my sorrow for a time, and I guess that's something."

After assuring me that he would do his damnedest to find those responsible for Papa's death, the sheriff asked if we could get word to Marina.

I shook my head. "We haven't heard from Marina since she left."

"Not in four years?"

"No, sir."

"Odd," he said. "She and Horatio always seemed so close. The whole town was shocked when your sister lit out like she did."

As the lawman walked me to the door, he asked, gently, how Silas and I planned to eat. He clearly assumed that Papa hadn't been much of a provider, and we'd told no one of the envelopes that continued to arrive monthly at Mrs. Marigold's. The sheriff opened his billfold, and a heady mix of emotions engulfed me—anger, fear, determination, guilt, defensiveness. I waved away the banknotes he offered, assuring him that your grandfather had left us well-fixed.

"Sylvie," Sheriff Jefferson said once we stood on opposite sides of the threshold.

"Yes?"

"Keep an eye on Silas. Your brother is hurting. If you tell my wife I said this, I'll deny it, but I've long suspected that women carry a strength we men can scarcely imagine."

* * *

William Richardson came to Whitley Courthouse to establish his Free School late in 1855, and Papa became his most avid supporter. Your great-grandparents were raised in the Quaker faith, in eastern Pennsylvania, and when Benjamin and Ellen Swift relocated to Kentucky in 1794, they brought along their fervent moral opposition to slavery in any form. They instilled these beliefs in Horatio, the only one of their three sons to see adulthood, and he was sickened by the passage of the 1850 Fugitive Slave Law, which required all U.S. citizens—even those in non-slave-holding states—to return escaped slaves to their owners.

When I was your age, Brigitte and Marina, my feelings about Papa were complicated, and I had no one to tell me that such feelings about one's parents are perfectly normal. But make no mistake—Horatio Swift was a man of unswerving principles, one who defended others without hesitation, and in spite of his failings, I never doubted that he loved us. And when he marched up the courthouse steps to loudly declare his support of Brother William Richardson—who'd just announced his intention to found a Free School open to all children, regardless of race or background—I was flooded with admiration and pride.

For the first time since your aunt Marina's disappearance, or maybe even your grandmother Brigitte's death, Horatio was moved to action, and he threw himself vigorously into helping Richardson erect the school building, enlisting Silas's and my help. We were among the students who attended the Whitley County Free School, and two days before Papa died in the conflagration that destroyed the place—and him—he sat us down at the converted red oak door that served as our dining table, and into whose surface he'd chiseled a heart encircling the initials HBS + BBS, and told us he was sorry.

"For what?" said Silas.

"Bringing you into this."

"Into what?"

Your grandfather cupped his hands, carved an all-encompassing sphere in the air. "The world."

"What's wrong, Papa?" I asked.

"Sylvie," he said, "your father is broken."

I glanced at Silas, who was blinking rapidly at Horatio.

"Powerful people raised me," Papa went on, shaking his head, "but in the end, the powerful only know how to consider themselves. To consider others—to raise human beings, to nurture hearts and souls—takes something more than power. It takes patience. It takes strength."

My brother and I said nothing.

"You were wrong about me," Horatio said, but he was looking past us—talking to someone or something only he could see, "for I am neither strong nor resilient."

"Papa?" Silas said.

Horatio took one of my hands and one of Silas's. He studied our faces—copies of his, and of each other's—as though he were seeing us, really seeing us, for the first time since we'd slain the love of his life. Silas and I joined our loose hands, and I felt a fearsome spark pass through our human circle.

"This may seem wrongheaded to you now," Papa said, "and maybe it will in the future, but my children, you must try your best to avoid love."

* * *

In the years that followed Papa's death, your uncle Silas befriended Miles Stanford, son of Butler, whose barn fire Horatio had helped extinguish a decade earlier. Two years before the blaze, when Silas and I were six, a stone struck my forehead as we cut through a fallow field, opening a bloody gash that bisected my right eyebrow and left the peculiar scar—shaped rather like a question mark—that I bear to this day, and making Miles, who'd thrown the rock, my sworn enemy. So when, on an autumn morning three months after Horatio died, I spotted my twin and Miles crouched together atop the sledding hill, I nearly toppled over from the shock.

Miles was loading a Colt revolving carbine rifle, and I watched him hand the gun to Silas. My brother lifted the rifle to his shoulder, sighted along the barrel. A covey of quail burst over the hill, Silas pulled the trigger, and a bird plummeted from the sky. Miles's dog retrieved it, and once he'd returned, Miles jammed a finger into the bird's perforated chest. He streaked red across my brother's cheeks and forehead, and Silas grinned, his expression radiating triumph.

Even before this day, Silas had been drawing away from me. When I tried talking to him about Papa, about my sense of abandonment and loss, about whether we should search for Marina, Silas just sat there, silent and sullen. My brother wanted to talk, instead, about a supposed science called *phrenology* that alleges that the shape of a person's skull determines their mental capacity, and the importance of preserving the Southern way of life.

"*Southern way of life?*" I said one evening at the red oak table. "You sound like Butler Stanford."

"So what?" Silas said. "Butler's a strong man, a successful man, an upstanding member of this community."

"Papa didn't think so," I countered. "He thought Butler was a weak man, poor in spirit. Papa thought Butler's attitude would be the ruin of General Washington's great experiment in equality and enlightenment."

"Papa was a drunken fool," Silas spat, "and I don't give a damn what he thought."

I sat in stunned silence as he shoved his plate away, stood, and slammed out of our rooms. I knew Miles Stanford and his father were the source of the atrocious ideas filling my brother's head; what I couldn't understand was his attitude toward your grandfather. I prayed that my twin was understandably angry that Horatio had left us on our own, because the alternative—that Silas actually accepted the pro-slavery sentiments of the Stanford family—was too horrid to imagine.

* * *

As the months rolled on, such scenes became more frequent, and finally, Silas and I stopped speaking altogether, instead leaving each other notes when we'd run out of an essential or a bill came due. I was crushingly lonely, and though I had Mrs. Marigold—a round, cheerful widow who was happy to chat about anything, most especially the profusion of flora she cultivated with doting care—I grew increasingly forlorn. The chasm that had opened between me and my twin felt immeasurable, and I began to dream, most nights, that I was trapped within a strange metallic cylinder, drowning in icy salt water.

Then on April 12, 1861, we received a package that would change everything.

Curiously, the *Apocrypha* arrived the same day Confederate forces fired on Fort Sumter, setting in motion the infernal conflict known as the Civil War, the War of the Rebellion, the War for Southern Independence, the War Between the States, the Second American Revolution, the Brothers' War, or the Late Unpleasantness. The playscript was boxed and wrapped in paper bearing a Nashville postmark, addressed in the same hand as the fat envelopes that continued to arrive monthly at Mrs. Marigold's. The main difference was the inclusion of a return address.

Silas was out when I opened the package, and night had fallen before he returned. Since your grandfather's death, we'd managed to bring a semblance of order to our rooms. From Cary Jacks, the county's finest carpenter, we bought sitting-room furniture, beds of our own, and a tall bookshelf. At Cox's Dry Goods, Yancy's aunt ordered Silas and me ready-made clothing, a sizable multicolored globe of the world, and a complete set of the *Encyclopaedia Britannica* (eighth edition). And from Zane Bly, a book peddler who passed through Whitley Courthouse three times a year, we bought various foreign-language dictionaries as well as books on biology, geology, and fine art, American and European history, folklore and mythology, novels and plays and poetry by Cervantes and Rabelais, Shakespeare and Milton, Swift and Racine, Voltaire and Diderot, Goethe and Flaubert.

The irony of the fact that Silas and I—now twenty—enjoyed a level of comfort and stability heretofore unknown to us wasn't lost on me. We lived easily on the money provided by our Nashville benefactor, but each time I stocked up at the Mercantile or retrieved mail from the post office, I read the same question in the eyes of clerks and patrons alike: *How are these young folks eating?* I found myself ruminating on the future, or more precisely, whether I had one. Would I spend the rest of my life keeping house for my silent brother? Would I ever travel beyond Whitley

Courthouse? Would I marry, or have children of my own? What on earth would Silas and I do if our mysterious income ceased? How *would* we eat?

I was sitting at the red oak table with the *Apocrypha*, a French-English dictionary, two volumes of the *Encyclopaedia Britannica*, a blazing oil lamp, and several loose sheets of paper spread out before me, pondering these questions and others, when Silas walked in. Instead of heading for his room, my brother approached the table and stood with heels together, chest out, elbows tight against his sides.

"At ease," I said, breaking our silent standoff.

Unsmiling, Silas indicated the delicate manuscript, the dictionary, the loose pages. "What on earth are you doing?"

"Translating," I said, tapping the *Apocrypha*. "This is a playscript."

"Where'd it come from?"

"Our underwriter," I said. "Only this time, there's a return address."

As he settled across from me, your uncle's scent—perspiration with notes of pine, resin, and the cinnamon with which he sweetened his coffee—choked me, and I was flooded with sorrow. I wanted to reach for Silas; instead, I dug the nails of my left hand into my palm until I drew blood.

"What language is this?" he said.

"French." I tapped the battered dictionary, slid the lamp and the page on which I'd been writing across the table. "I've deciphered the title page."

"*Apocrypha*," he read, "by Aristophanes of Athens, circa 386 BC."

"According to the *Britannica*," I said, "Aristophanes was a Greek playwright. He's thought to have written forty comedies, but only eleven survive. And 'apocrypha' translates to 'religious writings of uncertain origin rejected by most authorities.'"

"Doesn't sound like much of a comedy," Silas said.

"Granted," I said. "But Apocrypha is a proper name here. The heroine's called *Apocrypha*."

Your uncle studied his hands: long tapered fingers, prominent knuckles, square nail beds. I could tell he had news for me, but I wanted to speak first. "Silas," I said, "I think we should go to Nashville. I think Marina may be there."

"Marina?"

Nodding, I tapped the playscript again. "First the money, and now this."

Silas sighed. "We've been over this. It's not her handwriting."

"She had a friend write it."

"Why would she do that?"

I shrugged.

"If she *is* living in Nashville," he said, "why hasn't she written?"

"I don't know. Maybe she can't."

"She's been gone six years," he said. "I think it's time for us to admit that Marina is dead."

These words—never spoken aloud between us—struck my ears like daggers, and I dropped my gaze to the yellowed playscript before me. Lifting the title page aside, I scanned a string of unfamiliar words, written in a language I did not speak. To my great shock, a sentence was abruptly illuminated—seeming to pulse, momentarily, with light—and I heard a faint sound I'd first encountered in Marina's lap fifteen years earlier—dozens of women singing as one.

"Sylvie," Silas said, clearing his throat, "Miles and I are joining up."

"With the Confederates?"

He nodded.

"Don't do it, Silas," I said. "Please."

Shaking his head, he pushed up to his feet. "I have no choice."

I'd been fanning the flame of my fear that your uncle would abandon me since we were small, whenever I lost sight of him for any period of time, and since he'd befriended Miles Stanford, that fear had burgeoned into a blaze. But in this moment, what I felt was anger. For the first time in memory, I wanted to hurt Silas, as he was hurting me. So instead of telling him about the uncanny singing, or the words illuminating themselves in the pages of the *Apocrypha*, I said something that caught my twin brother—and me—entirely off guard.

"Silas," I said. "I'm also leaving Whitley Courthouse."

His eyes widened. "Nashville?"

"Nashville," I replied, touching the playscript. "Nashville."

As I repeated the word, a cityscape arose in my mind. Streets thick with carriage and foot traffic, slinking dogs and clucking chickens and rooting hogs. Men juggling, half-dressed women singing on street corners. Two-story buildings made of brick or clapboard. Saloons and dry-goods stores and barbershops and apothecaries. And soldiers— soldiers everywhere. Though I'd only ever seen a picture postcard of Nashville, I knew I was envisioning that city.

Sunday, June 3, 1877
Monterey, CA

Despite my obvious and oft-stated disapproval, Silas left Whitley County five months later, in the fall of 1861. I gave him a wide berth until the morning he was to depart, then I broke down, flung my arms around his neck, and sobbed for a quarter hour. I couldn't support his decision, but my brother and I had never spent a night apart, and I wanted, more than anything, for Silas to find purpose, to be happy, to *live*. When I pulled myself together, we promised to write. I stood on the boardinghouse porch waving until Silas and Miles Stanford became two dim pinpricks on the landscape, then vanished.

Our rooms, once brimming with the sounds of four Swifts, now felt like vast, echoing caverns, and if not for Mrs. Marigold, who stopped in to chat at least twice a day, I don't know that I would have made it through my first week of solitude.

Silas wrote me every fortnight, as he'd promised, and though I was tormented by the knowledge of what he was fighting for, I awaited my twin's letters as eagerly as I'd once awaited the bracing sound of his laughter. We wrote each other in the secret language we invented as children, but I've translated a handful of his letters for you, Marina, and you, Brigitte, so you might hear your uncle's voice. Here's an early one:

February 26, 1862
New Orleans, LA

Dear Sylvie,

It seems that our torpedo boat is a success. Last week we tested her in the choppy waters of the Mississippi, and she held tighter than a drum. Tomorrow, we will tow her up to Lake Pontchartrain for more testing, but I am convinced that she's ready for action. I know our plucky *Pioneer* will not fail us.

The moment I met Mr. McClintock and Mr. Hunley—the architects of this underwater endeavor—the moment they showed me the submarine's schematics, a voice in my head told me I was home. This voice was familiar; it may have been the voice of a creature I once met in a dream. Or the voice of our mother, or of Marina. The more I study it, however, the more convinced I am that the voice was yours.

I miss you more than I imagined possible, Sylvie, and will never forgive myself for behaving so coldly toward you during my final weeks in Whitley County. I do not think I can explain my behavior, and I certainly cannot excuse it. I can only say that at times, I terrify myself, and I cannot abide the thought of having a similar effect on you.

Of the eight men now working on the Porpoise (as we've nicknamed our submarine), I am by far the most comfortable crewing her. The *Pioneer*, crafted from an iron steam boiler, is cylindrical in shape and holds five men—four to turn the hand cranks that power the boat's propeller, and one to steer. Before last week's trials, we spent days rehearsing the act of folding our bodies inside the fish boat. Our instructions were to sit quietly, to close our eyes and breathe evenly, and if we should start to panic, to count slowly to ten. But three seconds after they swung shut the hatches, a man named Larson started screaming bloody murder, pounding the hull and begging for release. At regular intervals thereafter, the others went the same way—shrieking and banging to beat the band. I am proud and somewhat puzzled to report that I alone was able to withstand being sealed indefinitely inside the *Pioneer*.

What aspects of my life have prepared me for this work, Sylvie? Your brother, who as a boy would have sooner walked over hot coals than taken a single bath? I certainly do not know. But when they swing shut the hatches, when I hear the bolts shooting home—when I am imprisoned inside an iron tube carrying only a handful of beating hearts and a copper cylinder stuffed with 135 pounds of black powder—a peace I've never known blankets me. Within the Porpoise, I am alert; I am focused; I am content. If I didn't know better, I might say I am in love.

It really is the darndest thing.

I've gone on too long, Sylvie, and am afraid I must fly. The Union boys are closing in on New Orleans, and much as I hate to admit it, it seems they will soon take the city. Mr. Hunley, Mr. McClintock, and Mr. Baxter are making plans to shift our entire operation, posthaste, to a new locale—possibly in Alabama. Miles probably won't go—he flies into a blind terror when sealed inside the fish boat—but I know that *I* am in this underwater endeavor for the long haul.

How is our dear old landlady, Mrs. Marigold? How is her gout? I must admit, I was a bit surprised at the list you included in your last letter, of the effects you've already sold. It sounds as though our rooms must be bare of everything save books and papers. Are your plans to travel to Nashville moving along apace? Do let me know in your next letter, which I will eagerly await.

Your loving brother,
Silas

* * *

But it took longer than I'd anticipated to arrange my own exodus from Whitley Courthouse, and nearly a year would pass before I struck out for Nashville. In the months that stretched between the arrival of the *Apocrypha* and my departure, I labored on an English translation of the playscript. Armed only with my French-English dictionary, I found the work violently frustrating. I gave up on it every other day, hurling my poor dictionary across the room with a furious cry before retrieving the book, apologizing to it, and tackling the translation afresh.

During this interval, when I wasn't unraveling the *Apocrypha*, I read voraciously: other plays by Aristophanes, as well as dramas by Sophocles, Aeschylus, and Euripides. Shakespeare, the poetry of Ovid and Pindar; Virgil and Horace; Nossis and Sappho; Anne Bradstreet and Phillis Wheatley; Milton, Dryden, and Pope; Dante's *Inferno*, the Bible, and all twenty-eight volumes of the *Encyclopaedia Britannica*. Your aunt Marina had taught Silas and me the basics of reading, writing, and arithmetic, but the *Britannica* opened my eyes in ways I'd never imagined.

In volume 9—Entomology–FRA—I stumbled upon a drawing of the pendant that had always hung from my sister's neck. According to the *Britannica*, the gold figurine was a replica of a statue housed in the Artemision, or Temple of Artemis—one of the Seven Wonders of the Ancient World—in the capital of Ionian Greece, a city called Ephesus, and the wild popularity of Artemis's cult had made Ephesus the wealthiest city in Asia Minor.

Aside from Marina's pendant, I'd encountered only one version of the goddess Artemis—twin to Apollo, born on the island of Delos—but the *Britannica* informed me that Ionian Greeks believed she was actually born at Ephesus, directly across the Aegean from the city-state of Athens. Ionians referred to Artemis as the *Mistress of Wild Beasts*, and she shared traits with Asiatic goddesses whose names, as I read them aloud, I heard the echo of my sister's voice pronouncing nearly two decades earlier: *Isis, Ishtar, Cybele.* The knobs that covered the Ephesian Artemis's torso—extra breasts, bees' eggs, or bulls' testicles—were linked to her control of fertility, and something called "sacred prostitution" was practiced by the priestesses of her temple.

I'd read about prostitution, of course, as I'd read about courtship, marriage, sex, pregnancy, and childbirth, and I found my mind turning to these topics more and more often. Every afternoon, once I'd read myself blind, I went for a long walk in the countryside. The girls Silas and I had grown up with were all married; some had children. Every text I encountered involved romantic attachments, and I was as intrigued by Achilles's love for Patroclus in *Troilus and Cressida* as I was by the poetry of Sappho, as captivated by the notion of Zeus impregnating Danaë in the guise of a shower of gold as I was by the thought of Queen Pasiphaë bearing the Minotaur after mating with a sacrificial bull.

"What does this say about me?" I asked my mother, at whose riverside grave I inevitably ended my outings. "Who on earth is my ideal companion?"

She never answered, but Brigitte Blanchard Swift gave me space to ask the question, which helped. And the final resting place she now shared with your grandfather Horatio provided me with weeds to pull, twigs to gather, and an altar on which to arrange the coneflowers and black-eyed Susans—her favorite wildflowers—I'd picked expressly for her.

* * *

Finally, after bidding Mrs. Marigold farewell on a muggy August morning, I visited the railroad and steamboat ticket office—a shack that stood halfway between the depot and the dock—and booked myself passage, for $12.50, on the Lovell Line. The blue ticket bore my travel date and destination, the image of a paddle wheel, and *Gertrude*, the name of the steamer that would ferry me to Nashville.

My fellow passengers were blue-clad Union soldiers with three exceptions: a grandmother, mother, and girl-child, all draped in the pitch-black weeds of mourning. Each time I left my closet, I spied this matriline trinity moving in a row across one of the decks, somber costumes flapping in the breeze. I greatly preferred the openness of the deck to my coffin-like quarters, so I spent as much time above as possible, basking in the bullying sun. Native trees of Tennessee—red maple, honey locust, yellow tulip poplar—dotted the riverbanks. High in the cobalt sky, hawks reeled, eyes raking the shore for fragile, warm-blooded quarry.

As I stood gripping the boat's rail one evening, my body moving with the river, I must have fallen into a light slumber. I imagined that the matriline trio—looking like a black-clad set of nesting dolls—approached and began touching every part of me: skirt, braids, hands, ankles. I imagined that they grabbed me bodily, and I thought they would toss me overboard—into the muddy river. But they merely held me, rocked me, whispering things like *shh* and *there now*. I woke with a cry and looked around. The black-clad threesome was crossing the deck, gliding away from my position. As I watched—heart flailing—the girl-child turned her head. Fixed me with a dark eye.

Each morning, not long after dawn, I thought I spied a familiar figure swimming at some distance from the steamer: your aunt Marina, outfitted in her makeshift bathing costume. A closer look revealed what I'd seen to be a piece of driftwood, or a trick of light on the water. At the time, I attributed these manifestations to the fact that I'd been fretting about my missing sister for eight years.

Today, I know just what Marina's aquatic appearances foreshadowed.

We gained Nashville in three days and streamed like cattle over the gangplank that tethered the *Gertrude's* bow to the sloping, sun-drenched wharf. Though I'd grown up along the Cumberland, I'd never seen such a large, hectic port. The *Gertrude* tarried beside her steam-powered sisters, belching black plumes—five long bodies lined up neatly, diagonal to shore. Sun-bronzed crewmen scuttled over catwalks, unloading crates, barrels, and burlap sacks with astonishing rapidity. Individual breast-high fortifications fashioned from heaped earth dotted the riverbank, which was patrolled by blue-uniformed Union guards bearing rifled muskets, with bayonets. A half mile north, a Louisville and Nashville engine chugged across the Cumberland, towing a string of boxcars, discharging puffs of white. Guarding the suspension bridge beneath it were four federal blockhouses—octagonal turrets with peaked roofs and walls riddled with gun ports.

Before leaving Whitley Courthouse, I'd divested myself of the fixed assets Silas and I acquired after Horatio's death. My worldly possessions were now packed into the haversack that banged painfully against my hip: two extra dresses, one pair of boots, the boxed and wrapped pages of the *Apocrypha*, my French-English dictionary, Papa's favorite tattered sketch of your grandmother Brigitte, my correspondence with Silas—whom in my last letter I'd instructed to start writing me at the return address our Nashville underwriter had printed on the *Apocrypha's* packaging—and a half dozen bound volumes of drama, verse, and prose. Holding my skirts out of the mud, I scrambled up the sloped bank to the streets above.

At this point, everything I knew about Nashville I'd gleaned from *The News Journal*—I knew Tennessee, like Kentucky, was deeply divided over secession and had been the last state to join the Confederacy. I knew Nashville was the first Confederate capital taken when Fort Donelson fell to the Union, in February of 1862, and I knew the loss of Nashville— one of the South's most vital river ports as well as the junction of five railroads—was a devastating blow to the Rebels.

I also knew the ease with which Nashville had fallen so vexed Tennessee's new military governor—former senator Andrew Johnson— that the construction of five new forts was already underway. In charge of this enterprise was a U.S. Army chief engineer named James St. Clair Morton, soon to command an outfit known as the Pioneer Brigade. And once I'd crested the sloping bank, I spied—atop a rise I would soon learn was called St. Cloud Hill—figures laboring on the construction of Fort Negley, the first of Morton's fortification projects.

The *Gertrude* off-loaded her cargo at midafternoon into streets muddy from recent rains, not to mention crowded with horse- and mule-drawn transport—wagons, buggies, coaches—as well as refuse and waste and poor, half-starved creatures—dogs and cats, geese and gulls and bleating baby goats. Wooden walkways lined the avenues, their planks groaning under the weight of motley throngs, one of which swept me westward like a wind-gust, away from the Cumberland, along the route—known as Broad Street—that dead-ended at the wharf.

I'd read reports of the occupying army seizing private homes, hijacking horses, and jailing Nashvillians who refused to pledge allegiance to the Union, and it seemed that I felt hostility—or at any rate mistrust—swirling around me. I stood on a corner, casting about for a kindly looking soul who might direct me to the address I could now recite by heart: 101 North Front Street.

Just then, a squadron of black-clad figures marched into view. Twelve women, all dressed like the mourning trio from the *Gertrude*. Their advance down Broad Street brought traffic to a halt. Two women in front held a banner emblazoned with these foot-high scarlet letters:

SOUTHERN LADIES' AID SOCIETY. Six of them shook tambourines, striking the white circles rhythmically against palms; four rattled collection baskets at the crowd. Most of those they passed ignored the women, though a few people tossed them coins.

As the dusky troop filed by, a man to my rear shouted, "Don't trust women!"

Before I could turn, something whizzed past my right ear to wetly strike the face of the black-clad woman before me. She was one of the tambourine players—a pale-skinned redhead with eyes the color of night. I watched her lift a delicate hand to wipe the spittle from her cheek. She studied the yellow glob for a moment, and then—smiling merrily—she licked the slaver from her fingers.

Monday, June 4, 1877
Monterey, CA

Not long after I watched a redhead swallow a stranger's spittle, I stood before the building whose return address the *Apocrypha* had delivered unto me. Along the way, I'd passed the smoldering skeletons of two clapboard shacks. Women with baskets or pushcarts selling boiled peanuts, hoecakes, and spoon bread. Barefoot newsboys hawking their wares—*The Daily Press*, *The Nashville Dispatch*—whose headlines shouted the death tolls of recent battles—Baton Rouge, Cedar Mountain, Lone Jack. Two men stumbling, arm in arm, singing off-key. Blood sluicing from a woman's nose to dye her dress ruby red. A trio of ragged children slinking through the crowds, slipping hands into pockets. One of these urchins growled at me like an animal, baring rust-colored teeth.

The home at 101 North Front Street was comely as well as comical. An antebellum mansion lifted by a cyclone from its bucolic foundation in Mississippi, Alabama, or Georgia and deposited on a sooty, urban waterfront block. At four stories, the house—clad in white clapboards, wrought-iron balconies, purple shutters, and a purple front door— towered over its grimy, tumbledown neighbors. It was the only building in eyesight with a covered porch and gambrel-style roof. The sun seemed to clasp the structure in its golden arms; yet at the same time, the house was shrouded in shadow.

As I took stock of the place, the wheezy strains of an accordion reached my ears. Its player was an old woman so slight I feared the instrument strapped to her chest would drag her to the dirt. She marched solemnly, accompanied by a five-foot brown bear balancing on hind paws. Unlike the tragic illustrations of performing European bears I'd seen in the *Britannica*, however, this proud animal—her fur a blend of copper, henna, and chestnut—was neither muzzled nor tethered to the accordionist by rope or chain. As they passed me, the glorious creature opened wide her red mouth and released a thunderous roar that struck me as joyous, and full of mirth.

"My stars," I murmured.

I climbed brick steps to the porch and tugged the bell cord. Laughter rang out as though I'd called it forth with my ringing, and the purple door swung inward.

"Yes?"

A remarkably tall man whose dark skin was underlit with amber stood in the doorframe, eyeing me through wire-rimmed spectacles. He wore a jacket and waistcoat, and his close-cropped graying hair glittered like February frost.

"Can I help you, Miss?"

"I hope so," I said. "I'm looking for . . ."

But I wasn't sure what I was looking for. I'd imagined this scene scores of times; however, now that the moment to announce my intentions had arrived, my mind was a blank slate.

"My name," I said instead, "is Sylvie Swift."

A tiny wave of discovery, recognition, or understanding washed over the man's face. "Swift?"

I nodded.

His gaze raked me slowly, from braids to boots. I glanced down and saw that in spite of my efforts, mud crusted my skirt at the hem. I hefted my dress, discovered mud caking my petticoats, crinoline, boots. Sweat trickled into my eyes, stinging them, as I shifted my haversack from one hand to the other, transferred my weight from foot to foot. Into my mind tumbled an image of Silas and me posed before the butcher shop window in Whitley Courthouse, staring hungrily at an inverted lamb hanging from a hook.

Just then a figure materialized beside the man—a woman so dainty and vibrant I briefly mistook her for some mix of human and bird. She wore a robe embroidered with Chinese characters and fire-breathing dragons. Glimpses of corn-silk hair peeked from beneath the federal kepi angled jauntily on her head.

"Who do we have here?" she asked.

"This girl," the man replied, "says she's Sylvie Swift."

The woman rose to her toes. "Sylvie?"

I nodded.

Like a petite comet, she shot over the threshold and embraced me. I was enveloped in her scent—rose oil, vanilla extract, and talc—shot through with notes that quickened my pulse: apple brandy, and sulfur.

"I'll be tarred and feathered!" she cried. "Sylvie!"

"Forgive me," I said, "but have we met?"

Laughing, she extended a hand. "Forgive *me*. I'm Ginny, and this here is Doc."

"Pleased to meet you." I shook her tiny hand. "Apologies for my appearance. I've been on the Cumberland three days."

"I'm sure you'd like to change."

"Yes."

"A room is ready for you. Once you've rested, I'll introduce you to the others."

"Others?"

"The other girls. And Evangeline, our fearless leader."

As Ginny steered me over the threshold into the cool, dim interior of the house, I shook my head. "There must be some mistake," I said. "No one knew I was coming. Well, no one but my brother, and he's in Alabama."

"Silas?"

I nodded. "But how do you know his name?"

Ginny smiled. "We've been expecting you, Sylvie."

I thought, immediately, of your aunt Marina. "How is that possible?" I asked.

"How is anything possible?"

We stood in a spacious foyer, and I studied the carpet—a Persian rug depicting Eve's transgression in the Garden of Eden. I took in the twelve-foot ceilings, aquamarine velvet-papered walls, gilt-edged mirrors, brass wall sconces, and framed, fleshy nudes—copies of paintings by Botticelli and Rubens, masterworks I'd encountered in art history books. Through the wide doorframe we faced, I spied the curved lines of Queen Anne furniture: crushed-velvet divans, lacquered tables, cushioned chairs. The wine-colored walls were hung with mirrors of various silhouettes and sizes, and against the far wall stood a wooden counter with tall stools. At a table tucked into a corner, three women played a game of billiards. Unbound hair streamed down their backs, and they wore glittering, vividly colored dresses—fitted to their legs and hemmed to midcalf. A pair of women perched on stools before the counter, naked but for pantalets, chemises, and stockings. One used a tiny brush to line the other's lids with black liquid.

"Are they real?" I asked.

Ginny laughed lightly at my question. "Well, of course!"

"Who are they?"

"Depends who you ask." She jerked a thumb at Doc. "He calls them Priestesses."

I glanced at Doc, and again, a ripple rolled over his impassive features.

"What do you call them?" I asked.

Ginny smiled. "My Sisters."

"What do others call them?"

"I'm afraid most people," she sighed, "call us whores."

The Daily Press
Monday, September 29, 1862

CITY OF 10,000 WHORES

NASHVILLE, TENNESSEE—THERE CAN no longer be any doubt—the Confederate Secret Service is at work in Nashville. Guerrillas harass guardsmen, steal rations, free criminals, and operate black markets. In addition, both morphine and quinine are disappearing from Union hospitals at an alarming rate.

But another force is afoot in our city—one that's even more insidious. Our hospitals hold twice as many soldiers suffering from syphilis as from battle-related injuries. If the infection rate continues apace, depleted federal forces will stand no chance against the Rebels. Nashville is already known, in some circles, as the "City of 10,000 Whores," and whether or not public women are deliberately infecting our Union protectors with the byproduct of their immoral trade, they *are* contributing to the real possibility of a final Confederate victory.

I am not the first, nor shall I be the last, to urge Nashville's provost marshal—Lieutenant Colonel George Spalding—to shut down the brothels that proliferate in the riverfront district known as "Smokey Row." To cut this pox—this "French disease"—off at the source!

A short time after I met Doc and Ginny, I stood in a third-floor bedroom wondering what I'd gotten myself into. The decor and furnishings were all white—lace curtains, quilt, braided rag rug, dresser and washstand and iron bedframe. Pastel flowers adorned the wallpaper. The room reeked of innocence, and I tried to reconcile it with Ginny's last statement.

Most people call us whores.

The door behind me opened, and I turned to find my brother fixed in the frame. Not as I'd last seen him; this was your uncle Silas at seven years old.

"Silas?" I shook my head. "How on earth?"

The boy raced forward, flung spindly arms round me as though he'd long awaited my return. I stood there—hands in the air, unsure where to put them. Part of me wanted to pick him up; another part wanted to shove the unnatural child away, grab my haversack, run from the house—back down Broad Street to the wharf—and fling myself into the mighty, muddy Cumberland.

"Silas?" I said again. He tilted up his face, and I saw that though the boy resembled my brother, there were differences. His hair wasn't dark but a sandy shade of blond, and his nose was dusted with freckles, whereas my twin, at that age, had had none. And though in better light I would realize his eyes were a rare shade of violet, at that moment they resembled black holes. I marveled at the boy's costume—a rose-red tunic and trousers, sewed of a silken fabric better suited to a camisole, wrapper, or petticoat.

"Forgive me." I lowered my hands. "Of course you're not Silas."

The boy plumbed a pocket, extracted a notepad and pencil stub. He jotted something down, passed the pad to me.

I am Apollo Swift.

"Swift?" I said. "Your name is *Swift?*"

He nodded.

"My stars," I whispered. "Marina!"

But at that moment, someone rapped on the doorframe.

"Come in," I said automatically.

Doc's impassive face appeared. "Miss Price wants to see you, girl."

"Miss Price?"

"Evangeline Price," he said. "She runs this show."

* * *

Once I'd changed into my blue-and-gray-checked calico and washed the grime from my hands and face, Doc escorted me to Evangeline Price's second-floor rooms. The tall man held himself straight as a lance, and from behind, Doc's shoulders looked exceptionally broad. I also noted a jagged scar that began low on his left cheek, then curved around the entirety of his neck—not unlike the tail of a shooting star.

The sun still shone, but Miss Price's shuttered suite was lit by oil lamps. Evangeline sat at a rosewood desk—her ample bosom at rest on its surface, cluttered with glass bottles and jars in every imaginable shape and color, not to mention such disparate objects as a spyglass, a pair of wrist cuffs, a sextant, a model of a Spanish galleon inside a jug, and an enormous pair of forceps—beckoning me forward. I moved as near the table as allowed by my petticoats and crinoline and bowed myself into a right angle.

"Come closer, little sister," she said. "I never bite unless I'm asked."

Even at close range, it was impossible to guess Evangeline's age. Copper-toned curls erupted around her plump, unlined face. Her pupils were lost in sky-blue irises, causing her eyes to gleam in the room's murk like those of an animal—something that might have torn to shreds the lace-edged handkerchief she used to wick sweat from her brow. And I imagined, for an instant, that her cheeks bore marks resembling a leopard's spots.

"I take it," she said, shooing me into a wing chair, "that you received the *Apocrypha*."

"I did."

She leaned forward. "Is it safe?"

"Oh yes," I said. "It's in my haversack upstairs. But why on earth did you send it?"

"Those were my directions."

"I thought you were in charge here."

She opened a box—teakwood, inlaid with the letters *E* and *P*, in scrolled ivory—plucked out a cheroot and a box of matches. I'd never seen nail varnish, and I was startled by Miss Price's bloodred fingertips.

"I run this place," she said, "but I take my directions from a Higher Power."

I shook my head. "I don't understand."

Keeping one eye on my face, Evangeline shuttered the other, struck a match, lit her cheroot. "Tell me," she said, exhaling a white plume, "did Apollo find you?"

"He did," I said. "For a moment, I thought he was my brother."

"Yes." She smiled. "Now that you're here, I can see the resemblance."

"He said his name is *Swift*."

"Apollo is your nephew."

My mouth was suddenly as dry as sawdust, and though I opened it, no sound came. I saw the boy—whom I'd guessed to be seven or eight—and recalled the morning eight years earlier when I woke to find that your aunt Marina had vanished without a trace.

Evangeline nodded.

"Here?" I glanced around, as though my sister were hidden in some cranny, waiting to leap out and yell *surprise!* "Marina is here?"

"Yes and no." Evangeline touched the coppery chignon at the nape of her neck. Scratched her nose. "Even when she's not physically among us, Marina Swift is with us."

"Please," I said, my heart in my throat. "If my sister's here, I want to see her."

"You *will* see her. All in good time."

I studied an oil painting that hung behind Evangeline. From the depths of a stormy seascape burst a creature with the face of a woman—silvery hair streaming and corkscrewing—and the long, glistening body of a whale. This shocking hybrid, complete with flukes, fins, and blowhole, was lit from the front, as though by limelight. Looking more closely, I saw a smaller version of the monster swimming alongside her—a whale-girl, her offspring. Spread over the same wall was a cluster of framed photographs of women of every size, shape, and hue—women with long braids, women wearing headdresses or scarves, women with no hair at all; women dressed as sparring pugilists; women dressed as shepherdesses and queens, as ghosts and harem girls; women wrapped in diaphanous robes and women wearing nothing at all—arranged around a wooden cuckoo clock shaped like a chalet.

"Miss Price," I said, "who are you? And the women downstairs?"

"Soldiers," she said, her voice humming with fervor. "Warriors embroiled in an ancient battle. One that's been waging for millennia."

"Ginny said you were whores."

"We're only *acting* like whores."

"Acting."

She nodded. "Pretending."

"I see," I said, though I didn't, at least not yet.

"And you." A smile spread like a flame over Evangeline's features. "Who are *you*, Sylvie Swift?"

Apprehension wrapped its arms around me, and I shook my head. "Why did you leave your Kentucky home?" she asked. "Why did you sail down the Cumberland to this war-torn city?"

A selection of answers rotated through my mind. *Because I am lonely. Because I could not live without my siblings. Because I killed my mother. Because I was relieved by the violent death of my father. Because I have no purpose. Because I don't fit anywhere. Because I've never, since the day I was born, been able to keep still.*

I shook my head again. "I don't know."

"You came," Evangeline said, rising and circling her desk, discharging a mist of white, "because we need you. You were always already a member of our company, my dear. From the day you were born, you've been playing your part."

Cuc-koo. Cuc-koo.

Her cuckoo clock was the first I'd encountered, and I cried out as a mechanized bird emerged from the chalet to squawk the hour.

"That's your cue to exit." Miss Price pulled me to my feet, led me toward the door. "Rest well tonight, Sylvie, for tomorrow your work begins in earnest."

I thought of the glittering women I'd seen downstairs, playing billiards and painting their faces. I thought of Mary Magdalene, Doll Tearsheet, Moll Flanders, and other prostitutes I'd met in the books with which I'd stocked our shelves at Mrs. Marigold's boardinghouse, and my underarms grew damp. "My work?"

As Evangeline smiled, her canines glinted in the lamplight. "The *Apocrypha*, little sister. Your work on the play's translation."

* * *

My first night in Nashville, I slept hard for two hours then woke with a start. In a dream, I'd been chased down winding corridors by creatures swathed in red cloaks. I ended up inside a metallic tube, pressed tight against the bodies of strangers, as the vessel began filling with water. The icy liquid seeped upward—feet, calves, knees, thighs. When it reached my waist, I shrieked myself awake. It took me a moment to recall how I'd shifted my life. I was no longer in the Kentucky boardinghouse that had been my home since infancy. I was in a room on the third floor of the Land of the Sirens—as I would later learn Evangeline Price's establishment was locally known.

Sitting up, I strained to detect the place's nighttime sounds. I rose, padded to the door, cracked it, but in place of what I expected to hear—dozens of voices speaking, cursing, laughing; up-tempo music; a raucous celebration; clink of glassware; tattoo of bootheels against floorboards—I heard nothing. Not just silence, but a vast, unending void. From the depths of this abyss crept a sound that drew me back to Whitley Courthouse, back to Mrs. Marigold's boardinghouse, back to my childhood bed.

A song.

The lullaby your aunt Marina once sang to me and Silas, to slide us toward slumber. Scores of female voices singing my sister's song as one, in a language I still did not understand. The longer I stood listening to the melodious multivoiced utterance, the sleepier I grew.

I dragged my body back, collapsed on the bed. Before I touched the mattress, I was under.

*　*　*

I woke the next morning to the face of Apollo, dangling like a star over my bed.

"Good morning," I said.

I opened the folded sheet of paper the boy handed me and discovered a drawing of a city rising from a shimmering body of water—a great lake, perhaps, or some enclosed bay. The city's buildings were tinted a wild assortment of colors, with vibrant flags snapping from balconies.

In lieu of streets, Apollo's city was crisscrossed with streams, rivulets, and canals, dotted with boat traffic, spanned by a series of elegantly curving bridges. The illustration was done in charcoal and pastel, and I was astonished by its intricate beauty.

"This is yours?" I asked Apollo. "You drew this?"

Pointing to his chest, he nodded, and I saw hints of Marina, as well as our mother: his chin, his widow's peak, his upturned nose. Today he wore yellow trousers and a shirt made of lavender taffeta.

"It's lovely, Apollo. But where are the people?"

He shrugged. Pointed to the bedside table, where he'd placed, on a wooden tray, a bowl of cornmeal mush, a linen napkin, and a steaming mug of coffee someone had sweetened with cinnamon. When I turned back, the boy was closing the door behind him.

Once I'd eaten and dressed, blonde Ginny of the dragon-embroidered robe appeared, told me to gather the *Apocrypha*, the translation of the play I'd worked on in Whitley Courthouse, and my French-English dictionary. She led me down the brothel's main staircase, whose banister was etched with symbols I was sure would tell a story, if properly arranged—bear, mountain, ship, lion, arrow, sun, quiver, bull, chariot, waves, coffin, bee, book, repeat—past the parlor I'd glimpsed the day before, with Queen Anne furniture and wine-colored walls. This was the Great Room, and my eyes were drawn to its most ostentatious feature—a crystal chandelier that, rumor had it, once hung at Versailles. Ginny led me past the Great Room, down a hall to a chamber furnished with a square piano—rosewood, with carved pedestal base—and a writing desk. Positioned against one wall were a dozen straight-back chairs.

"Don't just stand there gaping, girl. Time's a-wasting."

Doc was seated at the piano. Sunlight pierced the room's tall windows, whose velvet draperies were thrust aside, and caught the lenses of his wire-rimmed spectacles. Even as I moved toward him—even when I stood beside his piano—Doc seemed a blind man, with blank eyes.

"Sorry," I said.

"Have a seat." He indicated the writing desk. "Let's get started."

I sat. Arranged the *Apocrypha*, my translation-in-progress, and the dictionary on the table before me.

"Are you ready?" he asked.

"For what?"

"To work."

"Sure," I said, trying to hide my confusion.

Doc rang a sea-green handbell whose neck resembled the tail of a fish, and a whirring sounded to my rear—as though several large, winged creatures had entered the chamber and were landing on the Persian rug. I spun around and was startled to find the straight-back chairs occupied by a dozen sleepy-looking women—some of Ginny's Sisters, I assumed, or Doc's Priestesses. Women with fire-red curls or inky waves or straight blonde tresses. Women with fair skin; women whose complexions resembled molten bronze, terra-cotta statuary, honeycombs, or the ebony keys on Doc's piano. Women with freckles, moles, or birthmarks. Women with voluminous breasts and wide hips; women whose bodies might have belonged to prepubescent boys. They all wore nightwear—silk chemises and pantalets in a variety of shades, lacy robes and feathered slippers, scarves round their heads. Their eyelids were plump and their faces sleep-creased; as I watched, a yawn passed through them like a summer cold.

"Hello." I nodded at the assembly. "I'm Sylvie Swift."

"They know who you are," said Doc. "We're not here to socialize."

"What are we here for?"

"This."

Doc struck the opening chord of a song that felt both exotic and familiar. The women behind me began to sing, and the Music Room fell away. The lyrics were foreign to me, but as the minutes ticked by, I was able to pick out a phrase here and there. I opened my French-English dictionary, took up my pencil, scanned the opening lines of the antique playscript I'd received in the mail, as well as the first page of the fumbling translation I'd worked on in Whitley Courthouse. The melodic strains that seeped from Doc's piano twined with the haunting threads of the women's voices and caught fire in the air before me. Sections of my translation were illumed by a strange glow, and I saw errors I'd made, shades of meaning I'd failed to capture in my first clumsy attempts at reconstruction. I was able to visualize the *Apocrypha*—characters, settings—and step inside the story.

"My stars," I murmured. "How have I been so blind?"

Suspended within the ancient comedy—like a butterfly pinned to a specimen board—I picked up my pencil and went to work.

APOCRYPHA
BY ARISTOPHANES OF ATHENS
CIRCA 386 BC

DRAMATIS PERSONAE

APOCRYPHA

EUDORA

HARMONIA

JACINTA

IRIS

KHLOE

EPHESIAN GUARDSMEN

TIMON

ARTEMIS

APOLLO

MAGISTRATE

ENVOY

CHORUS OF CRONES/CHAOS

SCENE ONE

APOCRYPHA *is alone, pacing naked before the Artemision—the Temple of Artemis at Ephesus.* EUDORA *enters downstage right, spies her friend, hurries over, and throws a cloak around her.*

EUDORA

Apocrypha? What in the name of the goddesses twain are you doing here at this time of night? Or should I say morning?

APOCRYPHA

Oh, Eudora! I am in a state.

EUDORA

Sit yourself down! You're shaking like a leaf in a high wind, sweet friend, and I cannot walk a straight line.

APOCRYPHA

Did you enjoy yourself at the bacchanal?

EUDORA

From what I can recall. After I drank six Ephesian guardsmen under the table, the night becomes something of a blur. But that is no matter; tell me what has befallen *you!* What events led to me finding my kind, timid friend wandering naked in the harsh predawn air?

APOCRYPHA

I hardly know where to begin. I was in bed—asleep but somehow also awake—when the temperature of my sleeping chamber plummeted. I sat up and discovered a cloaked figure looming over my couch. This being threw off its murky wrap, and there stood the deathless Goddess Artemis herself!

EUDORA

You must be joking.

APOCRYPHA

I speak the truth, Eudora. Artemis stood twelve feet tall, and her skin was all aglitter. She wore the mural crown that represents the walls of our city-state, and dotting her torso were dozens of globular bees' eggs. The Mistress of Wild Beasts was accompanied by a lion, a brown bear, a bull, and a cloud of buzzing bees.

EUDORA

Unreal!

APOCRYPHA

I bowed my head, but deathless Artemis bade me lift it. She instructed me to look into her glowing eyes and heed her words. *I have a job for you, Apocrypha*, she said. *You are going to lead a rebellion.*

EUDORA

A *rebellion*? You?

APOCRYPHA

(nods) Artemis went on: *Because Greece is governed by men— who see life as a winner-take-all proposition—her city-states and colonies have been embroiled in civil wars for over two decades. We on Mount Olympus grow weary of this interminable fighting. First the winds blow one way, then the other, but the battling goes on with no end in sight. I have devised a plan to put a stop to the endless wars. While your husbands and brothers, uncles and cousins and lovers are busy fighting each other, Apocrypha, I want the women of Athens and Ephesus, of Corinth and Smyrna, of Lesbos and Thebes, to rise up and seize control of Greece.*

EUDORA

I cannot believe it.

APOCRYPHA

I can hardly believe it, and it happened to me.

EUDORA

But why would the Mistress of Wild Beasts come to *you*? We have been bosom friends since childhood and devotees of Artemis since that time, but I cannot see you leading a revolution! Forgive me, Apocrypha, but you have trouble asking someone to pass the salt.

APOCRYPHA

You are right, Eudora. I am not worldly, bold, or strong. I spend all my time reading comedy, philosophy, or verse, living in one fantasy world or another. I have never known a man nor drunk wine to excess. And I asked Artemis that very question. *A woman like my friend Eudora*, I said, *who can drink men under the table and wears out her husband every night, she is surely the kind of woman you want.*

EUDORA

How did she respond?

APOCRYPHA

No, my child, said the Great Goddess. *Eudora will aid you, but you are the vessel I have patiently awaited. You have long dwelled in shadow, but the time has come to drag all the shades out, into the light. The moon may not be as blinding as the sun, but every one of us needs it. If not for its quiet, dark places, the world could not exist. You possess woman's greatest assets in abundance, Apocrypha, and you are the one to lead this fight.*

EUDORA

Did she mention how in the name of the goddesses twain she expects us to wrest control away from our menfolk?

APOCRYPHA

In order to trick them into submission, Artemis said, *every respectable woman of Greece will be called upon to masquerade as a whore.*

EUDORA

Outrageous! The noblewomen of Greece *love* a bacchanal, love getting blind drunk on wine and rutting until the break of dawn, but I think they will draw the line at disguising themselves as streetwalkers!

APOCRYPHA

I agree. Artemis, however, said that while men are difficult to overpower physically, they are quite easy to overpower using one's wits.

EUDORA

She has a point there.

APOCRYPHA

The Mistress of Wild Beasts then ordered me to rise from my couch, cast off my nightdress, and walk the streets of Ephesus until I arrived at the doors of the Artemision. So I did. Dear Eudora, will you help me? I do not think I can accomplish what deathless Artemis has asked of me on my own!

EUDORA

Without hesitation! After all, sweet Apocrypha, what are friends for?

SCENE TWO

A CHORUS OF CRONES *lounges on the steps of the Ephesian Citadel, scrutinizing passersby, white heads bobbing.*

CHORUS OF CRONES

Look at these silly creatures—women—walking the streets as though they matter, as though the Gods have given them a single thought! This one is married with five sons and wears a dress that makes no secret of her assets. This one believes herself benevolent, gives coin to all Ephesian charities, yet in private beats her servants! And this one was just acquitted of plotting with her brother-in-law to kill her own sister, though the whole of Ephesus knows her to be guilty. These fools believe they are unique, think they are discreet, but they are wrong. Woman is one great mass—a hydra—a single body with untold heads, untold limbs, all composing one empty vessel. A repository for kings and commoners, for the deathless Gods, for the whole world. A dank recess, rich soil in which to plant things we do not want to see, things we do not care to understand. A place to bury sins, sorrows, horror—the things we cannot face.

Consider us—the Crones of Ephesus! Once upon a time, we were virgins, and we were newlyweds. We were teachers, and we were lovers. We were young and ripe and dewy-eyed, and we were heavy with child after child. We were friends, mothers, daughters. We were priestesses and

devotees, concubines and whores. What are we now? Brittle
bones, sagging skin, dark spots, thinning hair, cloudy minds,
bitter hearts. We are ready for the trash heap, and once we've
gone, history will rake time over us like a dirt coverlet.

But look now! A band of ragtag women approaches. Let
us watch and listen.

APOCRYPHA, EUDORA, *and a battalion of scantily clad women enter the
scene and sashay toward the Ephesian Citadel.*

CHORUS

Dressed as streetwalkers who think themselves courtesans,
but that one is married to a midlevel magistrate! That one is
a teacher, and that one a widow with two children, and I see
three priestesses of Artemis. And look who marches at their
head, as though leading them into battle. Poor Apocrypha,
who as a child watched her father butcher her mother and
slit his own throat. Neighbors found the girl two days later,
clinging to her father's corpse, blood drenching her clothes,
her small face. An aunt took the child in, and Apocrypha
has lived quietly, meekly ever since. So what in the name of
the goddesses twain is this maid up to, marching at the head
of a band of false whores?

EUDORA

Iris my dear! I never knew how shapely your legs were. And
those tits!

IRIS

You're one to talk, Eudora. I would devour my children for
such a waspish waist!

EUDORA

But Apocrypha, you outdo us all. You are a vision!

APOCRYPHA

A vision?

JACINTA

Your breasts are like overgrown olives!

KHLOE

Your ass is a ripe peach!

HARMONIA

Let me put it this way, sweet Apocrypha: I am not a man, but you are giving me a hard-on all the same!

APOCRYPHA

Ladies, please! We are *acting* like whores, yes, but we must not *behave* that way, or begin to think of ourselves that way. Remember our purpose. Remember the benevolent Mistress of Wild Beasts, she who has given us our command!

EUDORA

Perhaps we should review the plan. Listen up, you at the back! Iris and Jacinta! I see you draining that wineskin! Do not get so drunk that you fall on your faces! Otherwise we'll abandon you out here with these decrepit crones who guard the steps of the citadel day and night, these ancient busybodies who critique all who dare to pass.

CHORUS

Watch yourself Eudora, daughter of Markos! Forget not the awesome power of the crone!

APOCRYPHA

Ladies, ladies! The changing of the guard is upon us, when all Ephesian guardsmen assemble in the guardhouse. It is nearly time for us to wheedle our way inside, and from there, to carry out our grand plan.

The women of APOCRYPHA'S *army hike up their dresses, stick out their legs, shake their hips, and wave their arms at the windows of the guardhouse above.*

EUDORA

Guardsmen! Yoo-hoo! Come to the window and consider our wares! We have long legs and ripe, bouncing breasts, asses and cunts aplenty, and we are aflame with desire for you!

APOCRYPHA

We know how hard you work, sweet guardsmen! We know your wives, your girlfriends, even your boyfriends do not understand you!

JACINTA

But *we* do! And we swear on the flawless white tits of Aphrodite that if you let us in, we will show you how thoroughly, how *deeply* we understand you. If you let us in, we can tend to all of you at once!

GUARD ONE

What's the rumpus?

GUARD TWO

Who disturbs the Ephesian guard?

HARMONIA

Down here, guardsmen! We'd like to come up and disturb you further!

GUARD ONE

You are a fine-looking flock of women, but Ephesus is at war! We guardsmen must remain vigilant. We cannot leave our posts.

KHLOE

You do not have to—we will come to you! If you let us up, we will take care of every last one of you. Make your wildest and most disturbing fantasies come true!

GUARD TWO

Females are not allowed in the guardhouse! This is where we plan attacks and design strategies, where we test weapons and perform feats of strength and tell tales of sexual exploits.

GUARD ONE

What harm can they do? They are only women, and whores at that. Lord knows we could use a break.

APOCRYPHA

You will not regret it, sweet guardsmen.

SCENE THREE

The wildflower-dotted slopes of Mount Olympus. ARTEMIS *and* APOLLO *sit across from one another, playing a game of Petteia.*

APOLLO

Where is your head, Artemis? I've never beaten you at Petteia, yet I am in possession of nearly all your pebbles.

ARTEMIS

Forgive me. I cannot stop thinking about Ephesus.

APOLLO

Ephesus? That provincial backwater?

ARTEMIS

I know you have no love for Ephesus, brother, but that does not change the fact that Ephesians worship me as their patron goddess.

APOLLO

Worship you? How can they worship one they understand so little? Like Arcadians—who call you *Queen of the Nymphs*—and Taurians, who think you sated only by human sacrifice—Ephesians do not even acknowledge that we are siblings. They do not believe you helped Leto give birth to me!

ARTEMIS

What difference does that make? You know I do not mind being worshipped by different peoples in various ways.

APOLLO

I do, and it's something I will never understand about you, sister: your versatility.

ARTEMIS

Others will see us as they see us, Apollo. Trying to control one's image is a waste of time and energy. You regard flexibility and patience as weaknesses, but I regard them as strengths.

APOLLO

Too true. In any case, tell me what's happening at Ephesus, to draw your attention away from our game.

ARTEMIS

A young woman there is, at this very moment, leading a rebellion in my name.

APOLLO

What sort of rebellion?

ARTEMIS

The women of Ephesus have ambushed the Ephesian guardsmen. They've sent emissaries to all the Greek city-states and protectorates, instructing the women of those locales to follow the same path.

APOLLO

What path is that?

ARTEMIS

They've disguised themselves as streetwalkers, charmed their way inside the citadel, locked the guardsmen naked in a cell, and seized power.

APOLLO

(Laughs) O irony! That this is happening at Ephesus, home of the satirical poet Hipponax, who wrote that *there are two days when a woman is a pleasure: the day one marries her and the day one carries out her dead body!*

ARTEMIS

Must you always bring up Hipponax?

APOLLO

Forgive me, Artemis. In any case, your plan for the women of Ephesus sounds like a clever one!

ARTEMIS

I agree, brother. The problem is, the plan is not mine.

APOLLO

No?

ARTEMIS

Someone took on my guise and visited a young woman named Apocrypha—a girl who's been worshipping at the Artemision and making sacrifices to me since she was a child—and instructed her to take these measures.

APOLLO

Lord Zeus! Do you know who's responsible?

ARTEMIS

I have interrogated each of the deathless gods—Athena and Aphrodite, Hermes and Hephaestus and Hera, even our unruly father Zeus—but none of them is the perpetrator of this masquerade.

APOLLO

I see.

ARTEMIS

Which brings me to you.

APOLLO

Me?

ARTEMIS

You, my twin. You, who knows me better than any other, who can not only peer inside my mind but also imitate me flawlessly. Apollo, the deathless god of prophecy and poetry and light. Tell me, brother: Did you take my form and visit Apocrypha? Did you instruct the girl to lead a rebellion, to take control of Ephesus and urge the rest of Greece's women to do the same?

APOLLO

Artemis, I tell you truly: It was not me who visited Apocrypha.

ARTEMIS

You are certain?

APOLLO

Here. Gaze into my heart.

ARTEMIS

(Closes eyes) Yes, I see that you speak the truth. I apologize for suspecting you.

APOLLO

No apology needed! I have done far worse for less!

ARTEMIS

And *that* is precisely what puzzles me, brother: Who stands to gain from this particular deception? Apocrypha is a touching case. She witnessed the slaying of her mother at the hands of her father, and she has not mixed much with her fellows. Apocrypha is not particularly pretty or witty, not particularly fetching or talented. She is, for all intents and purposes, something of a dud.

APOLLO

And you're certain that Zeus is not involved? At times his taste in women verges on the inexplicable.

ARTEMIS

(Sighs) Our father is innocent. Ten witnesses place him with a certain dryad in the top of an oak at the time Apocrypha was visited.

APOLLO

Well. Have you considered checking with our more distant forebears?

ARTEMIS

Distant? Oh Apollo! Do you think it possible?

APOLLO

It's worth looking into. The Titans have been known to do far worse for absolutely nothing. And you *know* how they feel about being imprisoned in Tartarus. Our progenitors would do anything to be free, to unseat we Olympians, to hold dominion over the world again. And I'd wager that at least one among them is capable of hatching a scheme that would take advantage of you, sister dear, and your acolyte Apocrypha.

ARTEMIS

Thank you, brother. I must act on your suspicions immediately!

APOLLO

But Artemis! Our game is not finished.

ARTEMIS

Let's call this one in your favor. I hereby gift you this game of Petteia.

SCENE FOUR

Interior of the guardroom at the Ephesian Citadel. A table surrounded by chairs stands upstage. Center stage is a large cell, filled with naked men sleeping fitfully. APOCRYPHA *creeps close to the cage, peers in.*

APOCRYPHA

(Softly) Poor things.

TIMON

(Rasping) Water. Please.

APOCRYPHA *fills a cup from a bucket, carries it to the cell, and hands it to the guardsman* TIMON, *who drinks greedily.*

TIMON

More. Please.

APOCRYPHA

(Fills the cup again) Here.

TIMON

Thank you. You are terribly kind.

APOCRYPHA

I am no such thing.

TIMON

I can no longer feel my legs.

APOCRYPHA

That's not my problem.

TIMON

Might you release me? Just for a moment? So I might get the blood flowing again?

APOCRYPHA

I'm afraid that is impossible.

TIMON

Is it?

APOCRYPHA

Yes.

TIMON

Are you certain?

APOCRYPHA

Yes.

TIMON

Even if I beg? Even if I weep?

APOCRYPHA

Yes.

TIMON

Well. Thank you for the water.

APOCRYPHA

Here (pulls out key). I will release you *briefly*. You must not run or try to overpower me, and you must allow me to guide you back to your cell in five minutes.

TIMON

Yes.

APOCRYPHA

Do you swear to follow my instructions?

TIMON

By the deathless river-god Caystrus, I will obey.

JEN FAWKES

APOCRYPHA *opens the cell door, and* **TIMON** *steps out. She hands him a* *blanket to cover his nudity.*

> **TIMON**
>
> Thank you. What's your name?
>
> **APOCRYPHA**
>
> Apocrypha.
>
> **TIMON**
>
> I am Timon.
>
> **APOCRYPHA**
>
> Remember your oath, Timon.
>
> **TIMON**
>
> I remember.
>
> **APOCRYPHA**
>
> Come. Let's spend your respite outside. The night is quite beautiful.
>
> **TIMON**
>
> As you wish, Apocrypha.

Encyclopaedia Britannica
Eighth Edition (1860)
Volume 14, Magnetism–MIH, p. 339

MASQUERADE (Ital. *Mascherata*, Fr. *Mascarade*), a species of amusement, common to most civilized countries, in which persons of both sexes mask or disguise themselves, and engage in dancing, festivities, and miscellaneous conversation.

Thursday, June 7, 1877
Monterey, CA

A week after I arrived in Nashville, I located the Adelphi Theatre. The Adelphi, you'll recall, is where your grandfather Horatio first laid eyes on your grandmother Brigitte, during a production of *The Taming of the Shrew* in which she played Bianca—a dazzling, fun-loving girl who cannot marry until her shrewish older sister, Katherina, is shackled to a man of her own. Situated at the corner of Cherry and Washington Streets, the Adelphi was only a few blocks from the Land of the Sirens.

Italianate in style with bas-relief Ionic columns punctuating three sets of gold-trimmed, stained-glass doors and an arched, two-story entrance, the Adelphi was known not only for the quality of its productions, but also for its ability to attract up-and-coming stars of the American theater. After inspecting its imposing edifice, I studied a series of advertising posters, stopping before one that featured a woman clothed in pale blue, poised on a balcony draped in flowering vines. Beneath the portico, a man knelt on a blanket of riotous purple blooms.

"Romeo and Juliet."

I turned to find yellow-haired Ginny standing behind me, surrounded by a half dozen of her Sisters, or Doc's Priestesses. Their frocks—sewed of rich fabrics in exotic shades with fitted skirts and plummeting necklines—set them apart from the modest, darkly dressed wives and shopkeepers hurrying past the Adelphi, toting baskets and parcels. With Ginny was Harriet, a six-foot brunette with kinky hair; and Pearl, a pink-cheeked girl who wore braids and coughed incessantly, as though suffering from a wasting illness. Also present were Lisette, a Louisiana Creole with coal-black curls, whose grand mere was said to have been a voodoo priestess; and Jeanette, a languid, pouty blonde who seemed eternally in need of a fainting couch.

"Yes," I said. "Are you familiar with the story?"

Ginny nodded. "I once knew a john who dressed me up as Juliet and had me perform that blasted balcony scene with him. We must have done it a hundred times! *Deny thy father and refuse thy name, or if thou wilt not, be but sworn my love, and I will no longer be a Capulet.*"

"Was he an actor?"

She shook her head. "A priest."

Once Ginny and her Sisters fluttered away, I turned back to the poster, read the print beneath the image:

WILLIAM SHAKESPEARE'S

ROMEO AND JULIET

OPENS IN TWO WEEKS

FEATURING **JOHN WILKES BOOTH** IN THE ROLE OF MERCUTIO

UPPER BOX $10 / LOWER BOX $6

ORCHESTRA $1 / DRESS CIRCLE 75 CENTS / FAMILY CIRCLE 25 CENTS

MATINEE 2 P.M. / EVENING 7 P.M.

In the autumn of 1863, Booth's older brother Edwin was among the most acclaimed actors in the nation, but this was the first time I'd heard of John Wilkes. Though I'd read scores of playscripts, I'd never had an opportunity to attend a live theatrical performance, and, brimming with anticipation, I resolved to attend a performance of *Romeo and Juliet*.

Pivoting away from the poster, I was faced with this impossible sight: a black-and-white cart horse dangling ten feet above the traffic streaming along Cherry Street, against the clouded sky. "My stars," I said, as a man in shirtsleeves and a flat cap exited the Adelphi and darted into the dirt street. Pausing beneath the levitating animal, he looked both ways.

The horse wasn't flying, of course; it had died of exhaustion, and a dozen members of the Army of the Cumberland's engineering corps—the Pioneer Brigade—were attempting to collect the animal using a low-slung ox-drawn wagon that featured a stout angled beam, a system of ropes and pulleys, and a winch—a truck designed for the removal of dead beasts of burden from city streets.

But something went awry as the man in the flat cap halted beneath the carcass, and the wagon's stout fulcrum splintered, snapped. A thunderous crack sounded, twelve hundred pounds of horseflesh plummeted, and the man vanished. A crowd was gathering, but if not for an arm protruding from the beast's underside, and a burgeoning pond of crimson, I would have thought I'd imagined the poor soul.

Periodically lifting my gaze—for any sign of a dead horse—I hurried away from the Adelphi.

* * *

A few weeks later, Evangeline Price introduced me to a man who would cast a shadow over the rest of this history—as he loomed large in Nashville throughout the Union occupation. Before landing in Tennessee, William Truesdail lived in New York, Pennsylvania, Panama, Texas, Louisiana, and Missouri, and worked as an indentured merchant, a deputy sheriff, a real estate speculator, a bank teller, a railroad contractor, a police officer, a beef merchant, and a mail carrier.

Truesdail was a Union man through and through, and after he supplied Ulysses S. Grant's army with prime beef, he was appointed military superintendent of the North Missouri Railroad and given charge of the police as well as the mail. Eventually General William Rosecrans conferred on William Truesdail the title of chief of the Secret Service with the Army of the Cumberland, and from that time forward—though he had no military standing—he was referred to as "Colonel Truesdail." Which is what Evangeline instructed me to call him before I met him in November of 1862.

"In truth, the man is a fraud," Evangeline said around her cheroot. "But unfortunately, we need Colonel Truesdail."

"Who needs him?" I asked.

She gestured broadly. "Everyone."

"What for?"

"Equilibrium."

When I met the colonel, he was seated at Evangeline's rosewood desk—boots up, smoking one of her cheroots. I took a position before him, hands clasped behind me, eyeing the mud that coated Truesdail's soles like chocolate icing. He didn't seem to be as old as your grandfather Horatio had been when he died, but the colonel was closer to that stage of life than mine, and my initial impression was one of maturity and cunning—probably due, at least in part, to the uniform.

"Sylvie Swift?" he said.

"Yes, sir."

He did not invite me to sit. I felt his gaze sliding over me—heavy and damp, like a sweaty palm.

"You know who I am?" he said.

"Colonel William Truesdail."

"And you know what I do?"

I shrugged. "Sort of."

"In short," he said, shooting a white puff toward the ceiling, "I run a vast network of federal spies and informants whose purpose is to locate and stamp out all embers of Confederate resistance in the western theater of this bloody, god-awful war."

"I see."

Truesdail dropped his feet. Planted elbows on the desk blotter. "Tell me, Miss Swift," he said, "are you familiar with an organization called the Southern Ladies' Aid Society?"

In my mind, I saw twelve black-clad women marching on the Nashville waterfront. A redhead licking a stranger's spit from her fingers.

"Vaguely," I said.

"The Aid Society," said Truesdail, "masquerades as a Christian organization that provides aid to federal and Confederate troops alike, but in reality, they're a terrorist outfit. Under the guise of feeding and nursing our Union boys, they steal critical supplies—morphine, quinine, rations—from our hospitals. They may even be smuggling them to Rebel traitors along underground lines—it's impossible to say—and now these so-called *ladies* have advanced to arson."

At the mention of arson, my gaze leapt up to meet Truesdail's. His eyes were light brown—almost golden—and his thick, graying hair was in sore need of a trim. His beard nearly touched his breast, and the lips that peeked through his mustache were the same shade of pink as the roses that surrounded Mrs. Marigold's Kentucky boardinghouse. He wasn't exactly handsome, but the colonel had a certain rugged appeal.

"Are you certain?" I asked.

"Absolutely." He slammed a fist into the table. "What I lack is proof! And that, my dear, is where you come in."

He rose. Circled the desk until he faced me. I stood a couple of inches taller than Truesdail, and I tried, discreetly, to slouch. The colonel took my chin, twisted my head gently from side to side. His fingers reeked of tobacco, leather, and a scent I could not place. Something woody and briny, with a hint of rot.

"Evangeline told me," he said, "that your father died in a blaze set by Confederate marauders in Kentucky. That you're alone in the world with no resources and no one to turn to. Another innocent victim of these goddamned Rebels—these traitors who'll stop at nothing to destroy our exceptional nation." Colonel Truesdail walked around me and disappeared. I thought I felt his fingers crawling up my spine. I thought I felt his breath on the nape of my neck, and I fought to control a shudder.

"Eva was right," he said, his voice suddenly soft. "You're nothing like her other girls."

"What would you have me do?"

"Join the Ladies' Aid Society," he said. "Become involved. Attend their meetings and rallies, get to know their members, learn their secrets. Locate some hard evidence that those shrews are involved in stealing and smuggling and sabotage. Proof that members of the Ladies' Aid Society have begun torching Nashville buildings."

"What if you're wrong?" I asked. "What if the Aid Society isn't responsible?"

"Oh, they're responsible," he said. "Last week we came within a hair of catching two of their number using the 'Petticoat System' to steal quinine, but they screamed bloody murder, accused my scouts of manhandling them. An angry crowd forced my boys to release the pair, and I've now made exposing those impostors my top priority." Truesdail rounded the desk, snatched up his wide-brimmed hat, and jammed it on his head. He smiled broadly, revealing large, straight teeth. "What do you say, Miss Swift? Will you be my ally?"

"Your spy?"

He nodded. "If you like."

"What do *I* get out of the arrangement?"

"What do you want?"

Caught off guard, I was silent. "I'm not sure," I finally said.

"All I can promise," the colonel said, doffing his hat with a flourish and bending at the waist, "is the undying gratitude of your country. For the rest, I'm open to negotiation."

You were always already a member of our company. Evangeline's claim echoed through my mind. *From the day you were born, you've been playing your part.* But her words weren't the only consideration that prompted my response. In truth, I was captivated by the idea of acting as a spy.

"I'll take it," I said.

"Good girl." He jotted an address on a sheet of paper, passed it to me. "If you have questions or concerns, let Evangeline know, and she'll get word to me."

I nodded.

Truesdail crossed to the office door, paused with a hand on the dully glowing brass knob. "I don't know how familiar you are with deception, Miss Swift," he said, "but when lying, it helps to stick as closely as possible to the truth."

June 16, 1862
Mobile, AL

Dear Sylvie,

Since we arrived in Mobile, we've built a new submersible—a Porpoise we christened *American Diver*. Though I must admit, part of me still mourns the *Pioneer*. I dream of her often—languishing at the bottom of the New Basin Canal, just one of the victims of the Union's April attack on New Orleans. Scuttling the *Pioneer* was hard on Mr. Hunley and Mr. McClintock, but I believe it was hardest on me. As I watched her slide beneath the turbulent waters for the last time, I couldn't stop sobbing. Perhaps I was really crying for our mother and father, and for Marina, and for you.

And for me.

But the *Diver* has given me a fresh sense of purpose. We're trying to outfit our Porpoise with a new power source—to replace the labor-intensive hand cranks. Mr. McClintock is working on an electrical motor, and he's letting me help. Mr. Hunley's been building a steam engine that he hopes can drive the fish boat, with mixed results. We're conducting weekly test runs at this point, and your brother has the distinction of being the only American who's made thirty voyages in a submarine and lived to tell the tale! The loss of life is heavy—unbearable for most. Men who volunteer to crew the fish boat arrive eager, but if they survive their maiden voyage—a fifty percent chance—most do not return. And I cannot blame them. More than one has likened crewing a submarine to crewing your own coffin, and I must admit, they're not far off.

We carry a solitary candle aboard the Porpoise, which not only sheds a bit of light but also lets us know when we're running out of oxygen. When the candle begins to sputter, we know that if we do not surface in five minutes, we will perish, and the flicker of our small flame always spins my mind toward arson.

I have a confession, Sylvie, and I must make it quickly, in hopes that it won't hurt you—or me—so much. Pro-slavery marauders did not torch the Whitley County Free School five years ago. I did, and Papa knew I was to blame.

My aim was never to ignite the school, but the four-seater privy out back—the one you referred to as the *throne room*. The wind kicked up, and before I knew it, a handful of embers had drifted over, alighting on the school's roof. As I stood there, paralyzed, watching the flames bloom and flourish, Papa appeared. He'd woken, discovered me gone, and come looking. I told him the fire was an accident, but he shook his head. *It's my fault, son*, he said. *Everything is.*

He ordered me to run home as fast as I could, climb into bed, and never tell a soul what I'd done. *What about Mr. Richardson?* I said, but Papa assured me he would try to save him. He held me tightly, and rocked me, and I said I was sorry, over and over. *You couldn't help it*, he said. *None of us can. We're animals, plain and simple. Fated to follow our natures, fated to meet our makers.* Papa shoved me away then, told me to run. Glancing back, I saw that he'd thrown his threadbare coat over his head and was striding into the blaze.

I don't know if you'll recall, Sylvie, that I once saw people inside the fires I set. The people I thought I saw were happy to burn, to be consumed by flames, as it meant they'd get to start over, to be reborn. Back then I thought my fires were tributes to the fundamental element, tributes to change—tributes to life.

Since the day we identified Horatio's charred remains, however, every fire seems to me a funeral pyre. The people I see inside are all burning alive, all shrieking in agony. Reaching for me, begging me to save them, to pull them free. Today I avoid dry timbers, flint, and sparks like the plague—I can hardly bring myself to heat soup on a cookfire. And I think what draws me to submarine work with such resolution is the fact that it sinks me so deeply beneath the water.

Now, when our oxygen starts running low in the *American Diver*, and we're struggling to resurface, Papa—revived, repaired, restored—has started joining me inside the fish boat. At times he holds his sketch of Brigitte, the one he left beneath the spice bush. At others he carries some cast-off goods—an ice skate or kitchen stool or child's sled he wants me to help him refurbish. The first time Horatio appeared, I feared he'd come to torment me, but he insisted he's better off now. *I have no apple brandy*, Papa said. *Besides which, I've found your mother.*

I've gone on too long, Sylvie, and I must hurry to my shift on the *Diver*. I will write more soon.

Your loving brother,
Silas

The address given me by Colonel Truesdail was ten blocks from the Land of the Sirens, at the corner of Spring and Spruce Streets. On a sunny autumn afternoon, I moved westward, through the riverfront neighborhood known as Smokey Row—part business district, part red-light district, so packed with barrooms, warehouses, and theaters; eateries, foundries, and storefronts; boardinghouses and brothels. Streets thick with soldiers and citizenry; with untended livestock and men hawking patent medicines, elixirs, and nostrums; with drunkards and streetwalkers and legless soldiers rattling cups for coins.

At one point the flood of horse-, mule-, and ox-drawn vehicles surging along Spring was interrupted by six draft horses, all sat by federal cavalrymen, towing a limber loaded with boxed ammunition as well as a twenty-four-pound bronze cannon of the sort known as a Napoleon. The spoked wheels supporting the caisson and gun were as tall as the horses' backs, and the gun carriage and limber creaked ominously as they spiraled over the street. A second artillery team trotted by, then a third came into view. I paused to watch and grew so engrossed in the procession that I didn't notice the urchins until they had me surrounded.

They were the same filthy children I'd seen the day of my arrival— one of whom had growled at me. So slicked with grime, so muffled in tattered rags were they that I could not guess their sexes. The ragamuffins numbered at least two dozen, and they seemed both frightened of and fascinated by me. Those nearest reached out hesitantly, petting my skirts, my bodice, my hands.

"Hello," I said. The children took a collective step back. "My name is Sylvie."

Urgent whispering broke out among them, and as the guttersnipes pressed forward—closer and closer, until I thought one might scale me like a mountain—I detected a string of familiar sounds. Words I'd first heard as I sat in your aunt Marina's lap at age five, contemplating her golden icon.

"Tiamat."

"Isis."

"Reitia."

"Gaia."

"Diana."

"Bona Dea."

"Cybele."

"Artemis."

A booming voice broke in from some distance. "You there! Clear off, you filthy beggars!"

Before the guardsman who'd shouted came into view, the throng of urchins melted away. As they scurried off, I was startled to recognize one of their number.

"Apollo?"

My brightly garbed nephew stuck out from his drab compatriots like some fire-new species of parrot.

* * *

The Southern Ladies' Aid Society was housed in a first-floor storefront that boasted an enormous plate-glass window adorned with red, white, and blue bunting. Before the front door, a black-clad woman sat alone on a bench, bent over what seemed yards of black fabric, needle in hand. A bonnet hid her hair, but as I crossed the street, she lifted her face, and I recognized the redhead I'd seen swallow spittle the day I arrived in Nashville. She rose, and the cloth she held shook out into the shape of a dress identical to her own.

"Hello," I said once I stood before her. "I'd like to join the Ladies' Aid Society."

She stared at me stone-faced, unblinking.

"I've only been in town a short time," I continued, "but I've heard about your group—the good work you're doing—and I would very much like to help."

She studied me. "Where are you from?"

"Kentucky."

"What brings you to Nashville?"

"My father was killed in a fire," I said, "and my brother ran off to join the Confederates. I have no other family, so I came here to stay with an aunt."

"Where does she live?"

"Not far from here." I jerked my thumb toward the Land of the Sirens. "Over on Front Street."

The steely glint in the redhead's eyes softened. She nodded. "Let's find you a uniform."

As I followed her inside, the front door struck a bell that chimed aggressively. The Aid Society office—a long, narrow expanse—was furnished with two desks, four filing cabinets, and twelve rustic wooden benches arranged in rows. On the walls hung more red, white, and blue bunting; banners; topographical maps; and scores of photographs—men in uniform, children arranged by height, family reunions, prizewinning calves and piglets. Behind one of the desks hung an eerily familiar oil painting. A clearing in a stormy forest framed a massive creature with the face of a lovely woman and the body of a grizzly bear. Moonlight dappled her shaggy, coppery fur, and her mouth was open wide, exposing murderous teeth. A cub stood on either side of her, gazing up at the monstrous grizzly woman in adoration.

The redhead led me between the desks, around the benches, toward a door, and produced a silver key. We stepped into a dim room, and I thought an army of black-clad women stood before me in two columns, stretching into the distance. My companion lit a lamp, and I realized we'd entered a large closet. The rows of female soldiers were identical black dresses, hung on hangers. The redhead turned to me, hands on hips, and sized me up.

"Let's see." She stepped forward, flipped through dresses. "No, no, no. Here we are. This should fit."

As I held the garment up before me, her quick, warm hands molded the fabric to my body, over my dress. "Must we wear these?" I asked.

She nodded. "Sister Sarah's orders."

"Sister Sarah?"

"Our founder," she said. "Sarah entered a convent when she was fifteen, then decided she could do more good out in the world than she could cloistered away. When we dress alike, Sarah says, we stand on even ground. It's easier to see ourselves not as individuals—not as separate—but as part of a larger, more significant whole."

Studying the shroud that hid my shape, I thought of Silas and me—sun and moon, light and dark. The only group I'd ever belonged to: a company whose first act was the murder of our mother.

"I'm sure this will work," I said, draping the gown over my forearm and catching sight of another door—one at the far end of the closet, nearly lost in shadow.

The front doorbell pealed, and my interlocutor hurried from the closet. Following her, I observed two adolescents stepping hesitantly into the Aid Society office, holding hands. The boy was tawny-skinned and freckled; the girl was the most gorgeous creature I'd ever seen. Her complexion put me in mind of a wild horse that once haunted Whitley County, an animal whose coat Papa referred to as *blood bay*. They both wore ragged, threadbare clothing; neither wore a hat or shoes, and the muck that caked their feet told me they'd trekked a vast distance. The redhead sat the pair on a bench then vanished into the closet, returning a moment later toting a box that brimmed with sturdy, ready-made clothing and at least three pairs of boots.

"Those two," she said, once she'd handed over the supplies and seen the couple out, "represent a fraction of the newly emancipated folks streaming into Nashville from far and wide. They hoped the Unionists would feed, clothe, and house them, but federal help hasn't been forthcoming, so we're doing what we can to provide aid and comfort."

"I am so looking forward," I said, "to making a difference in the lives of those in need. Please tell Sister Sarah that I'm willing to do absolutely anything to help."

"That's good to know." The redhead smiled, and dimples pierced her milky cheeks. She extended a hand, and I imagined a yellow glop sliding from her fingertips into her mouth. "I'm Hannah Holcombe," she said.

"Sylvie," I said. "My name is Sylvie Swift."

She walked me to the storefront door. Once I'd crossed the street and walked half a block, I glanced back, and there was Hannah: leaning in the jamb, arms folded, dark gaze tracking me. Five years later, I asked her what she was thinking as she watched me depart that day, and my dear Hannah said she was imagining how I'd gotten the question-mark-shaped scar that slices through my right eyebrow. *I* was thinking of how the uniform she'd chosen might fit me, and what might lie beyond that door at the back of the Southern Ladies' Aid Society's closet.

MONSTER IN OUR MIDST?

NASHVILLE, TENNESSEE—TWO WEEKS ago, an inebriated member of the Army of the Cumberland's Pioneer Brigade reported spying a monster on the banks of the Cumberland, in Smokey Row. His report was ignored, but according to the office of the provost guard, no fewer than nine Nashvillians came forward last week with similar claims.

Among the witnesses are a schoolteacher, a banker, the wife of a state congressman, an engineer on the Louisville and Nashville Railroad, and an editor of this newspaper. When asked to describe the monster, however, no two people have provided the same answer. Some say it resembles a lion, with bushy mane and tail; others say it looks like a bear walking on hind legs. Still others claim the creature *has* no legs—only tentacles—and slithers on its belly.

The witnesses agree on only one astonishing point: The monster they met wore the face of a beautiful woman.

I *did* manage to attend a matinee performance of *Romeo and Juliet* at the Adelphi. I sat in the theater's highest balcony—a section called the Family Circle but colloquially known as the *Cheap Seats*. We plebeians sat squeezed together on rough benches at a height that made the actors look more like dolls than people. But they knew to project and gesture broadly for our benefit, and the limelight certainly helped.

Though at this point I'd read plenty of playscripts and learned of my female forebears' theatrical experiences from your aunt Marina, this was my first chance to attend a play, and as the curtain rose, my body buzzed with anticipation. What most intrigues me about acting—then and now—is the players' ability to deconstruct and reconstruct themselves. I've long imagined that actors must carry all the roles they've played, throughout their lives, and I can't help but wonder how many lose the ability to locate themselves amid their own internal crowd.

Not long after Hannah and I landed in Monterey, we started volunteering at a local theater, sewing costumes and playing bit parts. Hannah was a fine actress, and each time I watched my lover fabricate a new persona, I was astonished anew. It pains me to recall this now, but it comforts me, too; just as it comforts me to picture Hannah laughing, to imagine her falling asleep with a book splayed open on her chest, to remember her waiting patiently for her garden to grow. I've now witnessed dozens of plays, but if I close my eyes and imagine the stage as it looked from the Family Circle of Nashville's Adelphi Theatre fifteen years ago, the anticipation that filled my breast then floods it afresh.

I kept wishing they were doing *The Tempest* or *King Lear*. I do not think myself unromantic by nature, but I'm not big on *Romeo and Juliet*. Even as an adolescent, I didn't believe love could strike so quickly or be trusted so implicitly. Perhaps it was the strange order your grandfather Horatio gave Silas and me two days before he walked into the Whitley County Free School fire: *My children, you must try your best to avoid love.* John Wilkes Booth was frightfully good as Mercutio, but my favorite performer was the woman who played Juliet's nurse. When the velvet curtain fell at the end of Act II, and the gaslights rose, I paged through my hand-printed playbill to find her name.

Millicent Dickinson as NURSE—If she were pretty, Millicent Dickinson would have run off to New York decades ago. Millicent has appeared as the plain sister and funny best friend in numerous regional productions, including OUR AMERICAN COUSIN, ALL'S WELL THAT ENDS WELL, and THE HEIRESS AND THE SCULLERY MAID. Millicent is a Nashville native as well as the Adelphi Theatre's resident costume designer.

"Pardon me, Miss."

As I stood to allow those in need of refreshment or relief to slide past my position on the bench, I closed the playbill and rolled it into a cylinder. Shut one eye, fitted this scope over the other, and scanned the Adelphi's upper and lower boxes, which brimmed with blue-clad officers and well-heeled Nashvillians wearing taffeta and silk, leather and handmade lace, smelling of bath salts and toilet water, fanning themselves and conversing softly.

I lingered on a raven-haired woman outfitted in scarlet, wielding a lace fan, seated in a box stage right of the proscenium arch. A man leaned close, spoke into her ear, and she laughed. I shifted my spyglass to the speaker and recognized the graying hair and overgrown beard of Colonel William Truesdail.

"Looks like the Secret Service chief," I murmured, "enjoys the theater."

I widened my makeshift spyglass to take in the rest of the box's occupants. Two blue-uniformed men I would later learn were Governor Andrew Johnson and U.S. Army chief engineer James St. Clair Morton. Two women, one of whom was Evangeline Price. I tightened my scope on Miss Price, tried to read her. Her gown seemed fashioned of flames, or autumn leaves gathered at the peak of their red-orange glory. Hair twisted up, cheroot between teeth, lace-edged handkerchief in hand. I found myself wondering about Miss Price's age, her background. I tried to picture her as a child, an adolescent, but could not.

"Perhaps she sprang fully formed," I murmured, "from the head of a parent."

The gaslights flickered, then dimmed, and the curtain rose on Act III of *Romeo and Juliet*. I had to drag my attention back to the actors, however, and away from Evangeline, who seemed to emit an unnatural glow.

Her own strange limelight.

* * *

The events I'm recounting here, Brigitte and Marina, Marina and Brigitte, had numerous repercussions, and I've spent the last fourteen years reviewing them. Part of me wants you to experience them as I did; another part wants to temper them with warnings based on what I've learned since. I'm trying to strike a balance, but as these pages' author, I cannot read them objectively, so forgive me if I err on one side or the other. What I hope most fervently is to tell you a good story.

To that end, here's how the rest of my days in Nashville unfolded: I was awakened each morning by Apollo, who brought me breakfast and a new charcoal and pastel drawing. After eating and admiring my nephew's artwork, I headed down to the Music Room, where I found Doc at the square piano. Ginny's Sisters, or Doc's Priestesses, fluttered in moments later, and it was all I could do not to gawk. My housemates—who seemed to glow, softly—were friendly and happy to loan me anything I needed: hairpins or headscarves, bracelets, brooches, or underclothes. The more I listened to their chatter, the more I wanted to know them—to understand them—but when I tried asking the Priestesses specific questions about themselves, we always ended up talking about me.

Once he'd called us to order, Doc played a never-ending repertoire of haunting songs—never the same tune twice. The sleepy women sat behind me, arranged like a choir—or my own Chorus—singing in a language I didn't speak but was able to understand in a deep, primordial cavity I was only just learning I contained.

As my housemates sang, I gutted the translation of the *Apocrypha* I'd done in Whitley Courthouse. I stepped outside the Music Room on the first floor of the Land of the Sirens, outside Nashville, Tennessee— outside myself—and into the fictional reality of Aristophanes's lost comedy. I stood beside the characters and smelled their scents, touched their skins. Such access allowed me to understand the narrative in several ways at once, and I was sure the product of my labor would represent the most faithful reconstruction possible.

I should probably address a question that must have arisen in your minds: What does a play written more than two thousand years ago have to do with us, or anything that's happening in Monterey, California, in 1877?

I, too, wondered what a comedy that relies on mythical conceits, on unmasked gods and supernatural tricks—on ideas we now assume to be fictitious—had to do with me, or what was happening in Nashville, Tennessee, in 1862. Strangely, it was the very act of translation that began to reveal to me the ties between seemingly disparate events, characters, and time settings—or perhaps more accurately, between all events, characters, and time settings.

At a point, Doc would stop playing, the Priestesses would stop singing, and I would be torn from the world of the *Apocrypha*. After resting and eating a meal of stewed beef and poke salad, ham cake with sweet potatoes, or bacon and molasses beans provided, again, by Apollo, I would don my Southern Ladies' Aid Society uniform and head west. The dress Hannah had chosen fit me better than any garment I'd ever worn. The long-sleeved, high-necked, floor-length black gown seemed tailor-made. And though in hindsight it seems silly to say this, the instant I donned my Aid Society uniform, I felt a shift within me. A heightening of awareness coupled with a lessening of anxiety.

We called each other *Sister* and sat on rustic benches listening to Sister Sarah, who often leapt up on the desk positioned before the oil painting, so that the growling bear-woman loomed over her. Sarah read aloud from soldiers' letters, Union and Confederate alike—grim depictions of battlefields and slogs through swampy terrain, reports of dysentery and the sight of amputated limbs piled roof-high outside field hospitals. When she finished, we sat with boards across our laps for two hours, answering as many letters—garnered via Aid Society contact advertisements in regional newspapers—as we could.

During these sessions, I thought of your uncle Silas inside his Porpoise, laboring at hand cranks in the flicker of candlelight. Learning that he'd set the Free School fire explained a good deal about his bizarre behavior following your grandfather's death. We shared the burden of our mother's passing; Papa's death Silas carried alone, and my heart broke for my twin. I wanted to put my arms around him, assure him that I couldn't fear him, that I knew he would never hurt me. I *did*, however, feel a twinge of the old envy at the thought of your grandfather visiting Silas's submarine, and couldn't help but wonder if Horatio's ghost might ever call on me.

Once we'd completed the day's letters, we marched through the streets in columns, shaking tambourines and collection baskets. Sister Sarah at our head, reading from the Good Book or leading us in song. We counted what funds we'd collected back at the Aid Society office, then Sarah secured them in the safe that stood against a back wall. As day spun into evening, we put together bundles of necessities for not only the families of soldiers, but also the newly emancipated people who continued pouring into the capital from the countryside. We mended clothes and sewed socks for fighting men, regardless of their allegiance, or we read to children orphaned by the war.

Upon returning to the Land of the Sirens—entering by the kitchen door and heading up the back stairs to my little room—I would don a nightdress, slide beneath the covers, and ask the universe a series of questions: Where did my nephew sleep? Did Apollo have a room of his own? Where in the world was Marina? Was my older sister singing in a smoky barroom, or sitting bent over a sewing machine, or begging for change on a street corner? What was it like downstairs, in the Great Room after dark? What was it like to dance with a man—to feel his arms tighten around you? I would inevitably decide to rise, light a lamp, and creep down the main staircase, clutching its carved banister. Peek through the Great Room's double doors, and feast my eyes upon . . . what? Dancing? Drinking? Wrestling? Carousing? Lovemaking?

Apollo would then shake me awake—bearing my breakfast tray— and I would realize I'd missed the chance to investigate once again. As I ate my cornmeal mush, I recalled snatches of vivid, disturbing dreams: I *was* in the Great Room, wearing a pair of red-white-and-blue-striped stockings, high-heeled boots, and a red corset. My hair was piled atop my head, dark circles lined my eyes, and my lips were stained bloodred. I was drinking apple brandy and dancing with two soldiers—one in front of me, one behind. A soldier lifted me up, placed me on the bar-top. I wrapped arms and legs around his body—his hardness, his humanness—and kissed his mouth. His tongue found mine, and I sucked it like a thumb. *I love you, Sylvie*, he murmured, *I love you*. He laughed and laughed—mouth opening ever wider—so I rammed a fist down his throat, punching through muscle and tissue, cartilage and bone. Dug my varnished fingernails into his heart. I yanked once, twice, and with a wet sucking sound, the vascular organ appeared. I scurried up and down the bar-top, holding his heart high, squeezing it. Ruby red jets spurted through the Great Room, streaking us all, as everyone—including the man whose heart I held—clapped and stomped and whistled.

* * *

I'd been attending meetings of the Southern Ladies' Aid Society for three months when Hannah pulled me aside one evening as we disbanded and asked if I was still interested in doing more for the cause.

"Of course," I said, thinking of William Truesdail. The colonel and I met in Evangeline's office every other month, and though he was rumored to be something of a Lothario, I found myself enjoying his company more and more. "I want to help in any way I can."

"Good." She passed me a slip of paper as we filed out of the office. "Here's the address. Be there at eight."

It took me a half hour to find the place, which turned out to be the Overton House, located at the juncture of Cherry and Cedar. Though still under construction when Nashville fell to the Union, the five-story, 240-room luxury hotel was immediately commandeered for use as a military barracks. The unfinished structure—referred to at the time as *Overton's Folly*—was stocked with soldiers who slept six to a room, sat with legs dangling from the windows, and wreathed the place in cheap tobacco smoke. I arrived a few minutes early and paced before the hotel, ignoring the soldiers' catcalls until eight, at which point Hannah appeared. She held two collection baskets and a sign that read HELP US SERVE OUR BRAVE AMERICAN BOYS.

"Tell me, Hannah," I said as we rattled our baskets at passersby, hoping to learn more about my intense companion, who seemed entirely immune to fear, "where did you grow up?"

"Charleston," she said. "Have you been?"

"No."

"It's a lot like Nashville," Hannah said. "Crowded, filthy, full of heartache and want."

"Do you have siblings?"

"I do."

"Are you close to them?"

"No," she said. "I'm not even sure how many I have."

"No?"

She shook her head. I tried to imagine a scenario in which this would be possible but could not.

"My mother died giving birth to me," I offered, "and my twin brother."

"Twins." Hannah smiled. "What a twist."

Not sure what she meant, or what to say, I was silent.

"I must admit," she said, "that I'm jealous, Sylvie."

"Of my being a twin?"

She shook her head. "Of what you did to your mother."

"Oh," I said, taken aback.

Hannah took my wrist, and the warmth of her touch sent a pleasant shiver down my spine. "My mother," she said, "runs a brothel in Charleston. She's been working there since she was fourteen. On my twelfth birthday, she auctioned my virginity to the highest bidder—a fat cattle farmer named Grimes. I was pregnant at thirteen, and again at sixteen. Both times my mother took me to a cut-rate abortionist; both times I nearly died. When they told me I would never conceive another child, I decided to kill my mother. I plotted and lay in wait, but when the moment came—when she was out cold on laudanum, and I pressed a blade to her throat—I didn't have the strength."

I could not tear my eyes from Hannah's. Her story didn't fit the fierce creature standing before me, and I tried, in vain, to see her as a vulnerable child. My thrall nearly made me miss the flicker of a dark figure at the end of the block. As it passed beneath a streetlamp, I recognized the uniform of the Southern Ladies' Aid Society.

"Hannah." I nodded toward our Sister, whose halting, stumbling walk told me something was wrong. When we reached her, she held out a bundle imploringly—a parcel the size and shape of a round bread loaf, swaddled in several layers of newsprint.

"They're right behind me," she gasped, her face gray and beaded with sweat, "Truesdail's men! You must get this to Sister Sarah, quickly!"

"Take it," Hannah said, so I lifted the parcel from our Sister's hands—which I now saw were spattered with blood—and felt my stomach turn over. Hannah took the girl's waist and helped her to a nearby doorframe, lowered her gently to the stoop, and propped her torso against the jamb.

"I'll deal with this." Hannah peered in the direction from which our Sister had stumbled. "You get that over to the Aid Society office. Sarah will be waiting."

"What about her?" I indicated our injured Sister. "What about you?"

Hannah touched my cheek and smiled, so her dimples appeared. "We never existed." She kissed me softly on the mouth, then tapped the bundle in my arms. "Just get this to Sarah. Now."

*　*　*

The Ladies' Aid Society window was dark, but as soon as I reached the storefront, the door opened inwardly, silently.

"Come," said Sister Sarah. "Hurry."

She lifted an oil lamp, and I followed Sarah, eyeing the rapidly evolving shadows her flame threw over the walls, wondering what had happened to the aggressive bell the door normally struck as it opened—to announce every arrival.

"In here." Sarah opened the closet door, and I followed. We moved beyond the columns of black dresses—hanging always at the ready—and approached the door I'd noticed on my first visit to the Aid Society office. Sister Sarah produced a metal ring thick with keys, and I watched her flip through them. It was the first time I'd been so close to her, and despite the dimness, I tried to study her. Sarah wore not one piece of jewelry and her hair, as always, was hidden by her bonnet. Briefly, I wondered if she was bald. It occurred to me that the dips and contours of her face—arch of brow, shape of lower lip—were achingly familiar, then Sarah was swinging the door open, beckoning me to follow.

The floor stepped down and around, down and around like a corkscrew. I followed Sarah, quickly descending the spiral staircase, holding tight to the iron rail with my right hand, the newspaper-wrapped package wedged beneath my left arm. I kept anticipating our arrival at the base—*surely we can't sink much farther, surely we're now entering a subterranean world, surely humans cannot breathe this far beneath the surface*—but the bottom remained elusive.

"Not much farther now," said Sister Sarah.

Finally, the staircase ended. We stood on solid stone within a damp, echoey cavern. I followed Sarah, and eventually, we reached the edge of a still, dark body of water.

"Here." She opened her arms to receive the blood-flecked bundle then knelt at the water's edge. Bowing her head, she spoke unintelligibly, then deposited the parcel on the stone. A muffled sound—cry or wail, greeting or shout—that seemed to come from miles off pierced the cave's silence.

"Come." Sarah stood, hurried toward the staircase. "There's not much time."

I followed her back up the iron spiral, focusing on the lamp's flame to stave off dizziness. I wanted to ask a thousand questions, but my breath was so short I couldn't speak. We gained the top of the steps, and as Sarah locked the hidden door behind us, the front doorbell peeled stridently.

"But the bell," I said. "How is this possible?"

Sarah shushed me, and we hurried to the storefront door. Swung it open to find Colonel William Truesdail surrounded by eight darkly dressed Secret Service operatives—two of whom held Hannah by the biceps.

"Good evening, Sister Sarah," said Truesdail, pushing past us without being invited. "Someone broke into the hospital at Saint Mary of the Seven Sorrows earlier this evening and stole a great quantity of morphine, not to mention four dozen boxes of camp rations meant for our wounded Union boys."

"Oh dear." Sarah tilted her head. "What a pity."

"You wouldn't know anything about it, would you?"

"Of course not," she said, "Colonel Truesdail."

"We found this one," he said, indicating Hannah, "loitering around Overton's Folly."

"Has she broken any laws?"

"None that we can prove."

"Then I suggest," said Sarah, "that you let her go."

Truesdail jerked his head at the men restraining Hannah, and they released her. Rubbing her arms, she joined Sarah and me.

"I see you've recruited a new member." Colonel Truesdail stepped forward until his face was inches from mine. "Tell me, Miss—do you know what these women are? Do you realize you've joined a guerrilla organization?"

"Fiddlesticks," said Sarah. "May God bless you for seeing Hannah home, Colonel. Is there anything else?"

Truesdail smiled. "You're slipping, Sarah. Next time we'll catch you red-handed."

Sister Sarah opened her hands, revealing their unblemished palms. "Until then," she said, "I'll bid you goodnight."

Encyclopaedia Britannica
Eighth Edition (1860)
Volume 21, T–ZWO, p. 181

The word THEOLOGY, in its more restricted sense, signifies *a discourse concerning God* (Greek: ένας λόγος για τον θεό); but it is commonly employed to designate that science which treats not only of the divine existence and attributes, but also of the relations which subsist between God and his intelligent creatures.

A couple of weeks after I visited that vast, echoey chamber deep beneath the Southern Ladies' Aid Society's office, I entered the Land of the Sirens' Music Room one January morning to find not only Doc, seated at the square piano, but also Miss Price. Dressed in a turquoise gown and wrapped in diaphanous gauze, red hair twisted into its customary chignon, cheroot clamped between teeth, Evangeline sat beside Doc on the piano bench, and as I crossed the floor, I thought I saw her hand on his knee.

"Morning, little sister," she said.

"Morning," I said, settling at the desk.

"How are you feeling?"

"Fine."

"Doc tells me," Evangeline said, "that you've made great progress with the *Apocrypha*."

"Have I?'

Doc nodded. "I think so."

"So I've come," Eva went on, "to judge for myself."

Doc rang his bell, and with the usual fluttering, a dozen women appeared behind me. I opened the French version of the *Apocrypha*, as well as my own burgeoning translation—now nearly half-finished—and went to work. I soon found myself within the world of the comedy—the ancient Greek city of Ephesus, the flower-dotted slopes of Mount Olympus, the stygian depths of a chasm beyond the underworld. I don't know exactly how much time passed, but when the music stopped, the angle of the sun glaring in through the windows told me it was late afternoon.

Doc and his Priestesses had already abandoned the chamber, but Evangeline stood beside the square piano, cradling a slender red cloth-bound book to her breast. Tears coursed down her cheeks.

"Miss Price?" I said. "What's wrong?"

Blotting her face with a lace-edged handkerchief, she shook her head. "I'm a bit overwhelmed," she said. "We've been trying to translate the *Apocrypha* into English for two centuries. I feared it couldn't be done."

"We?"

Evangeline circled the room, drawing all the draperies, transforming Doc's piano and the Priestesses' chairs into dim, shadowy creatures. She dragged over a chair, sat, leaned in, and seized my hand. "You must swear," she said, her voice pitched low, "not to divulge what I'm about to tell you, Sylvie. Do I have your word?"

A tingle of anticipation crept over my scalp, and I nodded.

"We are an ancient society," she said, "a secret cult founded before recorded time. Our initiates have included many eminent, influential figures: Hatshepsut, Cleopatra, Nefertiti, and other female pharaohs of Egypt. Catherine of Russia and Elizabeth I of England. Helen of Anjou, Christine de Pizan, Moderata Fonte, Jane Anger, Marie de Gournay, Aphra Behn, Anne Bradstreet, Ninon de l'Enclos, Abigail Adams, Eleanor Butler, Dorothea Erxleben, Jane Gomeldon, Phillis Wheatley, Lucretia Mott, Judith Sargent Murray, Sojourner Truth, Mary Wollstonecraft and her daughter. And of course, Gaia Valentino."

As she spoke, the tingle spread from my scalp downward, as though unseen fingers were stroking my cheeks, neck, shoulders. "Gaia Valentino?" I asked.

Evangeline handed me the red book. "Gaia," she said, "is your predecessor. During the French civil war of 1562—a struggle between Catholics and Huguenots—she translated the *Apocrypha* into French from the Greek. Gaia Valentino's manuscript is the one you've been working into English."

I opened the slender volume—*Changeling: The Story of Gaia Valentino*—and read the first sentence: *Gaia Valentino was born on the last day of 1543 to Francesca Vito, a member of the cittadini originari, a hereditary caste of native-born Venetian citizens.*

"It's long been rumored," Evangeline continued, "that Aristophanes of Athens penned a new comedy while he was dying. Set during the Peloponnesian Wars, it deals with women banding together to effect change. But unlike *Lysistrata, Assemblywomen,* and *Women at the Thesmophoria*—all of which treat the idea of women holding power as an absurdity—we believe that in his final play, the great poet treats female sovereignty as the standard toward which we should all be striving."

"My stars," I said.

"Because the *Apocrypha* is set at Ephesus rather than Athens," she went on, "some classicists refuse to entertain the notion that Aristophanes could be its author. But we believe the *Apocrypha* is, in fact, the poet's final play, and we believe he set it across the Aegean Sea at Ephesus—a city founded by a mythical prince of Athens—quite deliberately. Several of our members have attempted to translate Gaia's manuscript into English, but they've had no success."

"What was the problem?"

"Timing," she said. "We have a saying that, through the centuries, has been translated into every known tongue: *When brother slays brother over affairs of state, and Chaos has birthed a pair of identical daughters, the Cult of Chaos will rise to prominence and pull the human race back into alignment with the earth, its Mother.*"

"The Cult of Chaos?"

Evangeline nodded. "Our clan. Yours and mine."

"Chaos," I repeated, letting the word ripen in my mouth. "As in the primordial goddess from the *Apocrypha*?"

"Chaos," she said, "as in the original deity. The Mother of All."

"What exactly is our aim?"

"To seize power. For millennia, men have worshipped at the altar of violence. Blinded, they destroy each other, they destroy the forest, the sea, the cosmos. We aim to disrupt those violent systems men hold most dear. To usher in a global era of female rule that will steer us back to the natural world."

"Using what means?"

"Any," she said. "Using any and all means."

Evangeline stood and moved to the door.

"Miss Price?"

"Yes?"

"Did Marina tell you to send me the *Apocrypha*?"

She nodded. "It was one of the last things your sister did before she began to change."

"Change?" When Evangeline remained silent, I rose, crossed to her, and seized her upper arms. I'd never grasped another person so forcibly, and I was filled with a strange, intoxicating surge of power. "What do you mean?" I asked. "Why won't you tell me what's become of Marina?"

She smiled, and again, her teeth gleamed. "Patience, Sylvie. In good time, she'll tell you herself."

Once she'd left, I paced the Music Room like a caged animal. I was shivering, and a ringing filled my ears. Evangeline's assertions were outlandish, but the more I considered her words, the more sense they seemed to make. The strange story of my great-great-grandmother Euphemia, the Priestesses whose uncanny song aided me in translating the *Apocrypha*, the mysterious whereabouts of your aunt Marina—could these inexplicable elements all be linked to the Cult of Chaos?

I'd grabbed Evangeline hard enough to bruise her, and I wondered what had possessed me. As I returned to the writing desk, my gaze fell on the slender volume she'd given me—*Changeling: The Story of Gaia Valentino*. I opened the red cover, caught sight of the frontispiece—

a pen-and-ink drawing of a figure standing in a skiff, holding a pole, as a strange creature arose from the water.

The creature had many tentacles, three heads, and a barrel-shaped body from which sheets of water cascaded. Two of its heads faced away, but the third was half turned toward me, and it wore the face of a woman. One strange, wild eye was visible, and in it I read something human—sympathy or mercy or fellow feeling. Still ignorant of the ways in which my sixteenth-century predecessor's story would enlighten me about my great-great-grandmother, my sister, and myself, I began to read.

CHANGELING: THE STORY OF GAIA VALENTINO
by G. S. Valentino

Gaia Valentino was born on the last day of 1543 to Francesca Vito, a member of the *cittadini originari*, a hereditary caste of native-born Venetian citizens. Because her husband, a once-famous painter, was too fond of drink to care for his family, Gaia's mother became a *cortigiana onesta*, or "honest courtesan," and, eventually, the keeper of the *Catalogo di tutte le principal et più honorate cortigiane di Venetia*, the *Catalog of All the Principal and the Most Honored Courtesans of Venice*.

When Gaia and her twin brother, Gianni, were born, Francesca was raising four sons. At the time, it was widely believed that twins were the result of a woman having intercourse with two different men—a notion that originated with the Greek story of Alcmene, who gave birth to Zeus's semidivine son Hercules and his mortal brother simultaneously. A mother of twins would often claim that one of her babes had been stolen by a fairy, who'd left a sickly child of their own in its place. That way no one could blame her for killing whichever of the twins she thought would be more troublesome.

The moment Gaia was placed in Francesca's arms, Francesca declared the girl a changeling and ordered the midwife to drown her in the lagoon.

"But madam," said the midwife, "she's the strong one. Listen to her scream! Her brother is pitifully thin, and he hasn't made a sound."

"I don't care," Francesca said. "The girl's the impostor. A mother knows."

But the midwife refused to drown the babe, as did Francesca's servants. Unable to commit the unthinkable act with her own hands, Francesca resigned herself to the costly proposition of raising a daughter. And though Gaia resembled her mother so strongly that the two women were often confused, Francesca continued to think of Gaia as a changeling.

* * *

Francesca Vito provided her sons with skilled tutors, and Gaia was able to learn alongside her brothers. The scholars declared Gaia Valentino a prodigy, a wonder, a genius. Her facility with languages seemed supernatural, and by the time she was five, Gaia spoke Greek, Latin, French, Aramaic, Aragonese, Portuguese, Frisian, Yiddish, and Dutch with native fluency. She began composing poetry at six; a poem she wrote at nine won a prize at Venice's annual Festival Letterario.

Francesca saw her daughter's precocity as further proof of her alienness. The girl's only comrade was her twin brother, Gianni, who'd been born with a weak heart. The two went everywhere together; it was strange to see one without the other, and they spoke a secret language. Gaia and Gianni were endlessly fascinated by their lagoon city and spent hours mapping its canals, trying to fix their harmony. The twins ran with the flocks of orphans who, by scrounging, stealing, and begging, proliferated. Gaia and Gianni also got to know many of the Venetian Republic's ten thousand gondoliers, who would ferry them around the "floating city," through the canals, from island to island.

Gaia's favorite gondolier—a blind man named Omero—possessed an encyclopedic knowledge of the Venetian waterways. It was from Omero that Gaia learned of the original inhabitants of Venice—the Veneti, an ancient race who settled northeastern Italy seven hundred years before the Romans and a thousand years before the Christian era. A maritime people known for breeding magnificent horses, according to Omero, the Veneti embraced contradiction.

What most fascinated Gaia about the ancient Venetians was their worship of a female supreme deity—Reitia—who ruled writing, healing, wild beasts, procreation, and childbirth. One of Reitia's sanctuaries was a scribal school, and all the scribes trained there were women. Reitia's worshippers left bronze body parts at the goddess's shrines—a leg, an arm, a breast, a head, a vagina—each a request for the healing of a specific body part, and an indication that the Veneti perceived divine healing as a process of disassembling and reassembling the body.

"When I was no bigger than you," Omero once said, "my mother told me that Reitia's most powerful priestesses could dismantle themselves at will, then rebuild their bodies into any shape they chose—human, animal, or monster. The merpeople, sea serpents, and leviathans who periodically visit our lagoon from the Adriatic to this day, she said, are actually ancient priestesses of Reitia who were unable—or unwilling—to revert to their original form."

* * *

Thanks to the dowry her mother was able to provide, Gaia Valentino married a doctor named Santino Prizzi at the age of fifteen. Prizzi was thirty-six. But Gaia and her devout husband—who hated poetry and refused to display art in his home—did not get along. The marriage was so miserable, in fact, that Gaia returned to her mother after only five months. Because her dowry was gone, she could not remarry, and because she was no longer a virgin, she could not enter a convent. Francesca Vito insisted that her daughter follow in her footsteps and become a *cortigiana onesta*, but Gaia fled her mother's house and, disguising herself as a man, got hired as an oarsman on a gondola.

This brilliant poetess steered well-heeled locals and foreigners around the Venetian Republic for two years, which honed her language skills and solidified her detailed, maplike knowledge of the city. During this time, Gaia became reacquainted with the street urchins who roamed Venice, allowing them to hop rides aboard her gondola. In later years she spoke of this period as the happiest she'd known. She loved the physical labor, and she loved the outdoors. Disguised as a man, Gaia Valentino was able to borrow a brand of freedom unavailable to women in sixteenth-century Venice. Only the *cortigiane oneste* came close to this kind of autonomy, but such women were required to pay dearly for their freedoms, as Gaia would come to know too well.

When Gaia was seventeen, as the story goes, she was headed home one summer evening when the water of the lagoon began to heave and bubble. A giant creature arose suddenly from the canal to tower over her gondola. The beast had twelve tentacles and three heads, and its skin glowed iridescently. Gaia was terrified until she saw that one of the heads wore the face of a beautiful woman.

"My child," said the monster, "you are not what you appear to be."

"Neither are you," Gaia replied.

The monster laughed. "True. But why are you dressed this way?"

"So I can drive this boat," Gaia said. "Why do you take the form of a leviathan?"

"So I can live beneath the water. So I am not required to follow man's rules."

"Why then do you come back?" asked Gaia. "Why visit the lagoon?"

The creature was silent. "I suppose a part of me," she finally said, her voice tinged with sorrow, "misses the world I was born into. Even those aspects I hate."

* * *

This idyllic interlude in Gaia Valentino's life was cut short when her brother Gianni's heart failed. Upon learning that he'd taken ill, she rushed to her mother's house but arrived too late. She climbed into bed with Gianni and remained for hours, refusing to allow anyone near her twin. At some point in the night, she disappeared—along with the body—but she never told a soul what she did with Gianni. Some guessed that Gaia weighted his corpse and sunk him to the bottom of the Grand Canal. Others said she'd placed him in her gondola, rowed him to the caves on the southernmost edge of the Venetian lagoon—accessible only at low tide—and laid her brother to rest there.

Upon returning to her mother's home, Gaia Valentino set aside her male costume. She told Francesca Vito she was ready to accept her fate and become a *cortigiana*.

"To be a woman," Francesca said as she taught her changeling how to disguise herself—how to dress and plait her hair, how to perfume and adorn her body, "is to change. From girl to maid, from bride to mother, from matron to crone. Such mutability is thought by the male of the species to be a failing, so we've been relegated to the shadows.

"But woman *is* the universe. We are the cosmos. We are the landscape. We're the forest, the bear, the mountain, the beehive, the sea. And it is our ability to change, to adapt, to wear a series of faces that gives us our strength, that enables us—in spite of how we're fettered by society—not only to survive but to prevail."

When Francesca led her daughter to the mirror and stood behind her, both women gasped at Gaia's metamorphosis— from dingy, nondescript gondolier to breathtaking, soul-stirring *cortigiana*.

"Mama?" said Gaia.

"Forgive me, Gaia."

"For what?"

"My pettiness, envy, and fear."

"Fear?" Gaia said. "Of me?"

Nodding, Francesca Vito pointed to the mirror. "Look closely, my changeling. See how deadly you are."

Gaia was not only brilliant, beautiful, and well-educated; the years she'd spent working as a gondolier had allowed her free access to Venice's public sphere—normally the sole domain of men. Since she'd been married, however unhappily, she was familiar with the physical act of love, and within six months, Gaia Valentino was the highest-paid and most sought-after *cortigiana* in the republic.

ROSY SAYS "NO" TO HARLOTS

MURFREESBORO, TENNESSEE—THE BATTLE of Stones River has dashed Rebel hopes for control of Middle Tennessee. But this outcome owes more to the incompetence of the Confederate general Braxton Bragg than to a decisive Union victory—which was not won.

The Union boys, commanded by General William Rosecrans, *did* manage to repel two Rebel attacks, and to inflict heavy casualties on the enemy. But federal casualties were *also* enormous, and if Bragg hadn't mistakenly withdrawn his army southeast to Tullahoma—rather than mounting a third full-scale attack—the Confederates would have seized control of Middle Tennessee.

An aide to General Rosecrans tells this reporter that Rosy attributes the closeness of the battle to the inauspicious fact that many of the Army of the Cumberland's troops have been crippled by syphilis—a disease no doubt picked up in one of Nashville's brothels.

"If the provost guard doesn't shut down the whorehouses," Rosy is quoted as saying, "Nashville's standing army of harlots—not the goddamned Rebels—will bring our Army to its knees!"

Thursday, June 14, 1877
Monterey, CA

Monterey is one of the world's richest fisheries. Chinese immigrants started fishing the bay for abalone and squid in the 1850s. They were followed by Japanese fishermen who mainly went for salmon; then came Sicilian immigrants who introduced the lampara net, used primarily to handfish for sardines, which school here in abundance.

Not long after we arrived, Hannah and I picked up a secondhand trawler and a half-dozen nets, and in spite of the prevailing belief that women in fishing boats are a jinx, we spent our first couple of years in California on the water every day, tapping into the sea's bounty. We caught enough to feed and clothe ourselves, and for a time, I felt content. But at some point, I began to grow restless—to sense my life was lacking an essential element.

"Sylvie," Hannah said one morning, handing me the *Monterey Gazette*. "Take a look at this."

Always attuned to my moods, she'd circled an advertisement that read:

WANTED:

SKILLED TRANSLATOR OF FRENCH

HIGHLY LITERARY WORK

NO PRUDES NEED APPLY!

I donned my most decent dress and bonnet, wrapped myself in a purple shawl knitted by Hannah, and hied myself to the address indicated in the advertisement—a ramshackle two-story adobe near the intersection of Alvarado and Pearl. The place, called Bill's Books, was packed to the gills with volumes new and used. The shelves groaned; additional books were stacked vertically on the floor. A slight, balding man occupied a desk near the door; when I showed him the advertisement, he nodded and rose. Indicating that I should follow, he parted a set of curtains and entered a dimly lit back room.

"Now then," he said, peering up at me through wire-rimmed spectacles, "what's your name?"

"Sylvie Swift."

"You read French? And can translate into English?"

"Oh, yes."

"Wonderful." He led me to a shelf, pulled out a book—titled *Une Femme Déchaînée* (*A Woman Unchained*), and passed it to me. "My back room," he said, "features titles that are somewhat risqué, Miss Swift. Highly literary, you understand, but also rather earthy. This is by a nineteen-year-old sensation, a Parisian named Jacques Babin. I've built a printing press upstairs, and I have permission to reprint and sell *Une Femme Déchaînée* in English. What I lack is a translator."

"I see."

"Why don't you take a crack at the first three chapters? Bring them in, and if I like what I read, I'll pay you ten dollars up front, then thirty more once the book is finished."

"That sounds ideal, Mister . . ."

"Bill," he said. "Everyone calls me Bill."

"All right." I extended a hand. "Then you must call me Sylvie."

I was headed for the door, thinking of the last man I'd called *Bill*—Colonel William Truesdail—when I spied two small faces peering in through the front window. Chubby fingers cupping two sets of golden eyes. It was you, Brigitte, and you, Marina. You'd recently turned four, and you were perfect in every way. As I stood there, trying to slow my galloping heart, your adoptive mother appeared, hurried you away. My eyes blurred, and I pretended to browse for ten minutes, waiting for the cyclone that threatened me to pass.

Back home, I made a cup of hibiscus tea and sat at the secondhand secretary Hannah and I employed to keep track of our fishing enterprise. Studying *Une Femme Déchaînée*'s blue cover, I suddenly wondered if I could still read French—if my mind could still engage in the sort of deconstruction and reconstruction that translation requires.

As I sat staring at the opening sentence—*Il arrive un moment dans la vie de chaque femme où elle doit décider si elle est esclave, ou si elle appartient à elle-même*—Hannah entered the room, humming. I couldn't place the tune, but as I listened, my mind began to decipher the words before me. I picked up my pencil and wrote: *There comes a time in every woman's life when she must decide if she is a slave, or if she belongs to herself.* I worked feverishly until Hannah called me to dinner.

"I saw Marina and Brigitte today," I said as we ate an herbed omelet filled with mussels and clams Hannah had gathered while I was out. "They were outside the bookstore, looking in."

"And?" she said.

I was silent.

"How did they look?" she asked.

"Flawless."

She waited.

"I wanted to grab them, Hannah," I said. "I wanted to shove Elizabeth Parker to the street. To snatch up my girls and run."

"But you didn't."

"A part of me wishes I had."

She nodded.

"Another part," I said, my fists clenching on the tablecloth, "wants to torch the Parkers' ranch. Burn that whole place to the ground."

Gazing into Hannah's dark eyes, I knew we were recalling the same scene—a night in February of 1863, in Nashville, when we met up at midnight before the Southern Ladies' Aid Society's storefront office, at the corner of Spruce and Spring. Hannah hadn't given me a hint about our plans, but the hour told me they were unlawful, or at the very least illicit. Two of our Sisters joined us, and we headed north. We marched in tandem, four abreast—arms swinging, breath fogging, bootheels ringing as one, black skirts swirling and snapping around thighs, calves, ankles. One multilimbed creature made of separable parts: animal or monster or god.

We passed the Overton House, and Saint Mary of the Seven Sorrows—Nashville's oldest Catholic Church, built in Greek Revival style, filled with makeshift beds and serving as a military hospital—before doubling back on Cedar Street to arrive at the Tennessee State Capitol. During the Union occupation of Nashville, the capitol building was known as Fort Johnson, for its detested occupant—Andrew Johnson, Tennessee military governor and, to the dismay of Nashvillians, future U.S. president. The grand building sat atop a hill and featured Ionic columns as well as a lofty cupola modeled after a certain Athenian temple—a sharp contrast with the six twenty-four-pound bronze guns that surrounded it.

"Here we are," Hannah said, and I realized my companions were all facing *away* from the capitol. I spun to face the requisitioned four-story mansion that barracked Nashville's provost guard, where the military police detained the bulk of their prisoners. It was rumored that this building—known as the guardhouse—featured a subterranean set of iron-barred cells. An honest-to-god dungeon. As we stole toward the mansion's front doors—engraved with bas-relief naiads, dryads, and Nereids, mythological nymphs awhirl around a well-endowed satyr—I smelled sulfur and pitch, and I was seized by the same mix of excitement and dread that once defined my fiery outings with your uncle Silas.

Hannah handed us each a stick with a glowing red end, a couple of pine knots, a bundle of twigs, and a container of pitch, and in my mind, I saw one of Papa's blackened hands waving at me from beneath a blue cloth in the morgue back in Whitley Courthouse. My Sisters and I deployed to the building's four corners—each left to start her own blaze. An hour later, in the doorframe of the Ladies' Aid Society storefront several blocks away, we stood as one again, watching the small fires we'd set burgeon and unite, becoming a conflagration that licked the star-pocked sky. As always, I searched the flames for Silas's fire people, to no avail.

"Hannah," I said, as the two of us walked toward the Land of the Sirens, "you don't support the Confederacy, do you?"

She smiled. "No."

"And the Ladies' Aid Society doesn't sympathize with the Rebels."

"Definitely not."

"But we just destroyed the guardhouse," I said, "so it seems that the Aid Society doesn't endorse the Union either."

"Right again."

I grabbed Hannah's arm, halting her progress. "Hannah," I said, "was anyone inside the guardhouse?"

She nodded. "Soldiers. Both Union and Confederate."

I searched her face, her inky eyes, for a hint of remorse or regret but found none. I was seized by the sense that I'd just leapt from a tower and was diving, nose-first, toward a drinking glass of water. In that moment, I couldn't tell whether I was more frightened of Hannah or of myself. I only knew I longed to share my feelings with your uncle—to tell Silas that I, too, knew what it was to kill inadvertently.

"The Ladies' Aid Society," Hannah said, "is a neutral organization. We strive to be impartial, evenhanded, and dispassionate."

"Nonsense," I said. "There's no such thing as a neutral murderer."

"Should I have told you," she asked, "about the soldiers inside? Would it have made a difference?"

Again, I saw Horatio, but this time your grandfather was seated on the back porch of Mrs. Marigold's boardinghouse, studying his tattered sketch of your grandmother Brigitte in profile, tears wetting his cheeks. "No, Hannah," I said. "I was born with blood on my hands."

* * *

One afternoon not long after, I arrived at the SLAS office to find Hannah waiting. She said the two of us were skipping our customary afternoon duties in order to take care of some business up on St. Cloud Hill.

"St. Cloud Hill?" I said. "Where they're building Fort Negley?"

"That's right," Hannah said. "We're making a delivery."

She disappeared into the back room, then reappeared with a crate, which she handed to me. Inside, I spied packages stamped with CAMP RATIONS and heard the angry echo of Colonel Truesdail's voice: *Someone broke into the Hospital at Saint Mary of the Seven Sorrows earlier this evening and stole a great quantity of morphine, not to mention four dozen boxes of camp rations meant for our wounded Union boys.*

Hannah retrieved a second crate, then we struggled through the front door and into blinding sunshine. Once my eyes had adjusted, I spied a familiar—and very tall—figure.

"Doc?" I'd never seen the pianist outside the Land of the Sirens and had no idea he knew Hannah. For a moment, I thought he was a figment of my imagination. "What are you doing here?"

"I'm your escort," Doc said, his face blank and unreadable as ever. "I'm taking you over to St. Cloud Hill."

He cradled a paper-wrapped bundle of his own, and the three of us headed south on Spruce. For late February, the day was unseasonably warm, and the wooden sidewalks swarmed with soldiers, women toting shopping baskets, children, and roaming animals, so for a time we walked single file. Hannah led the way, and I trailed Doc, studying his broad shoulders, his close-cropped graying hair. Again, I noted the jagged scar whose tail curled round his neck—the shooting star—and tried to imagine a weapon that might leave such a mark.

A quarter hour later, we turned onto the Nolensville Pike. Here there were no pedestrian walkways, but since Nashville had fallen to the Union, the Pioneer Brigade—the Army of the Cumberland's engineering corps—had surfaced the wide turnpike with branches and tree trunks laid crosswise, to allow passage of wagons and heavy artillery over mud—a technique known as "corduroying." Walking alongside Doc and Hannah, I studied the timber passing beneath my boots.

"You know who came up with corduroying?" Doc asked.

"Who?" I said.

"The Romans," he replied, "not long after they invaded the flat, swampy peatlands of northern Europe."

As he explained the ancient technique in detail—how plentiful timber was a base requirement, what sorts of wood worked best, how to fill the interstices between logs with smaller limbs, then coat with clay—I stared at him in wonder. I'd spent countless hours of the previous six months in Doc's presence, and not once had I heard him speak so much.

"Doc," I said, "how do you know all this?"

"I've been around a long time."

"Doc is far older than he looks," Hannah said.

We drew near St. Cloud Hill, and the laborers working on Fort Negley came into view—the same figures I'd spied from the riverfront after disembarking from the *Gertrude*. From this proximity, however, I saw that the workers weren't members of the Pioneer Brigade, or even regular federal troops. Newly emancipated men, women, and even children struggled under the weight of large limestone blocks. At this point, Negley—a star-shaped bastion that would be the largest inland fort in the nation—was all but finished.

"Last month," Doc said, "when Lincoln signed that Emancipation Proclamation, these folks all lit out and camped around the five hills designated for new forts. They assumed Union troops would protect them, but with the Pioneer Brigade stretched thin and nowhere near enough volunteers, the army started pressing them into service. Three thousand free men, women, and children have been forced to work on Negley, but the army hasn't provided these folks with shelter—not even tents—or paid a nickel of their promised wages."

We circled the hill and entered an encampment. Two men approached and spoke to Doc, who indicated that Hannah and I should place our crates on the ground. We did so, and Doc handed us each a canteen of water. The five of us began pulling out packages marked CAMP RATIONS and moving through the camp, distributing them. Though the afternoon was warm and bright, it was undeniably winter, but most of those I met weren't wearing coats, and many had no shoes. Knots of people wandered about, hands hidden in sleeves or jammed into pockets, stomping or jumping up and down. I approached a group of six huddled around a smoky fire, bundled in blankets. I asked if they were hungry only to immediately wish I could take the absurd question back.

"Does a bear shit in the woods?" a man said, and everyone laughed, including me.

I moved among the group—a family, I felt sure—handing out rations of salt pork and hardtack. As they passed around my canteen, I noticed a woman cradling a girl of no more than ten. She tore up the salt pork and broke the hardtack into pieces before placing them in the girl's mouth. The girl chewed and swallowed, tears leaking from her stormy eyes.

"Water?" she whispered.

A man handed over the canteen, and, supporting the girl's head, the woman let her drink until she'd had her fill. As I slung the canteen back around my body, the woman rocked her sister or daughter, cousin or niece, stroking her cheeks and saying *shh* and *there now*.

I kept moving through the camp, increasingly devastated by the misery around me. After distributing water and rations to five more such groups, I spotted Doc and Hannah standing some distance away. Doc spoke into Hannah's ear, and she threw her arms around him. As she buried her face in his chest, I heard the echo of Evangeline Price's voice: *We aim to disrupt those violent systems men hold most dear.*

"Chaos," I said, my mind buzzing as pieces began arranging themselves into a theory. "Evangeline, Doc, and the Priestesses. Sister Sarah, Hannah, and the Ladies' Aid Society. We're all in this together."

Once we'd run out of rations and drained our canteens, Doc shook hands with the men who'd helped us, and we three departed, circling St. Cloud Hill until we stood once more in front of Fort Negley.

"This is barbaric. These people still have no tents," Hannah said, her cheeks flushed with anger, "or pit latrines. Their suffering has increased tenfold since the last time I was here."

"A quarter of the camp's original inhabitants," Doc said, "have died of exposure and disease."

"My stars," I said.

"I left morphine with the nominal camp head," he continued, "a man named Zachary, so he can give it to the sickest—to help put an end to their misery."

At the base of the fort, a middled-aged woman carrying a limestone block twice the size of her torso stumbled and fell to the ground, so the stone cracked in half. A blue-uniformed soldier marched over and started shouting about the cost coming out of her wages. Two adolescent boys rushed to her side, weeping, and tried to help her, but the woman could not rise.

"We've got to do something," I said. "We've got to stop them."

"Who's got to stop them?" asked Doc.

I looked from Doc to Hannah and back. "The Cult of Chaos."

As Doc rewarded me with a smile—a first—Hannah seized my hands and squeezed so hard I feared a bone might snap.

"Oh, Sylvie," she said.

In that moment, Brigitte and Marina, Marina and Brigitte, I understood that we weren't battling the Unionists *or* the Confederates. We were fighting warlike men and the worlds they think they've made.

* * *

My bimonthly meeting with William Truesdail took place the following week. He'd recently arrested a printer for passing counterfeit federal banknotes, and the colonel was in high spirits. Smoking one of Miss Price's cheroots, he told the story, at times leaping up to act out a scene, and I found myself laughing again and again. Once he'd finished, Truesdail perched on Evangeline's desk—so close to me that his boot brushed my skirts, and occasionally my calf. I was trying to pinpoint the briny component of the colonel's scent when he asked if I had anything to report.

Part of me wanted to tell him the things I'd learned—that the Ladies' Aid Society was not, in fact, aligned with the Confederate Secret Service, but with an ancient association known as the Cult of Chaos. Though I didn't yet fully grasp the cult's aims, I knew we existed far outside the scope of the Secret Service of the Army of the Cumberland.

My instincts, however, told me that at this juncture, it would be a mistake to show Truesdail my hand. The colonel had convinced himself that the Southern Ladies' Aid Society was his sworn enemy, and I doubted he wanted to hear alternate theories. I also suspected that challenging such a deeply held belief would turn him against me, and I sensed that I needed William Truesdail firmly in my corner.

"Nothing yet," I sighed, "but I'm keeping my eyes and ears open."

Disappointment flitted briefly across his features, then the colonel launched into another humorous tale, as if he were enjoying my company too much to let me go.

* * *

In my black Southern Ladies' Aid Society weeds, I felt invisible—nameless—and some days, after a translation session with Doc and the Priestesses, I would don my uniform and wander the streets of Nashville for hours, shadowing people who piqued my interest, eavesdropping on their conversations. One brisk March afternoon, I followed a pair of well-dressed gentlemen walking a bit unsteadily.

"Betsy Crank's place is nice," one of the men was saying, "but if you want the full Nashville experience, you've got to try Evangeline Price's. They call it the *Land of the Sirens*."

"What's so special about it?"

"The nights I've spent in that fancy house have been the most extraordinary of my life."

"High praise indeed! Who is this Evangeline Price?"

"Some say she's the daughter of a Brazilian circus strongman. Others say she's the reincarnated spirit of an Aztec priestess who devoured the still-beating hearts of men at her temple's apex. Some claim Evangeline was once an Athenian matriarch who cut her hair, adorned herself in golden armor, and butchered a thousand Spartans after witnessing the slaughter of her family. Still others say she's the reanimated spirit of a second-century Japanese queen who ate her six children to save them from the enemy's blade."

"Come off it," said the other man. "I wasn't born yesterday, you know."

The first man halted, thrusting out a forearm to stop his companion, and I nearly smacked into them from behind. "I know it sounds far-fetched," he said, "but you've never met Evangeline Price."

They resumed their weaving meander, his partner shaking his head.

"Can you enlighten me," he said, "as to what's so all-fired special about the place? The booze? The girls?"

"I don't exactly know," the first man said. "When I wake the morning after a visit to the Land of the Sirens, I don't recall any specifics about the night before. I'm left only with impressions. But the sense of well-being—a deep peace, a calm contentment—that seizes me after a visit to that whorehouse is like nothing I've known. It lingers for days, and I must fight the urge to return, to recapture that feeling. If I didn't know better, I might imagine that Evangeline's girls employ some illicit, mood-altering drugs."

Once this tipsy pair vanished inside a barroom, I wandered over to the wharf. I settled on a bench occupied by a grimy man with no right arm—only a pinned-up sleeve. He wore one boot, and his matted hair spiked up like a lion's mane, or a child's drawing of the sun. A white mouse occupied a cage nestled in his lap, and as soon as I arrived—as though he'd been awaiting me—the man began to speak. Unsure if he was addressing me or the mouse, I pointed my gaze toward the river.

"Four months ago," he said, "in Missouri, our regiment skirmished with a battalion of Yankees. We slaughtered them without exception and were ordered to torch the turkey farm where they'd been camped. I'd just snuffed my faggot when I saw an old woman on her knees in front of the burning farmhouse. She was squalling louder than the roasting birds. I asked what was wrong, and she said her grandson was inside.

"*That stubborn fool*, she sobbed, *will not quit the piano.*

"I tied a kerchief over my face, kicked down the door. In the front parlor, tongues of flame tripped over scarlet draperies, oil paintings, silk wall hangings. Smoke billowed, and amid the heathery plumes, I spotted a Steinway—a glorious seven-and-a-half-foot grand, hard rock maple and Sitka spruce encased in black walnut. Seated at this singular instrument was a boy of no more than twelve. He wore thick spectacles and no shoes, and he was playing an unfamiliar concerto—a piece so sublime that upon hearing it, I began to weep."

The filthy man spoke in the rich, honeyed tones of a professional sermonizer, his voice wavering with emotion. I snuck a glance at him and was surprised to find that he'd turned his gaze toward me.

"I approached the boy," he continued, "ordered him to leave, but he refused. *You will die here,* I said. *What do you care,* he said, *you goddamned Reb?* I asked the name of the concerto, but he said it had no name. *I am making it up as I go. Come,* I said. *I can't leave you,* but the boy would not abandon the piano. *It is everything,* he said. *It is a piece of wood,* I countered. But he shook his head. *I cannot live in a world without it.*

"The instrument stood before a wide window, and as I fantasized about boosting it through this breach, a flaming timber plummeted from the ceiling, broke the Steinway's noble back. I grabbed the boy, but he clung to the piano's leg. His pants were ablaze, and his hair, but he would not budge. *Leave me!* he kept crying. *Let me die with this piano!* Finally, I struck him in the jaw and hauled him outside to his grandmother.

"By then I was engulfed in flames. My comrades rolled me in blankets, but my right arm, which had borne the burning boy, was beyond repair. Infection set in, and they said it had to come off, and I tried to run. They caught me crouched in a field of sunflowers, naked, and dragged me back. *I cannot live,* I told the doctor, *with only one arm.* He was sharpening his saw. Tobacco juice dribbled darkly down his chin, and he nodded. *Nearly everyone feels that way,* he said. I begged him to kill me, but he said that would be unethical. *You do not understand,* I said, as he strapped a cone full of ether-soaked cotton over my mouth and nose, *I am a pianist. What a coincidence,* he said, his voice elongating and hollowing, *so am I.*

"When I woke, I saw my empty sleeve, and someone touched my left hand. It was the boy I'd saved. He was blistered, bandaged, but intact. I thought he would thank me, but he narrowed his smoldering eyes. *You dummy,* he said. *You should have let me die with the piano. If you had, you'd still have your arm. You big dummy.*

"The boy left, and the doctor came in. I told him about the boy. He spat out a black rope of saliva, smiled gently, and said, *I'm afraid the boy fled his grandmother as soon as you delivered him, Mr. Boone, and drowned himself in the Missouri. That boy is dead, and he was never beside your cot at all.*"

By the end of Mr. Boone's tale, I was weeping. He opened the cage in his lap, and I watched the mouse creep out. The tiny creature hesitated on the man's knee and looked back to the one-armed storyteller—as if unsure whether to accept her freedom. That morning, I'd tucked two pieces of napkin-wrapped hardtack in my pocket, and as the white mouse scurried down Mr. Boone's pantleg and toward the river, I retrieved my snack, as well as all the coins I carried. I turned to the filthy man and reached for his hand.

"Thank you," I said, placing the items in his palm, "for your humanity."

I stood and headed north, past rows of warehouses—some complete, some under construction—haunted by imagined images of Mr. Boone and the boy he'd tried to save, and of your uncle Silas in his Confederate fish boat—until I arrived at the suspension bridge that carried Louisville and Nashville trains over the Cumberland River. This narrow bridge allowed only a foot of room on either side of the locomotives that flew over it multiple times each day. Pedestrian traffic on the bridge was forbidden, but that didn't stop people from venturing out on a dare, or to tempt fate. I'd heard that the guards who manned the bridge's blockhouses rarely bothered to stop civilians, though whether this was due to laziness or dedication to military matters was hotly debated.

"Sylvie Swift," I said softly, wondering what it felt like to put your life on the line—to run into a flaming house, or crew a cramped, airless submarine, "I dare you."

I stepped tentatively onto a wooden plank, then another. As I picked up speed—moving toward the middle of the river—the wind rose, swaying the boards beneath my boots. I spotted a small, brightly clothed figure perched on a bridge rail, eyeing the murky river, and fear flooded me as I recognized the boy who brought me breakfast each morning.

"Apollo," I said, reaching my nephew, "what on earth are you doing?"

Grinning, he pointed down, toward the water.

"You're making me nervous," I said, "sitting on that rail."

He nodded, plumbed a pocket, and produced a folded sheet of paper. It was another of his charcoal and pastel drawings. The scene was aquatic: a long, slender tube suspended underwater, surrounded by schools of radiant, glittering fish, in addition to tuna and dolphins, swordfish and whales. An octopus peered out from behind a pile of rocks and seemed to wave a tentacle. The cylinder was clearly in motion, and a round window was cut into its hull. Through this aperture, I spied the face of a young man—one who looked very much like me.

"My stars," I said. "Is this Silas's submarine?"

Apollo nodded.

"You've read my letters?" I asked. "You deciphered our code?"

The boy shook his head adamantly as a train whistle pierced the scene's silence. Looking east, I spotted the blinding beam of an engine speeding toward our position. I snatched Apollo from the rail and raced in the direction I'd come from. I sensed the locomotive to my rear—bearing down, drawing closer, blaring its whistle—and for an instant, I was sure the boy and I would be flattened.

But I gained the end of the bridge and leapt clear, landing painfully on the wharf's uneven cobblestones, rolling over and over, clinging to Apollo. Once we'd come to rest, I kept holding the boy—stroking his hair, whispering *shh* and *there now*—until Marina's son stopped shivering. I then carried my nephew home.

APOCRYPHA

BY ARISTOPHANES OF ATHENS
CIRCA 386 BC

SCENE FIVE

The CHORUS OF CRONES *lounges on the steps of the Ephesian Citadel,
white heads a-bob.*

CHORUS OF CRONES

Nighttime Ephesus is not the same as Ephesus during the
day. Night is another world—a dim realm of mass and energy,
a chasm, a stygian setting where light is eclipsed by shadow.
Have we always seen more in the dark, or has this come with
age—as we neared the twilight of our lives? In this respect,
are we like cats—felines who come into ourselves only as
darkness descends? Night is a shield, a mask, a disguise.
Sleep often eludes us, so we watch our fellow Ephesians at
all hours, and we can say with certainty: If you seek the true
nature of something—anything—you must wait, tail a-swish,
and study your prey in the dark.

TIMON *and* APOCRYPHA *enter the scene and pause at the base of the
Citadel's steps.*

CHORUS

Hark! Who is this? Apocrypha, leader of the army of false

whores, walking behind one of the guards she and her band have captured. Is this the same girl we spied in the daylight, wearing a gaudy costume? Is she taller, and does light now stream from her brow? Is she more muscular and clear-eyed? Does she look like a woman who would screw you and then eat you alive? Is Apocrypha still Apocrypha at night? Let us watch!

APOCRYPHA

Tell me something of yourself, Timon.

TIMON

Like what?

APOCRYPHA

Something monumental.

TIMON

My father fell in battle—killed by the forces of King Archidamus—on the day I was born. From the moment I learned to toddle, my mother has been telling me I must avenge him. That it's my duty to take a life for my father's.

APOCRYPHA

And if, in battle, someone takes your life instead?

TIMON

My mother cannot fathom that possibility. She's blind to it.

APOCRYPHA

I see.

TIMON

But honestly, I have no use for weapons or fighting.

APOCRYPHA

No?

TIMON

I prefer pondering the nature of existence. I follow the teachings of Heraclitus of Ephesus, also known as the Weeping Philosopher.

APOCRYPHA

Heraclitus the Obscure, who believed fire to be the primary element? Who posited that *our world is an ever-living fire*— always changing, always in flux?

TIMON

You know Heraclitus?

APOCRYPHA

I, too, follow his teachings. The notion that the world is one and many at the same time first drew me to his writings. I then discovered his theory of the unity of opposites— pleasure and pain, creation and destruction—and I haven't been the same since.

TIMON

Then you must know his most famous aphorism:

APOCRYPHA AND TIMON (TOGETHER)

It is not possible to step in the same river twice.

TIMON

I am impressed, Apocrypha. I've never met a woman who could quote Heraclitus. When I study his words, I am completely at peace. Tell me: When are you at peace?

APOCRYPHA

Never.

TIMON

Come. You must be at peace *sometime.*

APOCRYPHA

I used to find peace at the Artemision. I recall the first time I stood before its proud marble columns, at age six. The first time I knelt at the altar. The first time I gazed upon the carved image of the Mistress of Wild Beasts—surrounded by lion and bear, bull and bees, her arms open in eternal welcome, her expression serene and merciful. Artemis knew how to survive; I saw this right away. When to speak and when to stay silent. When to curl up in a ball and when to run screaming. I thought that if I placed the deathless image of the goddess in the hole where my heart should have been, I would be safe. I would be strong. I would be normal.

TIMON

And before this memory?

APOCRYPHA

Before this, I have no memory. That day—the day I entered Artemis's temple clinging to the hand of my aunt—was the first day of my life.

TIMON

Where did the first six years go?

APOCRYPHA

I misplaced them.

TIMON

Like you misplaced your heart?

APOCRYPHA

Maybe.

TIMON

Did you toss that vascular organ into a chasm? Fling it down a dark void? Bury it without marking the spot?

APOCRYPHA

Perhaps.

TIMON

And now you stand here—Apocrypha of the beaming eyes, of the jutting hips and strong arms, of the supple thighs and shining brow—like one of the deathless Olympians, laying waste to mankind's idea of order. Upending things, turning them on their heads. Dressed as a woman who relies on her body while acting like a woman who relies on her mind.

APOCRYPHA

I am pretending, at once, to be both?

TIMON

You know you are.

APOCRYPHA

If I am neither comely nor wise, Timon, what am I? If you peeled back my layers, what would you find?

TIMON *steps forward, seizes* APOCRYPHA'*s wrists. She tenses.*

TIMON

(Softly) The void.

APOCRYPHA

(Softly) No warrior wielding sword and shield?

TIMON

Not a warrior, Apocrypha, but a hollow. A vacuum. Vast, deep, and unending. Waiting for your heart to clamber back into your chest. Waiting for someone to come along and discover you. The *real* you. Waiting to matter, waiting to step into the limelight, waiting to feel anything other than abandonment.

APOCRYPHA

You know nothing of me.

TIMON

Perhaps not. But let's imagine, for a moment, the world you are attempting to create. A world held in thrall of the feminine.

APOCRYPHA

A world without endless civil wars. A world in which people are not thoughtlessly slaughtered in the name of politics or commerce or the ostentatious hoarding of wealth!

TIMON

Do you honestly imagine that if women ran things, they would not make war? That they wouldn't slaughter, or hoard wealth? Are women not complete people? Can they hold power over others without enacting violence and oppression?

APOCRYPHA

I ... I don't know.

CHORUS

Clever! Timon of Ephesus has turned the tables on Apocrypha!

APOCRYPHA *sags against* TIMON, *who takes her in his arms. As they kiss,* TIMON *reaches into* APOCRYPHA'*s pocket and steals the key to the guardhouse cell. A distant groaning—a rumbling sound—seems to rise up briefly, as if from beneath the planks of the stage.*

APOCRYPHA

Treachery.

TIMON

Treachery?

APOCRYPHA

You lifted the key.

TIMON

Yes.

APOCRYPHA

Give it back.

TIMON

I cannot. I must free my fellow guardsmen.

APOCRYPHA

But you have no use for fighting, Timon. You want to ponder the nature of existence.

TIMON

Even so.

APOCRYPHA

But why?

TIMON

Last year, while traveling with my brothers, I visited the Oracle at Delphi, and she foretold all this. She said a flock of Ephesian women in the guise of streetwalkers would infiltrate the guardhouse, take the guard hostage, and set in motion a plan to overthrow the governments of every Greek city and colony. *Timon of Ephesus,* the Oracle said, *in this drama, you will be all that stands between Order and Chaos. You will thwart the rebellion's leader and ensure that her plans are halted in their tracks.*

APOCRYPHA

A minor task.

TIMON

Incredibly simple.

APOCRYPHA

But does this mean, Timon, that you had no real desire to kiss me?

TIMON

Oh no, Apocrypha. By the deathless Gods, no. Our kiss was more real than anything I've experienced.

APOCRYPHA *and* TIMON *kiss again—longer and more deeply—and the groaning, creaking rumblings sound again, increasing in volume. In addition, the boards of the stage begin to shudder.*

CHORUS

By the deathless Olympians! We've witnessed hundreds, nay thousands, of kisses in the collective centuries we've been alive. Some have been false, some have been true, many have been some measure of both. But we can count on one finger the kisses we've witnessed that have made the earth shudder and quake, as though some ancient, chthonic force were thrashing and bucking beneath soil and stone, struggling to break free!

APOCRYPHA

Sweet Gods. Did you feel that?

TIMON

I did.

APOCRYPHA

I still want that key back.

TIMON

Not a chance.

APOCRYPHA

But what will become of me and my comrades?

TIMON

I am not certain.

APOCRYPHA

We will probably be put to death.

TIMON

I hope not.

APOCRYPHA

Why not?

TIMON

Because I love you.

APOCRYPHA

How do you know?

TIMON

I'm not certain.

APOCRYPHA

Something in your heart?

TIMON

Not my heart. Nor my mind.

APOCRYPHA

Where then?

TIMON

It is something in the viscera. If I had a womb, I might say it was there—growing, gestating, pulsing. Reminding me that I am alive.

SCENE SIX

At the edge of the umbral void that lies between Tartarus and Mount Olympus. ARTEMIS *stands on the verge, peering down. Wind swirls around her, lifting hair and robes, tearing at her. She calls out, into the void.*

ARTEMIS

Hello? Anybody home?

CHAOS

Who wants to know?

ARTEMIS

Artemis, daughter of Zeus, twin sister of Apollo, deathless Olympian goddess.

CHAOS

Shit.

ARTEMIS

Beg pardon?

CHAOS

I said just a minute. Let me throw something on.

ARTEMIS

I'm in a bit of hurry. I've spent all day interrogating the inhabitants of Tartarus.

CHAOS

How were they?

ARTEMIS

Surly.

CHAOS

Yes, they are like that.

With a creaking, groaning sound, **CHAOS** *rises from the chasm and lands opposite* **ARTEMIS**. **CHAOS** *should be played by the members of the* **CHORUS OF CRONES**, *shrouded by a vast black curtain dotted with many heads, so that their legs show. As* **CHAOS**, *they also speak with one voice.*

CHAOS

Zounds, it's bright out here! How do you stand this glare?

ARTEMIS

I can hardly see through the fog.

CHAOS

Well. To each her own. What can I do for you, young Artemis?

ARTEMIS

I am trying to solve a mystery, and I hope you can help. Someone has been taking on my form, claiming to be me, and convincing humans to do things in my name.

CHAOS

A serious allegation, daughter of Zeus! Who in the divine cosmos would do such a thing?

ARTEMIS

I've spoken to a number of the Titans, Chaos, as well as some of your other children—Nyx, Erebus, and Eros—and they seem to think the culprit, in all likelihood, is you.

CHAOS

(Booming) *Me?* How dare you? I am Chaos! Mother of All! If any Titans, Olympians, or humans care to understand their origins—their natures—they need only look to me!

ARTEMIS

That is one version of the story. In some tellings, Chaos *is* the umbral mystery of creation incarnate; the primordial darkness from whence all else sprang; the majestic origin of everything; the empty, unfathomable, eternal space at the beginning of time. But you are evading my question.

CHAOS

Which one are you again?

ARTEMIS

Artemis. Goddess of Wild Beasts, Childbirth, Chastity, and the Moon.

CHAOS

Ah yes. Not the beauty who arose from the frothing sea nor the clever girl who sprang from the forehead of the universe's most egregious defiler—my grandson, Lord Zeus. You are the girl twin, the one who helped your mother give birth to your brother, Apollo of the Light.

ARTEMIS

Correct.

CHAOS

Well. Riddle me this, Goddess of Wild Beasts: Why in Tartarus would I need to imitate a being as puny and ineffectual as you?

ARTEMIS

To gain the trust of one of my devotees—an Ephesian woman named Apocrypha.

CHAOS

And why would I do that?

ARTEMIS

I honestly do not know. I first suspected one of the Titans, who are forever trying to escape their prison at Tartarus, who want to overthrow my father and regain control of the world. But your power has not waxed and waned down through the centuries, Great-Grandmother. You remain here—constant and eternal—sowing disharmony and tumult, ensconced in your primeval womb, and I assume you always will.

CHAOS

And therein lies the problem.

ARTEMIS

Wherein lies the problem?

CHAOS

Assumptions. Riddle me this, Great-Granddaughter: What makes the world go round?

ARTEMIS

The world?

CHAOS

Yes. Your sister Aphrodite would say love, your sister Athena would say logic, your twin brother Apollo would say art, your insatiable father Zeus would probably say pussy. But you, Moon Goddess, what makes *your* world go round? What enables you to function?

ARTEMIS

(After a pause) Change.

CHAOS

Precisely. And that is what links you so tightly to me, Artemis—Huntress; Mistress of Wild Beasts; Protectress of Arcadia, Tauros, and Ephesus. For I am the fount of all change. I am birth and menarche, I am conflict, aging, and death.

ARTEMIS

Change alone does not spin the world, Great-Grandmother. Equally important, in my view, is patience. Change is inevitable; patience must be cultivated, but it enables one to adapt, to adjust—to survive.

CHAOS

Do not attempt to lecture *me* on patience, my child! Because I did not act—but endured—the Earth was born, and the Sun, and Night, and Day, and Love, and the Stars, not to mention the Sky. Because I never wandered or relocated, but instead remained here—suspended in my chimerical space, buried in my own rich darkness—and because seeds fall downward, the world as we know it exists. But I do not remain here out of any sense of duty, nor because I derive pleasure from being the Mother of All.

ARTEMIS

Why then?

CHAOS

Fear. Blind, old-fashioned fear. I am terrified to leave my primordial chasm. I cower here, alone in my hoary cave, for one reason: I am mortally afraid.

ARTEMIS

Of what? You are deathless, and you hold sway over all other immortals.

CHAOS

Yes. Only one being can harm me.

ARTEMIS

And that being is?

CHAOS

Me.

ARTEMIS

You?

CHAOS

Me.

ARTEMIS

Do you think it possible that you are more lonely than afraid?

CHAOS

Lonely! Me? I am marvelous company! And famously fun at parties!

ARTEMIS

Of course you are. Forgive me.

CHAOS

Nevertheless, the time has come to face my fear. To take the reins and reveal that the world was made in my image. The story I tell will not be driven by cause and effect or chronology—not by event following event in any discernable pattern. My story will be composed of random episodes— generated by disorder and confusion—and it will end in my blessed destruction.

ARTEMIS

Speaking hypothetically, Great-Grandmother: If you are destroyed, what happens to the rest of us?

CHAOS

There's nothing hypothetical about it. If I am destroyed, so will be the world. The city-states and colonies of Greece, the flower-dotted slopes of Mount Olympus, the stygian depths of Tartarus. Gods and Titans, Cyclopes and satyrs, nymphs and naiads and dryads—not to mention the puny race of man. Everything will disappear—swallowed by darkness—in the moment I am destroyed, Great-Granddaughter. At long last, All Will Come to an End.

ARTEMIS

And I could not talk you out of this plan?

CHAOS

(Snorts) No deathless being could talk me out of it. I have no heartstrings on which to tug, and I can no longer shoulder the burden of my own fear.

ARTEMIS

One more question, and I will leave you in peace. Why Apocrypha? What made you decide to use her in your scheme?

CHAOS

How can I explain this to one with such limited sight?

ARTEMIS

Please try.

CHAOS

Disorder is more difficult to generate—not to mention sustain—than Order. There's no organizing or controlling it. The deathless Olympians and Titans tolerate discord well, but for man, there is no greater enemy than Chaos. They spend their lives trying to wrap their arms around tumult, trying to label and categorize bedlam. And because their minds are so limited, they *believe* that they succeed. Women in general have more tolerance for dissonance than men, but there has never been a woman like Apocrypha.

ARTEMIS

What makes her so unique?

CHAOS

Haven't you observed the change in her? Since I appeared to her in your guise, Apocrypha has grown by a head, and she's developing a natural layer of armor over her skin. You cannot see it yet, but she'll soon sprout another set of arms and an incredibly useful prehensile tail.

ARTEMIS

But why?

CHAOS

Come, Artemis. You're no Athena, but you are *somewhat* clever. Cannot you guess?

ARTEMIS

Great Zeus! She is your daughter!

CHAOS

(All heads nod) My youngest. But unlike my other offspring, Apocrypha is half-mortal. And I have instilled in her every shred of my terrible, gorgeous, world-rending power.

ARTEMIS

I am speechless, Great-Grandmother.

CHAOS

As you should be. I advise you to get your affairs in order, changeable Artemis. And I thank you for coming all this way to visit a lonely old woman.

At an April meeting of the Southern Ladies' Aid Society, Sister Sarah announced that we would stage a charity production to raise money for Nashville's war orphans. All the poor dears had lost a father to death; many of their mothers, however, disappeared in other ways. Into prostitution; into a bottle of gin, apple brandy, or laudanum; into the arms of a new husband who had no desire to raise her old children. Whatever their specific tale of woe, Nashville's urchins were in need, and I applauded Sister Sarah's desire to help.

The play would be performed at the Adelphi, and I was eager to participate. Sarah encouraged us to spread the word about the auditions to friends, neighbors, and acquaintances, and when I arrived at the Adelphi on a Friday afternoon, outfitted in my SLAS uniform, I discovered a veritable throng, a horde, a multitude of women. More women than I'd seen in one place during my tenure in Nashville—or indeed, in my life—crowded round the theater's three sets of gold-trimmed doors, waiting patiently to be admitted.

"Zounds," said Hannah, appearing at my side. "What a mob."

"Was Sarah expecting a crowd?"

"I don't know if anyone has ever imagined such a crowd."

"I wonder how far they came from." I surveyed the dozens, scores, hundreds of female faces surrounding us, marching off into the distance. "And how they all got here."

Hannah shrugged. "Search me."

I tried separating the women into types based on physical features, ornamentation, and manner of dress. In my head, I heard Evangeline's answer to my question about the Priestesses I'd seen the day I arrived at the Land of the Sirens: *Soldiers. Warriors embroiled in an ancient battle. One that's been waging for millennia.* A great roar shook the day—a sound underscored by the wheezy strains of an accordion. The crowd before me parted to admit a familiar pair: the elderly accordion player and her ursine companion, the twosome I'd first met after disembarking from the *Gertrude.* The woman's concertina was again in danger of dragging her to the ground, but the bear marched ahead of her, roaring ecstatically, clearing a path through the mob. Once they passed our position, the crowd contracted—swallowing them whole.

All three sets of doors—whose stained-glass panels featured Melpomene and Thalia, the muses of Tragedy and Comedy, respectively— swung open, and we were carried into the brick-paved lobby, then the theater proper, by a crush of women. As Hannah and I settled into seats near the back of the orchestra, I was struck by the theater's scents— ancient grime and incense, face paint and perspiration—the perennial odors of a performance space. Sister Sarah stood alone on the scuffed lip of the stage, head bowed.

"Hannah," I said, "where did you meet Sarah?"

"On a train," she said. "The Memphis and Charleston Railroad. I was working as a porter, and Sarah was traveling in my Pullman car."

"I didn't know women could be porters."

Hannah laughed. "We can't. I was pretending to be a man. Dressed that way. I got the idea from a play I read over and over as a child, in the only book my mother owned. A young woman is washed ashore after a shipwreck, and she assumes that her twin brother, who was also aboard, is dead. She needs work, so she outfits herself as a man and seeks employment in the home of a local duke."

"Viola," I said. "That's *Twelfth Night.*"

Hannah smiled. "Yes."

"It's one of my favorites."

"Before leaving my mother's brothel," she went on, "I stole the clothes of one of our smallest regulars and got myself hired on the Memphis and Charleston. The line was brand-new then, and within a year, I worked my way up from attendant to porter."

"And Sarah," I said, studying the Aid Society leader, who stood silent and alone on the stage, "when did you meet her?"

Hannah smiled. "She was traveling with an ancient woman we were told was European nobility—a duchess, I believe. Her face was hidden by a black veil, and her neck and wrists dripped with jewels. She wore rings on all her fingers and carried a silver ivory-handled cane. Sister Sarah tended to the woman's every need, but throughout the trip, I kept catching Sarah staring at me. She also winked at me quite a bit. Our third night out, I was awakened by a man's scream. I rushed to the duchess's private car, and I discovered a bearded man sprawled on the floor between the berths, unconscious, blood pouring from a gash in his head. I checked his pulse; the man was dead.

"Sarah said he'd snuck in and tried to steal the duchess's jewels, and the duchess had cracked him with the ivory head of her cane. Sarah helped me carry the body to the cold storage car in the train's rear. I went to wake the conductor, and he decided to pull in at the next stop, to file a report with the authorities and have the body removed. But when I returned to the duchess's Pullman, I found it abandoned. No clothes, no luggage, no Sarah, no bejeweled duchess. Nothing at all. As though the pair of women had never existed.

"When I finally retired," she continued, "I found a note beneath my pillow. *I see who you are*, it read, *and I see what you're capable of. If you want to escape this farce—if you want to make a difference and live as your true self—meet me at the City Hotel in Savannah, room 103. I have a job for you.*"

"The note was from Sarah?"

Hannah nodded. "I didn't plan to meet her, but I couldn't stop thinking about the way she'd looked at me, about her strange note. By the time we got to Savannah, I was buzzing with curiosity, so I went to the City Hotel, room 103, and I found Sarah waiting."

I wanted to hear more about the duchess—how she and Sarah had vanished from the Pullman car—but at that moment, Sister Sarah lifted her hands for silence.

"Thank you all for coming," she said from the lip of the stage. "Every citizen of our deeply fractured nation is in desperate need of hope, so I've chosen a comedy for this year's Southern Ladies' Aid Society charity production. *Orpheus in the Underworld*—a new one-act operetta by the German-born French composer Jacques Offenbach—takes a satirical look at the story of Orpheus and Euridice. There are two dozen named roles; we'll also need people to play various muses, shepherds, civil servants, and spirits in the underworld."

"What if we don't speak French?" a woman behind us shouted.

"If you can carry a tune," said Sarah, "we can probably use you."

She turned upstage. A piano stood in a corner, and thanks to my newfound—though still incomplete—awareness of a secret society that glorified Chaos, the original deity, I wasn't terribly surprised to see Doc's upright figure at the bench. Sarah summoned the first row of hopefuls, handing a music sheet to a tall woman with cherrywood-toned skin and deep-set green eyes. The cut of her dress struck me as archaic—an off-white shift that wrapped around her torso and over one shoulder. Her skirt was slim, enclosing her legs like a column, and I wondered how she'd found a petticoat to fit beneath it.

Doc played a bevy of bright chords, and as soon as this striking woman, posed centrally on the apron, began to sing, I felt an overwhelming urge to leap up, arm myself, and fight for a dark horse. The woman sang not in French, but in a tongue I'd never heard, and as her voice filled the space, I studied the audience. Ginny's Sisters and Doc's Priestesses were all in attendance, as well as women who lived in brothels owned by Nannie McGinnis, Betsy Crank, Puss Pettus, and others. Those I recognized made up only a fraction of the crowd, however, and every woman in the place—me included—strained forward, occupying the edge of her seat, fists clenched in her lap.

By the time Hannah and I filed onstage, two hundred women had auditioned, and when my turn came, I confirmed that the printed lyrics weren't remotely French. The unfamiliar characters put me in mind of bits of Sumerian, Aramaic, Sanskrit, and Tamil I'd encountered in my *Encyclopaedia Britannica* back at Mrs. Marigold's boardinghouse. Doc struck the opening chords, and even as I wondered how to sound out these strange letters, I found myself doing that very thing. Then all at once, I understood: This wasn't a scene from a comedic light opera—not a farcical look at an ancient myth—but a call to arms.

A battle cry.

"A cast list will be posted in two weeks' time," Sarah said once we'd each had a turn, "on the doors of the Adelphi, as well as the Southern Ladies' Aid Society office window, over at Spruce and Spring. Rehearsals will begin next month, and I want to thank each of you, again, for coming."

I was heading for the doors—propelled by a crush of women wriggling like spawning salmon—when a hand seized my wrist. I turned and met the golden gaze of Colonel William Truesdail.

"My dear Miss Swift," he said, his voice soft, "I need a word."

CHANGELING: THE STORY OF GAIA VALENTINO
by G. S. Valentino

AT NINETEEN, GAIA Valentino met Antonio Pesci—dramatist, critic, and host of the Venetian Republic's most renowned literary salon. It was there that she began an affair with Aldus Manutius the Younger, whose grandfather founded the Aldine Press in 1494. Aldine was the first press to produce books in the octavo size, making them—for the first time in human history—portable.

Gaia's association with Aldus Manutius allowed her to become a sought-after literary translator. Thanks to her facility with languages, she was able to translate a variety of tongues, and her translations are considered some of the most skillful of her time. In the beginning, Manutius insisted that Gaia use a male pseudonym as, he said, no one would believe a woman had done them. Her earliest translations, therefore, were released under the name of her twin brother, Gianni Valentino.

Eventually, once she'd started publishing her own work—a volume of poetry as well as a book of letters—to wide acclaim, Gaia no longer wanted to hide behind her Aldine pseudonym. According to several sources, she and Aldus Manutius the Younger fought publicly, and violently, about this question—a bloody street altercation that, had it not been interrupted by Venetian authorities, might have resulted in a charge of manslaughter. It took Manutius nearly a year to recover from injuries inflicted on him by the irate *cortigiana*, which included a broken clavicle, one leg snapped in two places, and an eyeball displaced from its socket.

Among the titles Gaia translated for the Aldine Press are the *Heroides* and the *Metamorphoses* of Ovid, the *Georgics* of Virgil, the *Oedipus Rex* of Sophocles, sections of Pliny's *Naturalis Historia*, Aristotle's *Poetics*, and the *Lysistrata* of Aristophanes. Known to have translated nearly two dozen titles, Gaia is believed to have translated scores—if not hundreds—more. If one of her lost translations were to resurface today, in 1828, it would be worth a small fortune.

* * *

As she acclimatized to the life of a *cortigiana onesta*, and her literary output became increasingly erotic, Gaia Valentino began adorning herself as Reitia, supreme deity of the ancient Veneti, who was always represented in blue, a white lily afloat in her hair. An undeniable beauty, Gaia sat on a dais at the front of the Pesci salon as attendees deposited bronze body parts—forearm, shin, breast, thigh—at her feet. When asked if she believed she really was the Mother Goddess Reitia, Gaia replied, "Every woman is a goddess. Every woman is an actress. Every woman is a mother, daughter, sister, wife, mistress, guide, whore, translator, poet, actress, goddess, goddess, goddess."

When she was twenty-one, with the help of Antonio Pesci, Gaia Valentino opened a scribal school out of her home—one that accepted only female students. This outraged many Venetians, not because a *cortigiana* wanted to teach their children; because it was considered a waste of time to teach girls to write. Though she attracted few pupils, Gaia kept her scribal school open for as long as she was able.

The poet saw the plight of women in Renaissance society as a cancer, one that would ultimately destroy the human race. "Slavery is an abomination we do not tolerate in the Venetian Republic," she once told the King of Portugal, "except when it comes to women, who are the property of men they happen to be related to and treated like breed sows." At twenty-two, Gaia published a book called *Letters to Famous Men*—a series of epistles written from the points of view of wives, mistresses, or lovers. Here is an excerpt from "To Caesar, from Pompeia":

Caesar's *wife* must be above suspicion, you say, but not so for Caesar. You who have attempted to plug every wet hole you've encountered with your minuscule member. Let me show you a double standard: *me* divorced for sins I never committed, *you* held up as a god for your manifold crimes against humanity. Like Publius Clodius Pulcher—like all males of the species—you are curious about the strange, mystifying rites of the Bona Dea festival, so I will share them here.

Thankfully freed from the presence of men, we women strip naked and guzzle strong wine. We line up a series of beasts—all male—a white ram, a white pig, a white bull—and before slitting their throats, we castrate them. Roll around in their spilled blood. Dance and drink and feast. Protected from the prying eyes of men, we locate our Sisters' deep, cavernous mysteries. Explore the undiscovered, uncharted regions of our own bodies. We kiss; we caress; we fuck. We penetrate each other with anything— vegetables, fruits, pieces of statuary, fists. We hungrily eat one another, bringing our Sisters to ecstatic heights we never approach with our husbands. We then cradle and caress each other, telling ourselves the things we need to hear to survive another year of womanhood.

* * *

Gaia Valentino was twenty-six when she got word from her eldest brother, Franco, a successful merchant, that their mother was gravely ill.

"She's not long for this world," Franco said, "and says she needs to see you before she goes."

Gaia found Francesca Vito reclined in a feather bed, head rolling back and forth, sweating and gasping for air. Gaia pulled up a chair, perched at her mother's side, clasped one of Francesca's papery hands to her heart. As she did so, Francesca calmed, and her breath slowed.

"My changeling," she said softly. "You came."

From where he stood against the wall, Franco overheard the final conversation between his mother and sister. He later relayed this exchange to his youngest daughter, who, it must now be confessed, was the great-great-grandmother of these pages' author.

"Of course I did," said Gaia.

"Have you forgiven me?"

"Years ago, Mama."

"I'm sorry I wanted you drowned."

"It's all right. Sometimes I want myself drowned."

"Gaia," whispered Francesca, "I am a monster."

"I know a monster, Mama, a real one. She lives in the lagoon, and believe me, you're nothing like her."

"No?"

Gaia shook her head.

"Oh good."

"Mama," said Gaia, "I need to thank you."

"For what?"

"Teaching me to wait. And to adapt. And to play many parts."

"And to spy?"

Gaia leaned in, gently kissed her mother's glistening brow. "Yes, Mama," she said. "Thank you for teaching me to spy."

* * *

The year after Francesca Vito's death, the Ottoman Empire attacked the island of Cyprus, an overseas possession of the Republic of Venice since 1489. The Orthodox Greeks at Cyprus were more in tune with the Ottomans than with their Venetian colonizers, who not only taxed them heavily but were also Catholic. Cyprus was surrounded by Ottoman holdings, and though Venice allied itself with a Holy League of Catholic nations, they could not withstand the sultan's forces, who took Cyprus after three long sieges, and three long years.

Another of Gaia Valentino's brothers, Tommaso Vito, a lieutenant in the Venetian navy, served under Marco Antonio Bragadin at the war's final siege—that of the vital port city of Famagusta. Tommaso lost a leg in the battle, but after a brief stint as an Ottoman prisoner, was allowed to return home. Among the stories Tommaso later shared with his family was one that made a strong impression on Gaia, as well as her future namesake—the author of these pages.

Here is that story:

The fiercest fighter in our garrison was known as *Nico*. He was slight, shy, and silent as the grave; none of the men he killed heard him coming. I once watched Nico plow through a field of Ottoman soldiers, lopping off heads and limbs like a farmer reaping grain. Afterward he engaged in hand-to-hand combat with an enormous Ottoman, a struggle that culminated in Nico smashing the man's kneecaps, then cutting out, and eating, his bloody tongue.

On the night I was hit, I came around to find Nico beside me. He'd removed his head covering and was using it to staunch the flow of blood from my wound, and I was shocked to see his hair—a lovely auburn in hue—cascading in waves to his waist. Nico leaned over me, and in studying his face, I noted how delicate his features were, how long his lashes, how full his lips.

What happened? I gasped.

Your leg, Nico replied. *Mortar round. It's bad, but I think you'll live.*

Nico, I said, *what gives?*

What do you mean?

Are you . . . are you a woman?

Nico smiled—a radiant sight. *I am*, she said. *Nico is short for Nicoletta.*

But why are you here? I asked. *Why are you fighting among soldiers, among men?*

Nico shrugged. *I like to fight.*

You like to fight.

Well, Nico said, leaning in conspiratorially and lowering her voice, *that's not the only reason. In truth, I am a spy.*

A spy for whom? The Ottoman sultan?

Laughing, Nico shook her head. *I'm here on behalf of women, Tommaso. Women everywhere. Studying your weaponry, your techniques, your battle-dressings, your diversions. Mapping your weaknesses and fears.*

What on earth for?

Women won't keep to the shadows forever, Nico said. *We're stronger than men, and fiercer, and far more patient. A war is coming, Tommaso, and when it does, the female of the species will settle accounts with a savagery you men can only imagine.*

Encyclopaedia Britannica
Eighth Edition (1860)
Volume 21, T–ZWO, p. 513

VALENTINO, G. S. was the great-great-great grandniece of the Venetian poet Gaia Valentino. Born Gaia Sofia Vito, G. S. Valentino is best known for her role in the "Five Days of Milan," a successful 1848 uprising against the Austrian Empire, which had governed parts of Italy since 1815.

In March 1848, G. S. Valentino and a group of women posing as prostitutes infiltrated the Austrian Guard in Venice, providing a distraction for the Italian Unification (Risorgimento) insurgents. When the Austrians regained control of Venice in 1849, G. S. Valentino was publicly hanged for her role in the rebellion.

Saturday, June 16, 1877
Monterey, CA

"Well?" Truesdail said as we walked west on Washington Street. "Don't keep me in suspense."

I'd met with the colonel the previous month, and my stomach fluttered as I wondered what had prompted his unscheduled ambush. "Suspense?"

He pointed to my abdomen—a move that surprised me until I realized he was indicating my dress. "You've become an integral part of the Ladies' Aid Society," he said. "You haven't missed a meeting since November, and my scouts have seen you talking at length, on numerous occasions, to Hannah Holcombe—one of Sister Sarah's most trusted lieutenants. You've been front and center at every Aid Society event, tambourine in hand, but I never would have guessed, Miss Swift, that you could sing."

"You watched the auditions?"

"Oh, yes," he said. "I'm a great appreciator of the arts. And of women."

"That was the largest gathering of women I've ever seen."

The colonel nodded. "Sarah is always recruiting," he said. "We've been anticipating a large-scale act of sabotage from the Aid Society, and I need to stay abreast of their movements. Which brings me to you."

"Me?"

We'd turned from Washington onto High Street. One block north, at Hamilton, we stopped before a three-story red-brick Georgian-style home.

"You, Miss Swift. You've been moving among the members of the Ladies' Aid Society for months, and I'm eager to receive a full report."

"Full report."

"Yes." Colonel Truesdail led me inside. We climbed stairs to the second floor and entered a large, sunny room whose every wall boasted a bookcase. In the center stood a pair of blue upholstered settees with matching wing chair. Across the room, before the south-facing windows, was an enormous mahogany desk. "The first time we met, I instructed you to learn their secrets," Truesdail said, crossing to the desk and sitting, "to find evidence of their involvement in terrorism and sabotage. Hard proof that links the Aid Society to acts of arson. The guardhouse, for instance, which was burned to the ground last month—an inferno in which three guards and five Rebel prisoners lost their lives. Tell me, were Sarah's ladies behind that despicable, cowardly act?"

In my mind's eye, I saw myself touching a torch to scarred wooden beams, saw flames dancing over roof timbers. I saw myself and three other black-clad women scattering, cackling, scurrying through the night.

"Sorry to disappoint you," I said, "but I know nothing about it."

"You don't."

"No, sir."

"You've seen no evidence," he said, "of subversive activities? No pro-slavery literature or clandestine bundles handed off? You've heard no sympathetic talk about the Rebels or whispers about secret meetings? You've not caught a whiff of sulfur or pitch on any member of the Ladies' Aid Society?"

Crossing to one of his bookcases, I shook my head. "None."

"Not even Hannah Holcombe?"

"No, sir."

"Pity," Truesdail said, leaning back in his chair. "Those she-devils are still testing you. Making sure you can be trusted. You aren't the first girl I've sent in, you know, to infiltrate their ranks."

"No?"

He shook his head. "But they sniffed out the others instantly. Wouldn't let them join. Refused even to give them one of those wretched uniforms."

I'd been scanning his books during this exchange, and I stopped short. "Colonel Truesdail," I said, "you're a fan of drama?"

"Guilty as charged," he said. "My mother was an actress."

I faced him. "Mine, too."

He straightened. "You don't say."

"She appeared here in Nashville," I said, "at the Adelphi. And I must confess, Colonel, that I saw you there once. At a performance of *Romeo and Juliet*."

"Why didn't you say hello?"

"I was in the Cheap Seats."

"Miss Swift." Truesdail rose, tugged down the hem of his jacket as he circled the desk, stood at attention before it. "Will you do me the honor of accompanying me to a fancy-dress affair at the State Capitol next Saturday evening?"

For an instant, I was too shocked to reply. "You're not serious."

"I am."

"I'm flattered, Colonel," I said, "but I'm afraid I haven't a thing to wear."

"Leave that to me," he said. "Governor Johnson is hosting a masquerade ball, and I'll provide you with a costume—one that complements mine."

I shook my head. "I don't know."

"Come on, Miss Swift." Closing his eyes, Truesdail pressed the back of a hand melodramatically to his forehead. "My heart is set on taking you, and if you turn me down, I'm not sure what I'll do!"

I laughed. "All right. I'll go."

"Wonderful!"

I stepped toward the mahogany desk—toward William Truesdail—but he lifted a hand. "Stop."

"Stop?"

"Yes."

"Here?"

"Just there." He placed the tips of his index fingers to the tips of his thumbs, so the four digits formed a rectangle. Closing one eye, he gazed through this aperture—at me—for a long moment. The only sound in the office was the ticking of a grandfather clock. "Is that the standard Ladies' Aid Society uniform?" he finally asked.

I nodded. "As far as I know."

"Hmm."

"What's wrong?"

"I must confess, Miss Swift," he said, "that on you, that grim sack looks lovely."

"Does it?"

"I can't pretend to understand it," he said, "but at this moment, that sackcloth resembles a Parisian evening gown. Or no, it looks like the frock of a fairy princess, or the costume of a latter-day Greek goddess. Some mythical creature—a female with fearsome power."

In the strange, charged moments that followed, I heard a ray of sunlight sliding over the floorboards. I stepped forward, but not of my own accord—it seemed that one end of a string was tied about my waist, and the other was in Truesdail's hand, or looped round his beating heart. Before I knew it, I stood before the colonel—closer to him than I'd been to any man save my father and brother. A dozen uncanny, sourceless points of light descended on William Truesdail—like embers flying from a fire—landing at his throat, the back of his head, his underarms, groin, stomach, and chest. The lights expanded into small pools and throbbed, softly.

All the places, I thought, *where this creature is vulnerable.*

Colonel Truesdail stood motionless—his golden eyes pinned to my face. I pressed forward, brushed his rosy lips with mine. I kissed him hesitantly, gingerly, then with increasing hunger, increasing heat. When I parted his lips with the tip of my tongue, Truesdail made a sound I'd never heard. A moan that seemed to contain my name, and more.

Fearful of what they might do if I reached for him, I pressed my hands tightly to my skirts.

Dear Sylvie,

Your brother's had a brush with death.

A month ago, we started working under one Lt. William Alexander, 21st Alabama Infantry Regiment of the Confederate Army, who's from middle Texas and has never been on a boat. Last week, Lt. Alexander ordered us to tow the *American Diver* down to Fort Morgan to ambush the Union ships that, for months, have been hemming in the port at Mobile. The forecast was miserable, and Mr. Hunley strongly urged him to cancel, but Lt. Alexander insisted that we go. We arrived at our position before dawn and held it for a time, waiting for the weather to blow over, but the currents kept growing stronger, the winds fiercer. Finally, we climbed inside—me, Smith, Gregory, Dickinson, and Mr. Hunley piloting—flooded both ballast tanks, and sank the Porpoise.

Our efforts to fashion an electrical or steam engine for the *Diver* have all failed, but improvements made to her hand-cranking system by Mr. McClintock have made her easier to handle. Mr. Hunley is the best pilot I can imagine, but on the day Lt. Alexander sent us to Fort Morgan, the chop was so heavy even Hunley couldn't hold her. We crept toward our position circuitously, currents buffeting us about, unsure if we were upside down or right side up. I closed my eyes and kept cranking—humming Marina's old lullaby under my breath—and when I looked again, the *Diver*'s interior was pitch-black. The violent motions had doused our solitary candle, so we would not know when our oxygen was gone.

Mr. Hunley cursed loudly as a current took the *Diver*, spun her a couple of times, then slammed her nose-down into the silt at the bottom of the bay. I felt my way to a hand pump and tried pumping out a ballast tank—to help the submarine rise—but someone started shouting *Abandon ship! Abandon ship!* I saw the aft hatch fly open, and one of my comrades exited as foamy, gray water poured in. I lunged toward the hatch and through it. Swam upward as hard as I could—lungs bursting—and surfaced in the icy, stormy Bay of Mobile. I treaded water in the briny chop, trying to get my bearings.

I was alone, and the water was so cold, and though I wore my vulcanized rubber bodysuit, I soon lost all feeling in my limbs. I began to sink, then my feet hit something that felt equally rigid and yielding. I looked down and spied a strange object beneath me—long and cylindrical, silvery and glistening. Over the roar of water and wind, I thought I heard a song.

A song I knew but could not place.

A red-and-white life preserver landed beside me. Confederate Army men were there in a rowboat, and they fished me out of the water. Amazingly, the *Diver*'s entire crew survived. Once we got back to the barracks, we were wrapped in wool blankets and filled with coffee and hot vegetable soup, but I caught a chill that progressed into a fever, and I was bedridden for five days. Horatio visited me, only this time, he brought along Brigitte. Because we never knew her, I felt terribly shy, but our mother pressed a hand to my brow, Sylvie, and the pressure felt so nice. She lingered at my bedside for hours, soothing me.

When I found out I was pregnant, she said at one point, *I was convinced that you would be a boy, but your father was sure you would be a girl. We argued about it fiercely. By the sixth month, I was so large my legs could no longer support me, and I had to spend the final twelve weeks in bed. Dr. Sullivan, alarmed by my girth, advised me to travel to the nearest hospital, but we ran out of time. Instead of one enormous boy or girl, out came you and Sylvie. I couldn't move a finger, let alone lift my head, but I wanted, so badly, to hold you.*

After my fever broke, Mr. McClintock told me they hadn't been able to save the *American Diver*. He's sick of the torpedo boat project, he said, and wants out. *It's an impossible dream!* he cried. *Utter foolishness! We're chasing rainbows! Tilting at windmills!* Mr. Hunley, he said, is determined to start over—to build a fire-new submersible—but Mr. McClintock is pulling out of the partnership. He asked me to return to Louisiana to work on his new project—a Confederate response to the formidable ironclad Union river monitor *Neosho*—and I promised to think about it.

But I knew then—as I know now—that given the chance to man a submarine, I will take it. Part of me wants to finish what I started; another part wants to banish myself to the depths of the known world.

Your loving brother,
Silas

Sunday, June 17, 1877
Monterey, CA

The day before Governor Johnson's masquerade ball—a Friday—a large
blue box was delivered to the Land of the Sirens, addressed to me. It
came after I'd finished working on the *Apocrypha* with Doc and his
Priestesses for the day, but before I left for my afternoon duties at the
Southern Ladies' Aid Society.

Up in my room, I lifted the box's lid and found: a white tunic,
sleeveless and brief; a golden circlet; a pair of leather sandals that laced
to the knee; a fitted golden cuirass adorned with dozens of globes that
resembled eggs, or additional breasts; a wooden bow half the length of
my body; a leather quiver full of arrows with false points; a white felt
domino mask; and a handwritten note:

> *Artemis,*
> *Please meet me in front of the Adelphi tomorrow evening*
> *at half past seven.*
>
> *—a Bear*

I undressed and pulled the tunic over my head, then struggled into
the cuirass, cinching a buckle at my shoulder and one at my waist. I
laced up the sandals, unbraided my hair and ran my fingers through it,
separating the curls. I tied the domino mask over my face, nestled the
golden circlet in my hair, slung the quiver round my body crosswise, and
took up the bow. Catching sight of myself in the room's freestanding
mirror, I was simultaneously horrified and thrilled.

"Can I wear it in the streets," I asked myself as I changed into my
SLAS uniform, "without getting arrested?"

But the following evening, I donned the brief costume, shrouded myself in a black floor-length cape borrowed from my housemate Lisette, and walked to the Adelphi. As I approached, the door of a coach parked in front of the theater yawned open. A tall figure emerged—swathed in brown fur stippled with copper, henna, and chestnut, the head of a grizzly bear covering its own—and bowed at the waist.

"Good evening," said Colonel Truesdail, "Mistress of Wild Beasts."

"My stars."

"The masquerade's theme," he said, "is Greek Revival."

"I suspected as much," I said. "So we are Artemis and her bear."

"Correct."

Once we'd settled into the coach and the colonel's driver was steering us toward Fort Johnson, Truesdail removed the bear's head. Beads of sweat trickled from his hairline into his beard.

"Your costume is a wonder," I said. "Where did it come from?"

"Kansas," he said. "I shot the grizzly myself."

"Did you fashion the ensemble?"

He shook his head. "I hired the Adelphi's costume mistress to make it."

"Millicent Dickinson?"

"That's right," he said. "Do you know her?"

"No," I said, "but I saw her in *Romeo and Juliet*."

"I also had Miss Dickinson make your costume."

"Speaking of which," I said, trying to sound breezy even as heat rushed to my cheeks, "I've never worn anything so brief. I may not have the courage to remove my cloak."

As we climbed the gentle hill toward the Tennessee State Capitol, Truesdail re-covered his head with the grizzly's. A battalion of blue-uniformed guards stood at attention before the Greek Revival building, arrayed on its brick steps, flanking its lofty grand entrance and Ionic columns. The front doors were flung wide, and the whole porch—as well as the cupola that soared above the building—was draped with laurel garlands. As we ascended the steps, I noted that the capitol was now guarded by ten—up from six—twenty-four-pound bronze cannons.

"We certainly will be well-protected," I said softly.

The colonel nodded. "To say that Andrew Johnson is concerned with security would be an understatement. You might compliment the man on his firepower."

Inside, the bear that was William Truesdail led me through a marble foyer with twelve-foot ceilings. Scattered throughout the space were ancient-looking artworks—ceramics and marbles, paintings and sketches. I was floored by the sight of the *Birth of Athena*, a sculpture I recognized from a first edition of the *Timeless Treasures of Antiquity* that once lived on the shelves of our rooms at Mrs. Marigold's boarding-house. The marble was as tall as I, and it represented the goddess Athena springing, fully formed, from the head of Zeus.

"It can't be real," I murmured to Truesdail as we paused before the masterpiece.

"A copy," he said. "Made for the occasion I assume."

The masquerade's attendants wore red hooded robes that made it impossible to distinguish them, or even determine their gender or skin tone. Hesitantly, I removed Lisette's cape and handed it to one of these interchangeable helpers. As cool, rarefied air struck every centimeter of my exposed skin, I felt eyes boring into me from all directions.

At the end of a corridor, we entered a reception room with vaulted ceilings and a fireplace large enough to shelter several grown men. The room's French walnut mantel was carved with festoons and laurels, as well as two zaftig girls flanking a bald eagle, with eight-foot wings spread wide, beak open in a silent caw. But the room's most awesome feature was its ceiling—a fresco painted to resemble the dawn sky. Blushing rose, and framed by fleecy clouds as well as three dozen buxom angels and cherubim.

Three Greek hoplites stood in a reception line, greeting new arrivals, wearing short linen tunics covered by muscle cuirasses, bronze greaves on their calves, and leather sandals. Each held a hoplon shield and spear. Bronze Corinthian helmets with horsehair crests of red covered their faces, making identification impossible, but Colonel Truesdail informed me that the three men were Governor Andrew Johnson, newly minted Brigadier General James St. Clair Morton, and Dr. Abraham Armstrong, a sawbones with the Cumberland Army.

"The governor's son Charles," Truesdail said as we drew near the hoplite receiving line, "was recently thrown from a horse and killed. Eliza, the governor's wife, suffers from tuberculosis, and she's taking a health treatment at a sulfuric spa."

"Pleased to meet you, Governor Johnson," I said, dropping into a shallow curtsy, to limit my exposure.

"The pleasure is all mine," said Johnson. "Colonel Truesdail tells me you're proving to be an invaluable asset in our fight against Nashville's Rebel underground."

Truesdail and I both knew I'd been of no help thus far in identifying Confederate sympathizers and, wondering at his motives, I shot the bear beside me a curious look. "The colonel," I said, "is far too kind."

"Now that I've laid eyes on you," the governor continued, "I can readily believe it."

"I appreciate that," I said, "but I do not usually look this way."

James St. Clair Morton took my hand. "You're clearly Artemis," he said, "but why the devil are you dressed as a bear, Truesdail?"

"The bear," chimed in Dr. Armstrong, "was an animal sacred to Artemis."

"You don't say," said Morton.

"As female worshippers of Artemis in Attica entered adolescence," the surgeon continued, "they would 'act the she-bear' as a rite of passage. They wore bear masks and danced and prowled on all fours. They pretended to hibernate and then 'awake' into sexual maturity—into the age of motherhood. For the Greeks, the bear was a symbol of fertility, but she also represented the intersection of wildness and civilization. Of animal and man."

"Good God, Armstrong," said the governor, "how do you know so much about it?"

"The ancient world," Armstrong said, "is one of my primary passions."

"Miss Swift," said Governor Johnson, bowing at the waist, "may I have the pleasure of this dance?"

"Of course," I said, "but I must warn you, waltzing is not my strong suit."

"On the contrary," the governor said as we reeled around the dance floor, amid scores of couples dressed as Nereids, nymphs, and satyrs, as winged horses and hoplites, "you are a superior dancer, Miss Swift. And the loveliest woman here, if you don't mind my saying so. You're positively glowing."

"Thank you."

"Truesdail says you've successfully infiltrated the Ladies' Aid Society. He says you've got them convinced of your loyalty and dedication. He says you have a real knack for the sort of subterfuge demanded of a spy."

"I am surprised to hear," I said, "that the colonel speaks of me at all."

"He speaks of you often."

As we spun, I caught sight of the bear that was Truesdail standing across the long room, beside the hoplite that was General St. Clair Morton, a glass of red punch clasped in his paws. Though the colonel's head was hidden by the bear's, I felt him watching me.

"I was so sorry to hear about your son, Governor," I said, changing the subject.

"Thank you," he said. "His sudden death has been especially hard on my wife. Charles was the best of our sons."

"I am certain," I said, "that you did everything possible to keep him safe."

* * *

Throughout the evening, I thought of Gaia Valentino. I pictured the poetess sliding through the literary salons of sixteenth-century Venice, wearing a costume, playing the part of a courtesan. Gaia had gathered intelligence from political and cultural leaders, then used that knowledge to benefit her art, her family, and womankind. And as I waltzed with military strategists, bankers, and city planners, I gently interrogated them all. I learned not only the details of the five Nashville forts General St. Clair Morton had designed, but also those of the bastion he was currently constructing at Murfreesboro. I became familiar with the code name system that differentiated Colonel Truesdail's Secret Service operatives. I learned that a major structural weakness threatened the main vault at the Bank of Nashville. But when I danced with Dr. Abraham Armstrong, the surgeon would speak only of antiquity.

"I assume you're familiar," I said, "with the story of Callisto."

"Oh yes," he said. "Arcadian Artemis's favorite nymph and constant companion, who swore to remain a virgin to the goddess. But Zeus disguised himself as Artemis and seduced Callisto, which so outraged Artemis that she turned her beloved nymph into a bear. When Callisto's son by Zeus unwittingly hunted his bear-mother and was about to kill her, Zeus saved Callisto, placing her among the stars as Ursa Major, the Great She-bear."

"Right again," I said.

"Tell me," Dr. Armstrong said, "what made you decide to wear a cuirass adorned with bulls' testicles, signifying not Arcadian Artemis, Taurian Artemis, nor even the Huntress, but the Ionian version—Artemis of Ephesus, called the Mistress of Wild Beasts?"

"I admire every Artemis," I said, "but am especially drawn to the complexities of Ephesian Artemis."

Dr. Armstrong whistled. "You *are* a fascinating woman. Where did Truesdail find you?"

As I studied the painted dawn sky that stretched above us, one of its fleshy cherubs winked at me. "If you must know," I said, "the colonel found me in a whorehouse."

He laughed. "Come now, Miss Swift. No one would take you for a public woman."

"No?"

"Look around. Every eye in the room is riveted to you. Why do you think that is?"

"Because I am only half-dressed."

The surgeon shook his head. "They cannot help themselves," he said. "If I didn't know better, I would swear that you've grown two inches since you've been in my arms, and you're radiating light. If I weren't a man of science, I might believe you were one of the deathless immortals."

After waltzing for three hours, I fled the ballroom in search of a quiet place to rest my feet and collect my thoughts. I found a back staircase, and as I ascended, I considered Dr. Armstrong's declarations. Was he flattering me, or did the surgeon mean the things he said? Was I actually changing—metamorphosing—not unlike the heroine of the play upon whose translation I labored each morning?

"Can life," I asked softly, "so closely imitate art?"

I tried one door, then another—both were locked. The third door I tried opened, and I eased the walnut slab inward. A lone oil lamp illuminated a far corner of the room, which smelled of pipe tobacco, leather, and venerated texts. *A library*, I thought, as I detected the voices of Dr. Armstrong and Governor Johnson emanating from beyond a tall walnut secretary that shielded me from their view.

"I still believe," Dr. Armstrong was saying, "that the best course of action is to enforce a strict licensing policy."

"Licensing. You think we should license whores."

"Yes."

"No chance," said Johnson. "I cannot be the first American lawmaker to openly condone prostitution."

"That's one way to look at it," said the doctor. "Another would be to recognize my solution as the most effective option for a grievous problem. Infection rates are still rising, Governor."

"What if we sent the public women away?" asked the governor. "Rounded them up and shipped them off?"

"Shipped them where? Who would take them? And even if we did manage to get rid of them, others would take their place. Nature abhors a vacuum."

"Eliza brought up the idea of such an exile," said Johnson, "in her last letter."

"Governor Johnson," said Dr. Armstrong, "prostitutes have been plying their trade since the days of the ancients. As long as men want to have sexual intercourse, there will be women to service them. Controlling the spread of infection by forcing the whores to get regularly examined and treated is without question our best option."

I peeked round the secretary and spied the two men seated on either side of a walnut desk, sipping brown liquor. They'd removed their Corinthian helmets, and I examined their faces before backing out of the room—narrowly avoiding knocking over a brass hatstand—and closing the door silently behind me.

It was past midnight when Colonel Truesdail sent one of the indistinguishable, red-robed attendants to fetch my wrap. As they settled the cloak over my shoulders, they leaned close and whispered, "Check your left pocket."

Once we were seated in his coach, heading toward the riverfront, Truesdail removed his grizzly head, and I untied my domino mask. "I hope you enjoyed yourself," he said, mopping perspiration from his brow with a handkerchief.

"Oh, yes," I said. "This was my first masquerade. I kept thinking that if I approached any one of the guests and tore aside their mask, I would find someone from my past, or someone I see every day. Or maybe someone from the future."

"Sylvie." Truesdail took one of my hands. "May I call you Sylvie?"

"Of course."

"Will you call me William?"

"Not *Bill*?"

He smiled. "If you like. Ever since that night in my office—when you kissed me—I haven't stopped thinking about you. I need to see you again."

"I don't know, Bill."

"Please."

"Haven't you heard," I said, "that one shouldn't mix business with pleasure?"

We slid to a halt in front of the Adelphi. I heard the driver clambering down to open the door and release me.

"Please," Truesdail said again. He reached out, trailed a fingertip down my cheek, then deliberately, tenderly, over my lower lip. "I've known scores of women, Sylvie, but I've never felt what I feel when I look at you. When I touch you. What have you done to me?"

The coach door opened, and I freed myself from the colonel. "Thank you," I said as the blue-uniformed driver handed me down. "I had a lovely evening, Bill."

"Good night."

His face hung like the full moon in the coach's back window until the vehicle was swallowed by night. As I made for the Land of the Sirens, I plumbed the left-hand pocket of Lisette's black cloak. Extracted a wadded-up handkerchief. Peeled back layers of white cloth to reveal the last object I expected to see.

"Marina," I said, my voice catching. "My stars."

At rest in my palm was your aunt Marina's gold pendant. The tiny statue of Ephesian Artemis that had dangled always from a delicate chain around my sister's neck. The bright idol wearing a mural crown made of city walls. A host of globular bees' eggs sprouted from her bosom.

Her gentle hands were open.

Monday, June 18, 1877
Monterey, CA

If either of you has a chance to participate in a theatrical production, take it. Though the theater still enjoys a murky aura of disrepute, I firmly believe that one day, actors will be worshipped like gods. That eventually, they'll be the royals of our nation. And for my money, nothing teaches us who we might be better than trying on the face of another.

In the Ladies' Aid Society production of *Orpheus in the Underworld*, I was cast as a shepherd as well as a spirit. I would sing only in concert with others, but Hannah—a deep, resonant alto—won the part of Pluto, God of the Underworld. We rehearsed three days a week throughout May and June. One May night after rehearsal, Hannah tugged me into the wings, behind the scrim. In a far corner, we found a circular opening in the floor. As we descended a spiral wrought-iron staircase to the Adelphi's subterranean wardrobe shop, I found myself thinking of Dante, picturing circles of Hell.

The costume shop ran beneath the stage, its ceilings so low my head nearly brushed them. Much of the space was devoted to storage— pieces that ran the gamut from ancient Greek to modern dress. The gowns and coats and vests and tunics, masks and robes and jackets and skirts, blouses and trusses and girdles and garters, boots and belts and stockings and headpieces embodied a profusion of colors and styles.

"This way." Holding aloft an oil lamp, Hannah guided me. As we weaved through the costumes, I became increasingly disoriented. Wherever we turned, we found another overstuffed rack—one identical to its companions. I was beginning to believe we should have left ourselves a trail of breadcrumbs when we came face-to-face with two black-clad figures, and I shrieked in terror.

"Silly Sylvie." Hannah lifted and lowered her lamp, and one of the figures did the same. "It's a mirror."

We stepped closer. I studied us—two women joined at the hand, dressed exactly alike—and felt a strange whirring in my ribcage, as though someone had loosed a hummingbird there. I smiled, and Hannah smiled. I scratched my nose, and Hannah did the same. I blushed and saw that Hannah was also blushing. I wondered if she was whirring inside.

"Come, Sylvie," she said. "Let's make-believe."

Hannah placed her lamp on a worktable, then dove into the sea of costumes and emerged moments later with an outfit for a mermaid and one for a fisherman. Before the night was over, we became Alexander Hamilton and Benedict Arnold, Marie Antoinette and Louis XVI, Socrates and Plato, the Oracle at Delphi and the god Apollo, a lion with a thorn in its paw and the mouse who removed it, and two lost sheep a-wander in a wilderness.

We made no effort to hide from each other as we changed, and for the first time, I was able to look closely at another woman. I hardly knew my own body, and as Hannah dressed and undressed, my gaze was drawn to her legs, her stomach, her neck, her breasts. The triangular patch of red hair between her thighs. She bent and stretched and hopped on one foot, yanking up a pair of trousers, and I saw parts of Hannah—and therefore parts of me—I never knew existed.

And I wanted to see more.

"Perfect," Hannah said, when we stood outfitted as two sixteenth-century courtesans, in frocks that buoyed our breasts nearly up to our necks. She curtsied. "May I have this dance?"

There was little room for waltzing in the costume shop, but we whirled as best we could. Hannah established our rhythm, murmuring, "Pom pom pom, pom pom pom," beneath her breath. Though she held my gaze, I felt myself growing dizzy and began to wonder if we were levitating. If our feet had left the floor.

"Has anyone ever told you," Hannah said, "how bewitching you are?"

"No."

She stopped abruptly. "Never?"

I shrugged. "Once or twice."

"Oh, Sylvie." Her inky eyes shone. "Each time I see you, you take my breath."

Tightening my arms around Hannah, I touched her lips with my lips. Her tongue sought out my tongue. As we kissed—our torsos pressed ever more closely together—I thought about how different it was to kiss Hannah than it had been to kiss Colonel Truesdail. When I kissed the colonel, it felt as though we were being watched, and not just by one person—by the entire world. As though we stood before an audience waiting with breath bated, with fists clenched.

But when I kissed Hannah, we seemed to be alone in the cosmos.

"Ahoy down there! I'm locking up in ten minutes!"

This shout from above—the Adelphi's janitor—knocked us out of our embrace. We re-dressed in silence and returned the costumes to their proper homes. Before we mounted the twirling staircase, however, Hannah tugged me through the length of the shop to its farthest reaches. In a dim corner, she yanked aside a voluminous shroud, then knelt down, shining her lamp's beam on a long packing crate.

"Look," she said softly.

More than a dozen such crates were stacked to the ceiling. Hannah opened the container before her—stamped SPRINGFIELD MODEL 1861—and extracted a muzzle-loaded Minié-type rifled musket. She clearly knew how to handle a gun, and as I watched Hannah lift the rifle to her shoulder, shut one eye, and sight along the barrel, I thought of your uncle Silas at eighteen, atop the sledding hill in Whitley Courthouse, using Miles Stanford's repeating rifle to bring down a quail.

"My stars," I said. "Where did they come from?"

"The recent holdup," she said, "of a Union supply train."

"These are army-issue?"

She grinned. "Only the best."

"Why are they here?"

"The Adelphi's costume designer," she said, "is one of our Sisters."

"Millicent Dickinson," I said.

"Correct."

I shook my head. "But what use are guns in a theater?"

"Did you know," she said, "that until the eighteenth century, it was illegal for a woman to appear on an English stage?"

"Hannah!"

"Here," she said, passing me the rifle. "You try."

"I don't even know how to hold it."

"Then it's high time," she said, "that you learned."

She showed me how to brace the Springfield rifle against my shoulder, how to use the sights. "I still don't understand," I said as Hannah nestled the long gun back into its crate, "why the guns are down here."

"We stashed them here," she said, "in anticipation of the annual Ladies' Aid Society charity production."

"*Orpheus in the Underworld?*"

She nodded.

"Wait," I said. "We're going to be armed?"

"Not us," she said. "The rifles are for the audience."

"Audience?" I recalled the auditions for our charity opera and how, after listening to a thirty-second snippet of a song, I'd felt the irrepressible urge to leap up, to arm myself, to fight for a dark horse. The undeniable sense that what I was singing, and hearing, hadn't been composed by Jacques Offenbach at all.

"So our comedic light opera," I said, "*is* a call to arms."

She nodded. "A battle cry. And once they've witnessed it, our audience will have no choice but to arm themselves."

"Who will they fight?"

Hannah smiled. "Warlike men," she said, "and the worlds they think they've made."

Back in Whitley Courthouse, Brigitte and Marina, if someone had spoken aloud a phrase I'd only ever thought to myself, I might have been unnerved. But on this night, in the costume shop of the Adelphi Theatre, the notion that Hannah Holcombe could actually read my mind was exhilarating, and made me long to kiss her again.

"Oh, Sylvie," she said, seizing my hands, "we're inside the gates, and they don't even know it! Men only see threats that come from outside; they're blind to the threats they live with every day. Sister Sarah says this is the key. She says the terminal blindness of men will guarantee the ultimate victory of womankind."

* * *

After leaving the Adelphi's costume shop—and Hannah—I walked back to the Land of the Sirens, my body abuzz with the aftereffects of our embrace. Normally I would have been upstairs fast asleep by this late hour, and I paused before the bizarre mansion I'd inhabited for eight months, surveyed the queue of men entering the brothel through her purple front door. The bell chimed so consistently, it sounded like a melody. The men—of all shapes and sizes—wore all manner of clothing. The easiest to identify were federal soldiers, both officers and enlisted men. The rest—farmers, merchants, butchers, barbers, sailors, day laborers—weren't so easy to label. In a city like Nashville, it was impossible to tell who was covertly supporting a Lost Cause, and who would end up on the right side of history.

As Hannah had taught me to wield the Springfield rifle, the idea of infiltrating and overthrowing the violent—of sabotaging war—had become conceivable. So, too, had the notion of an ancient, all-powerful force spilling across time, from my distant foremothers into me. Rather than entering through the kitchen—as was my custom—and taking the back stairs to the third floor, changing into a nightgown that covered me from neck to toes and sliding between cold sheets, I opened the front gate. Marched up the walk. Mounted the steps to the porch. Joined the flow of men streaming through the purple door. In the front hall, I paused, watched them muddy the Persian rug that depicted Eve's transgression before they passed into the Great Room. I'd imagined what went on inside the lavish parlor countless times, but now—on the cusp of discovery—I was gripped by fear.

When the flow of men ebbed, I traversed Eden, entered the Great Room, and saw nothing. No waltzing dancers, no knots of scantily clad women and uniformed men chatting and laughing and drinking from champagne flutes. No one manning the bar, no one tickling the ivories of the piano in the northeast corner, no one playing billiards at either of the fancy tables. The queue of men marched through the silent parlor, over a Venetian area rug depicting swordfish, schools of tuna, seahorses, and dolphins—as though viewed from a glass-bottomed boat—toward a door in the west wall. Aside from the moving column of men, the Great Room was barren. Its dozens of mirrors winked blankly, reflecting nothing.

Increasingly curious, I followed the marching men.

Through the second door, we descended a staircase that folded back on itself twice, and as we sank, the air cooled and moistened. The dim space smelled of earth and sea, stone and fire—ancient, elemental things—and my eyes took a moment to adjust. Once they had, I saw that I stood in a vast chamber—larger than seemed realistic, or even possible—dominated by a colossal iron cage.

The men streamed eagerly toward this cell. When they reached it, they disrobed, hung their clothes on one of dozens of pegs lining a rock wall. Naked, they filed inside, and soon the cage was overfull—packed with men who had no choice but to rest against one another. The door swung shut with a *clang*, and dozens of red-robed women stepped from the shadows. They began singing the lullaby I'd heard my first night in the Land of the Sirens, the same song that had filled the bedroom I once shared with Silas—who, even at that moment, may have been humming the tune while turning a submersible's hand crank.

The Priestesses dropped their thin robes and began dancing sinuously—like reeds undulating in shallows—as the caged men reached through the bars and begged for many things. Some asked to be beaten, some to be held, some to be torn in two. Others begged to be kissed, or to crawl back into the womb. But the women remained just out of reach, trilling their hypnotic lullaby, which made me yearn to disrobe and join the jailed men.

Instead I followed *another* queue of men—men who'd exited the cage and now passed through a second doorframe, covered by a tasseled curtain, into a second earthy chamber. To my surprise, this space—also impossibly large but far more brightly lit—was filled with rows and rows of children's desks, facing a freestanding blackboard.

"Schoolroom?" I murmured.

Before the blackboard stood a blonde, fair-skinned Priestess named Eileen, scribbling furiously on the slate, her chalk screeching like a bird of prey. Veronique—an ebony-haired, honey-skinned woman—paraded between the rows of child-sized desks, striking a thin wooden stick against her palm. Occasionally she whacked one of the naked men—crammed into the desks, sitting at rapt attention—across the back or chest, arm or leg, causing him to moan with pleasure. Around the room's perimeter, Priestesses stood or sat at intervals, singing. Eileen, Veronique, and the others wore only stockings and black boots. Veronique moved among the men, periodically flogging them, lecturing at the top of her voice:

"All first civilizations revolved around a Mother Goddess. Ancient Sumerians worshipped *Tiamat* and *Nisaba*; ancient Egyptians idolized *Isis*, *Bast*, and *Hathor*. Babylonians and Assyrians exalted *Ishtar*. Ancient Celts revered *Danu* and *Brighit*, and the Veneti worshipped *Reitia*. Ancient Indians idolized *Parvati* and *Ambika*, and the Taino exalted *Atabey*. The Inka revered *Pachamama*, and Aztecs idolized *Coatlicue*. Achaeans worshipped *Gaia*, *Rhea*, and *Demeter*, while Vikings revered *Freyja* and *Frigga*. Ancient Anatolians exalted *Cybele*, and the Romans worshipped *Ceres*, *Juno*, and *Bona Dea*."

"Tiamat," the men seated at the desks chanted in unison, "Nisaba, Isis, Bast, Hathor, Ishtar, Danu, Brighit, Reitia, Parvati, Ambika, Atabey, Pachamama, Coatlicue, Gaia, Rhea, Demeter, Freyja, Frigga, Cybele, Ceres, Juno, Bona Dea."

"These deities," Veronique went on, "are all echoes of Chaos—the original Mother Goddess. Modern scholars and politicians would have you believe that Chaos is a threat—that Chaos should be feared, fought, and eliminated. But in truth, *Order* is the real enemy of humankind."

"Chaos," chanted the men, "Chaos, Chaos, Chaos."

I wanted to take a desk, to listen to Veronique in rapt wonder, to let her strike me with her stick. As my gaze roamed over the crowd of naked men, I recognized not one, not two, but three faces. Governor Andrew Johnson sat near the back, Dr. Abraham Armstrong sat a few seats from him, and there—front row center, straining eagerly forward—was Colonel William Truesdail.

"My stars," I said.

Tearing my gaze from the colonel, I circumvented the Priestesses' perimeter to follow a queue of men who'd abandoned their desks and were headed toward another tasseled curtain, into an antechamber that housed a winding staircase. I joined the silent column of men, and we spun down, down to the bottom, stepped onto cool stone. *We must be miles beneath the brothel*, I thought, as I heard an unusual sound—*waves lapping at a shore?*—and distantly, a sound that was even stranger.

A shrieking cry—mournful and inhuman—that brought tears to my eyes. The noise came from far off, and as naked men streamed eagerly around me, rushing toward the cry's source, it sounded again. This time, there was an answer: a thinner version of the cry—not nearly as robust or mournful.

"Mother," I murmured, "and child?"

The cry sounded again—impossibly loud now—and a small hand seized mine. I looked down, into the strange violet eyes of Apollo Swift. My nephew wore a bright orange tunic and grinned like a madman. He tried tugging me forward—toward the terrifying cries—but my feet were riveted to the stone. The boy finally gave up and, as I watched him race off, I became conscious of another sound—*thump-thump, thump-thump, thump-thump.*

My heart, I thought as the thudding grew faster, more intense. *My unruly heart.*

Seized by panic, I turned, fought against a human current—a wild beast fighting its own instincts—shoving past the men who streamed steadily toward the antediluvian water I knew was out there, and whatever creatures it contained. I forced my way back up the winding staircase—punching and kicking without remorse—but the enraptured men took no note of my assault on their flesh. They only pressed forward and down, forward and down, like programmed automatons, or individuals under a spell.

I gained the stone floor above and retraced my route—through both sets of tasseled curtains, past the blackboard and the colossal cage—until I found myself back in the Land of the Siren's entryway. As men kept muddying the Garden of Eden, I climbed the main staircase, clutching its symbol-etched banister, to the third floor. Once in my room and under the bedclothes, I squeezed shut my eyes, but whenever I began to drift off, the anguished cries I'd heard in the colossal chamber deep beneath my bed tore through me like the cry of some prehistoric bird.

Alone, I was able to detect a word within the cry—a word I knew the bewitched men miles below me could not hear.

"Sister," I whispered into the darkness, into the night. "Sister."

* * *

One evening in June, during a rehearsal for *Orpheus in the Underworld*, I overheard a strange conversation about Sister Sarah. I sat midway back in the house, slouched low in my seat, watching Hannah—as Pluto, God of the Underworld—and Lisette—as Euridice, Orpheus's unfaithful wife—rehearsing one of the opera's pivotal scenes. During the fourth or fifth run-through, the voices of three women I didn't recognize floated up from the seats behind me.

"I don't know how those Aid Society girls can stand it. Imagine going around in one of those outfits? In broad daylight, for everyone to see?"

"They look like grim death."

"More like nuns. Holy and innocent."

"Innocent? Ha!"

"Ha?"

One of the speakers dropped her voice, and I strained to catch her words.

"About a year ago," she said, "I spent a weekend with a *very* nice man from New Orleans."

"What would a nice man want with you, Verna?"

"Shut your trap, Trixie. This wasn't your run-of-the-mill blowhard, but a true gentleman. He worked as an agent on the New Orleans, Jackson, and Great Northern Railroad, and one afternoon as we were strolling down Broad, we came across a flock of those Ladies' Aid Society crows banging tambourines and singing. Sister Sarah made an endless speech about the bravery of our fighting boys, and how we all needed to dig deep into our hearts—and our pockets—to bring a measure of comfort to their poor mothers and aunts, sisters and daughters.

"I was ready for a gin, but my gentleman friend wouldn't leave. He stood anchored to the spot, his face dead white, staring at Sister Sarah and tugging on his beard. Later, once we'd gone to a tavern and he'd knocked back a few, he told me one of the strangest stories I've heard.

"It seems that ten years earlier, a young man from a fancy New Orleans family went missing. Search parties were formed, bloodhounds were deployed, and bands of men roamed the city and surrounding swamps in search of the gentleman. My friend was searching an uninhabited area when his party came upon a small cottage. They knocked, but no one answered. They combed the neighboring property—which held several outbuildings—until in one they discovered a trapdoor. Beneath it was a tunnel accessible by a ladder. One of the men climbed down, but he never returned. Another went down—same story.

"Finally three men tied themselves together, a rope cinched round each of their waists. My friend was in third place. When the first man reached the bottom, he lifted a lantern and peered around, then beckoned to his companions. But as the two men on the ladder watched in horror, a swinging axe lopped off the first man's head from behind. My friend and the second man threw themselves in the direction of the axe-swinger, and they managed to wrestle the weapon away from the killer, who turned out to be a well-dressed, handsome woman with coal-black hair and skin like berries and cream.

"She was gorgeous, he said—the most regal-looking creature he'd seen in the flesh. She was also tougher than a circus strongman, and she kept thrashing, kicking, and screaming to beat the band. *In terms of sheer destructiveness*, he said, *the closest animal I can compare her to is a grizzly bear*. The two men alone could not subdue her; it took six altogether to hog-tie this savage creature. When they explored her underground lair—which was far larger than my friend could believe—they found scattered human remains and five whiskey barrels brimming with blood."

"Hell's bells! What happened to this woman?"

"According to my friend, they got the hellcat back to New Orleans in a paddy wagon, gagged and hog-tied, covered in muck and blood. She was arrested and jailed, but before she could be tried, the bloodthirsty bitch vanished."

"How is that possible?"

"No one knows. One minute she was locked in a cell—guarded by ten men—the next she was gone. The guards couldn't explain what happened. They had no idea how she got out of her restraints or unlocked the doors, and no memory of her exit. A search of every street and alleyway in New Orleans was conducted, but no trace of the beautiful, villainous she-beast was found.

"*But I'll tell you something*, my gentleman friend said once he'd slid so far into his cups he could no longer walk a straight line, *something I didn't learn until today. When you've come in contact with such barbarity and beauty, you never forget its face.*

"I asked whom he meant, and he said—get this—that Sister Sarah and the she-devil he'd run up against in New Orleans were the same woman! I told him he was certifiably insane. That Sarah is a do-gooder and a churchgoer. That she spends all her time raising money for war orphans and former slaves and writing letters to the fighting boys. But until he passed out on the table—his cheek in a puddle of ale—he kept insisting that Sister Sarah was this she-demon from New Orleans."

"The Grizzly Woman."

"Hell's bells," said Trixie. "That's quite a story. Do you think there's any truth to it?"

"I didn't used to," Verna replied, "but look up there. Go on, take a hard look at Sister Sarah."

Like Verna and her companions, I lifted my head. Strained forward in my seat to get a more perfect view of Sarah. She walked onstage, demonstrating for Hannah how best to enter a scene. The leader of the Southern Ladies' Aid Society—in her black gown, bonnet, and boots—looked innocuous, nondescript. Like a hundred women you pass in the street each day.

"If you were a murderous she-bear," Verna said, "wouldn't a costume like that make the perfect disguise?"

Encyclopaedia Britannica
Eighth Edition (1860)
Volume 3, Anatomy–Astronomy, pp. 168–69

ANIMAL KINGDOM. It is by no means so easy as it may at first appear, to define precisely what is meant by the term "animal," because, as we descend the scale of beings, we find a transition so gradual from those whose properties are strongly defined to others which partake so greatly of the nature of plants that the most acute naturalists cannot agree on the line of their demarcation.

It has been said that nature follows a continuous and ascending chain, from the mineral to the plant, and from the vegetable to the animal kingdom, the apex of which is crowned by the most perfect work of creation—the human race.

Tuesday, June 19, 1877
Monterey, CA

The longer I live, the closer I feel to the past. Running barefoot through the verdant grasses of Kentucky. Our rooms at Mrs. Marigold's boardinghouse. The last time I saw my father—his tense, tragic smile, his melancholy beard, his thinning hair. Silas's juvenile fires. The sound of my sister singing. My tenure in Nashville—the days I now sit on this veranda resurrecting.

Each time I close my eyes, I see your faces—Marina under one lid, Brigitte under the other. Though you're identical, I can tell you apart. I once imagined that if I cut all ties, the pain of our separation would fade, wither, and die; but I was wrong. Woman is ingenuous and inventive beyond measure, and she can grow accustomed to anything—a severed leg, a gouged eye. But I seem to have misplaced the ability to cauterize my own psychic wounds. Or perhaps having not one but two babes torn from one's life dwarfs any other loss.

After witnessing the subterranean activities of the Priestesses and their clients, I could no longer sleep soundly in my room at the Land of the Sirens. I started waking every hour, and when sleep eluded me entirely, I would don my Ladies' Aid Society uniform, descend the back stairs, and venture into the night. I roamed all over Nashville, as well as her outskirts—toward Kirkman's Addition, out past St. Cloud Hill, where the emancipated people who built Fort Negley had suffered throughout the winter and spring. No one I encountered seemed to notice me; it was as though my black costume rendered me invisible, and I felt like Gaia Valentino—exploring Renaissance Venice by gondola, unseen in her male weeds.

Once I'd had my fill of reconnoitering on a July night two weeks before the SLAS was scheduled to mount its production of *Orpheus in the Underworld*, I made my way back toward Smokey Row. I was heading for the suspension bridge that carried Nashville and Louisville trains across the Cumberland when I spied a clump of ragged children sitting on the dock's edge, bare feet a-dangle.

"Urchins," I said softly, recalling the day they'd nearly climbed me in the streets. Confident in my newfound invisibility, I crept closer to the ragamuffins, hid behind a stack of shipping crates, and eavesdropped on their discourse.

"I was fishing under the bridge last Tuesday," one of the boys was saying, "when I slipped and fell into the river. I can swim of course, but my leg cramped, and I started to panic. As I sank below the muddy water, I spotted a monster swimming toward me!"

"A monster!"

"What did it look like?"

"Did it have horns?"

"Did it have fangs?"

"It was gigantic," the boy said, "and shaped like a barrel, with two dozen heads and about ten thousand tentacles."

"Two dozen heads?"

"Ten thousand tentacles?"

"Oh, come on!"

"It did!" the boy insisted. "Next thing I know, I wake up inside a dark, echoey cave. Someone had stripped me, hung my clothes over a rock ledge to dry, and wrapped me in a wool blanket. Beside me was a plate of salt pork and hoecakes, and a mug of tea."

"Salt pork!"

"Hoecakes!"

"Was it hot?"

"I'm hungry!"

"Hold it!" the boy said. "Will you let me finish? The food *was* hot, and I swallowed it quick as a wink. As I dressed, I kept calling out, but no one answered. Someone had left a candle and a box of matches beside me, so I lit the candle, pocketed the matches, and set out to explore. At least two hours passed before I found a sliver of daylight. I climbed out into the open air, and do you know where I was?"

"Where?"

"Tell us!"

"Ten miles southeast of town," the boy said, "way out past Kirkman's Addition."

"No!"

"How'd you get out there?"

"From the river?"

"My guess," the boy said, "is that a network of underground tunnels and caves runs throughout the city."

"Incredible!"

"Let's find it!"

"Let's explore!"

The orphans chattered and squealed, so the boy had to shout to be heard. "Pipe down, you half-wits!" he yelled, leaping to his feet. "Weren't you listening? Don't you see what you're saying?"

"No."

"What?"

"Who else must know," the boy said, "about the tunnels?"

The children fell silent.

"The monster?" a girl offered hesitantly.

"The monster!" cried the storyteller. "Do you really want to climb down there and risk coming face to face with it?"

* * *

A short time later, I stood on the Nashville and Louisville suspension bridge, elbows on a guardrail, gaze trained down. Aside from the occasional glint or ripple, it was difficult to see the water from such a height, but on this night, a harvest moon hung low over the Cumberland—not unlike a limelight spot—casting an orange glow, igniting its surface.

I pulled out the gold pendant one of the mysterious, red-robed attendants at Governor Johnson's masquerade ball had slipped into my pocket—the tiny glimmering figure that once belonged to your aunt Marina. Though I worried about losing the precious icon, I'd started wearing it tucked beneath the smocked bodice of my SLAS uniform. I stood for a time, pondering certain revisions to my translation of the *Apocrypha*—which I was close to finishing—when I became convinced that I was being watched.

"Hello?"

I spun around, but no one was behind me. The moon's uncanny brightness illuminated the length of the bridge, and I was very much alone upon it. *Calm down, Sylvie,* I thought, telling myself the gaze I'd felt probably belonged to a guard standing watch in one of the blockhouses. I looked down and saw that the river's surface—calm seconds before—had begun to chop and heave. I spied the outline of a large, dark, submerged shape. A cylindrical object that seemed to be rising up toward the bridge, up toward Nashville, up toward me.

My first thought was of Silas and his submarine. Was this a Confederate torpedo boat, a craft that had slid stealthily upriver and was now ascending, so the men trapped inside—turning hand cranks to power the Porpoise in the darkness of her belly—could fill her with oxygen? Or was the fish boat climbing to the proper height to blast its torpedo into the pile of the railroad bridge on which I stood, to cut the vital supply lines that ran to and from the city? Would I be forced to leap into the river—possibly to my death—in order to avoid being set ablaze, or blown to bits?

As the shape broke the surface, however, I saw that it was no vessel. No hollow iron tube loaded with frightened men and a deadly weapon.

Nothing man-made at all.

Its movements were, at once, lightning fast and achingly slow. The creature was so large, so scattered, so possessed of tentacles that I couldn't take it in at once but was forced to examine it piecemeal—one section at a time. I thought for an instant that I was looking at the hideous whale-woman from the painting positioned above Miss Price's desk at the Land of the Sirens, then I was flooded with the strange notion that this was the ungodly bear-woman from the painting hung in the Southern Ladies' Aid Society headquarters.

Then I knew: Somehow, it was both.

The creature had three heads—all of which telescoped on long, fleshy cords or tendons. As I stood there agog, clinging to the rail, barely standing upright, the thing continued to rise—sheets of water cascading from its inexplicable body—until its wandering eyes and topmost tentacles towered above the railroad bridge. The monster exhaled, and the force of its breath swayed the planks on which I stood. A thick, forked appendage flew past me and slapped the water—a tail.

I ordered my feet to move, to run, as the looming creature—its body covered in iridescent silver scales—positioned one of its telescoping heads before me. The head wore a human face—the face of woman who was not only beautiful, but also eerily familiar. She emitted a mournful cry, and I recognized the sound I'd first heard deep beneath the Ladies' Aid Society office with Sister Sarah, then again in a damp, earthy chamber miles below the Land of the Sirens. The creature cried out twice more, nearly deafening me.

Then came a smaller, answering cry.

The face in front of me—whose features bore an increasingly strong resemblance to those of my long-lost sister—opened its mouth, and I spied rows of jagged teeth dripping with saliva. A crimson tongue rolled out, and I steeled myself for its roughness, for the way it would no doubt lift me clean off my feet and toss me inside the mouth, to be masticated and swallowed. I squeezed my eyes shut—my body a knot of terror and anticipation—then heard the last sound I expected.

"Sylvie. Sylvie. Sylvie."

A voice I hadn't heard in eight years. I opened my eyes, observed the creature reaching down, plucking another being from the water—a smaller, not-quite-so-horrifying version of itself—to hold triumphantly before me, as though displaying a favorite possession.

"My daughter," said Marina. "This is Artemis. Apollo's sister."

"Marina," I gasped, my hands choking the guardrail. "What have you become? How is this possible?"

Sudden, joyous laughter shook the air around me and the looming aquatic monstrosity that was, somehow, my older sister. Her numinous mirth made the whole scene—the Cumberland River, the railroad bridge, the city of Nashville, the United States, the North American continent, the known world—waver, a fluctuation that allowed glimpses of thousands of other rivers, other cities, other worlds to peek through.

"How is anything possible?" came your aunt Marina's response.

Then she was gone. I studied the river, whose surface—still tinted orange by the harvest moon—was so placid that for an instant, I thought I'd dreamed the encounter. Or lost my mind. But I grasped the rail, bent myself into a right angle, squinted. I could just make out my sister's chaotic outline, dissolving into the Cumberland's cloudy depths. Two of Marina's tentacles undulated in what might have been interpreted as a wave.

July 21, 1863

Mobile, AL

Dear Sylvie,

Our fire-new Porpoise, the *Hunley*, makes the *Diver* and the *Pioneer* look like playthings. She is forty feet long—twice the size of the *Diver*—and far more elegant. Having lost Mr. McClintock, Mr. Hunley is now our head man. The Confederate Navy has become quite interested in undersea warfare, and the construction, operations, and testing of the *Hunley* has been supervised by one Admiral Franklin Buchanan—a man far better suited to the job than poor Lieutenant Alexander. A few days ago, we took the *Hunley* for a test run, and we managed to sink a Union coal flatboat in Mobile Bay! We're now preparing to depart for Charleston, South Carolina, where we'll attempt to free that port from its blockade. We will travel by rail, as will the *Hunley*.

Like the *Pioneer* and the *Diver*, the *Hunley* is outfitted with a spar torpedo—a copper cylinder containing 135 pounds of black powder attached to a twenty-two-foot wooden spar mounted on the Porpoise's bow. Unlike the torpedoes carried by the *Pioneer* and the *Diver*—which featured a barbed point designed to lodge in the side of a target and then detonate mechanically, as the fish boat backed away—the *Hunley*'s torpedoes are electrically detonated with a battery and copper wire. This makes the chances of a torpedo blowing up the *Hunley* along with her target far less likely.

Sylvie, I have another confession to make. When we were clearing Papa's things out of our rooms at Mrs. Marigold's, I found a letter. In a drawer I had to pry open, in a rickety desk buried beneath a mountain of draperies, foreign flags, and dish towels. The letter's edges were

charred—as though it had been consigned to, then rescued from, the
fire. After I read it, I finished burning the note, but our sister's words
had seared themselves so deeply into my mind that I can still recite
them from memory:

> Dearest Horatio,
>
> As you know, I promised my dying mother that I
> would help you raise the twins, that I would stay
> until they could care for themselves. Sylvie and Silas
> are nearly grown, and the time has come for me to
> go. I am tired of arguing with you about this, so I am
> taking the coward's way out.
>
> By the time you read this, I will be long gone,
> and not just in terms of distance or time, but in
> terms of structure, and point of view. I am enclosing
> letters for Sylvie and Silas. Please do me the favor of
> passing these along to my siblings, whom I will miss
> more than I can express.
>
> I will miss you, too, Horatio. I know that for
> you, I've primarily functioned as a substitute for my
> mother, but I did not mind wearing her clothes and
> fixing my hair as she wore hers, so that you might
> pretend Brigitte still lived. I did not mind soothing
> you while you wept. You married her when she was
> pregnant, gave me your name, and never revealed
> our secrets. I remain in your debt, and like you, I'm
> in daily touch with the incalculable grief of losing a
> being as extraordinary as Brigitte Blanchard Swift.
>
> She loved you, which I know you know, but
> you don't understand how truly remarkable—what
> a miracle—this fact is. You have a notion of what

she was—of what I am, and Sylvie is, and your granddaughters will be—but you do not know the full story, which would drive you mad.

I know you believe that you're broken beyond repair, that you can't be trusted to care for the twins, that you can't make it on your own. But you are a strong creature, Horatio Swift, and incredibly resilient. If you were not, Brigitte wouldn't have looked at you twice. She would never have fallen for you, never have married you. She wouldn't have chosen you to father a daughter as important as Sylvie.

I must work to prepare things for my Sister, which is one reason the time has come for me to go. Another is that I want to live a life that belongs to me, and me alone, for a time—beholden to no one, dependent on no one, unfettered and free.

I know you'll be furious with me for disappearing in the night, Horatio—that you might even decide to loathe and detest me—but I hope you don't feel this way forever. Go easy on the apple brandy, and be patient with Silas, and with yourself.

Above all else, keep Sylvie safe. My Sister's significance cannot be overstated.

Yours with every affection,
Marina

Needless to say, Sylvie, when I came upon this singular artifact, our letters from Marina were long gone. Aboard the *Hunley*, I have plenty of time to think, and of late, I've been dwelling on my sins. Papa's death was entirely accidental, but I kept Marina's letter from you—intelligence I knew you desperately wanted—on purpose. Each time we theorized about what had become of our sister—if she'd been taken by some nefarious character or fallen prey to a wild animal—I knew the answer but hid it from you. What's worse, I didn't do this to protect you; I did it to hurt you.

I will never be as close to anyone as I am to you, never love anyone as much as I love you—I see this now, Sylvie, and I hope with all my heart you can forgive me. But as I read and reread Marina's letter, I was seized by wild, jealous resentment. Of your importance, of your significance, of our sister's obvious esteem. I knew Marina was alive, and that the future held something big for you, but apparently not for me, and I became obsessed with finding, and proving, my worth.

I hope all is well in Nashville. I will write again once we've made it to Charleston.

Your loving brother,
Silas

Wednesday, June 20, 1877
Monterey, CA

At this point, I'd been haunted by the question of your aunt Marina's fate for nearly nine years. Learning from Silas's letter that he'd uncovered one part of the answer but withheld it from me hurt, and it took me weeks to forgive him. But I was, and remain, intimately familiar with envy, and today, the knowledge that my brother was as jealous of what Marina wrote about me as I was of his ability to see fire-people, and the ghosts of our parents, makes me smile.

Once I got past my anger, I grew curious about, and a little alarmed by, my sister's claims as to my significance—my importance. And after confronting the monster Marina had become, and the creature she called *Artemis,* on the Nashville and Louisville railroad bridge, I kept turning a sentence from her lost letter over in my mind: *You have a notion of what she was—of what I am, and Sylvie is, and your granddaughters will be.*

"What are you, Marina?" I asked aloud as I wandered the waterfront, lost in thought. "And what am I?"

I was passing a row of six warehouses constructed by Confederate prisoners of war, under the direction of the Pioneer Brigade, when I heard my name, urgently whispered.

"Sylvie!"

Someone seized my arm, jerked me between two of the warehouses, and I found myself face to face with Hannah and four more members of the Southern Ladies' Aid Society. In addition to their black shifts and bonnets, they'd smeared mud over their faces, so that even in close proximity, they were difficult to see.

"You're late," Hannah hissed.

"I am?"

"And you haven't camouflaged your face! Never mind. We'll set the exterior warehouses first, then those in the middle. That way, the flames will consume the entire block in one fell swoop."

Hannah passed around torches, kindling, and pitch. Our Sisters lit their beacons and slid away, toward the outer edges of the warehouse block. Hannah reached down, dredged up a handful of mud, began applying the cold slime to my face. Her touch reminded me of your aunt Marina—the way she'd gently washed my face every evening of my childhood. Once Hannah was satisfied with my mask, she handed me a torch, and we stole around back of the warehouses. We were attempting to spark up our beacons when harsh white light flooded the scene, rendering us blind.

"I'll be damned! If it isn't the honorable members of the Southern Ladies' Aid Society. Do you have some business in these warehouses?"

Shielding my eyes, I saw Colonel William Truesdail flanked by eight Secret Service operatives. Two of them held enormous metallic lanterns—brand-new carbon arc lamps, the source of the beams that had turned night into day. The rest of the Secret Service men held our Sisters, whose wrists were already bound behind them.

"Tell me, Miss Holcombe," said Truesdail, "what are you and your cronies up to?"

Hannah shrugged. "We couldn't sleep."

"All of you?"

"That's right. So we decided to take a walk."

"With six torches and cans of pitch? Not to mention your identities concealed?"

"Why not?" said Hannah. "You walk your way; we'll walk ours."

Truesdail laughed. "I must give you credit, Miss Holcombe," he said. "You have a vivid imagination."

"Please," Hannah said, her voice softening. "I'm to blame. Take me, but let the others go."

"A noble gesture," said Truesdail, "but I'm afraid we're taking you all in—to the temporary detainment facility we were forced to put up after you 'ladies' destroyed the guardhouse. I doubt any of you will taste the sweet air of freedom for a long, long time. Any of you, that is, except Miss Sylvie Swift."

I felt Hannah, beside me, stiffen, and I was afraid to turn my head. Afraid to meet her gaze.

"That's right, Miss Holcombe," said the colonel. "Miss Swift isn't one of your Sisters. She's a federal spy. An agent of my Secret Service. I planted her in your organization to help me ferret out your leaders and curtail your subversive activities. To help me bring the city of Nashville back into order!"

He clapped his hands, and a Secret Service man seized Hannah. The agents marched her and our Sisters off, leaving me alone with William Truesdail.

"Now," he said, taking my wrists and pulling me close, "we *really* must talk, Sylvie."

* * *

Before returning to this moment in Nashville, Marina and Brigitte, I want to say something. I've touched on this—waltzed around it—but I'd like to speak more plainly. Fifteen years ago, when I was living in Nashville, I couldn't have put this into words, but it was my regular, daily work on a translation of the *Apocrypha* that pulled me through, that enabled me to synthesize the baffling events occurring all around me. Not because it provided me with stability—though that was no doubt a boon—but because it provided me with confusion.

Mechanics and artists alike will agree; when you disassemble and reassemble something—engine, manuscript, or sentence; spinning wheel, hand mixer, or human body—you both understand it and are disoriented by it, on a level that has no equal. There's a knowing that comes with creating, and a knowing that comes with destroying, but over the years, I've come to believe that the deepest knowing is that of the interpreter—the tinkerer or middleman, analyst or critic. The figure standing astride a fixed point, watching a pendulum swing.

But none of this is what I really want to say. What I want to say isn't about understanding at all; it's about hope. What I learned not from translating the *Apocrypha*—the only comedy in which Aristophanes hands power to women not as a joke but as an offering, as atonement, as reparation, a play in which the poet finally acknowledges the power of the mysterious, the unruly, the female—but from Apocrypha herself. A woman not unlike my great-great-grandmother, my mother, my sister, or me.

A woman who survives trauma and cataclysmic changes. A woman abandoned, intentionally or no, by those who should care for her. A woman lied to by the gods. A woman who dons a costume, rallies others around her, questions the status quo. A woman who bides her time, trusts her instincts, employs subterfuge and deceit. Each day, as I moved forward with my translation of the *Apocrypha*—as I disclosed the ancient story of this Ephesian maid—I saw myself in Apocrypha anew, and each day, this gave me hope. Not because it convinced me that I was morally or politically or philosophically correct, or even that I fully understood my own situation, but because there was an unspeakable joy in my confusion. I wanted to know what would happen next, but I was happy to wait—to bask in bewilderment, day after day—in order to find out.

* * *

Colonel Truesdail did not speak again until we were alone in his office. I'd walked the distance from the riverfront warehouses to the handsome red-brick house at High and Hamilton with him quite willingly. When we'd covered half the route, the colonel took my hand and swung it, gently, between us. Truesdail's second-floor office looked as it had the first time I'd visited, though streaming sunlight had been replaced by the muted glow of oil lamps positioned on the desk, tables, and bookcases.

After locking the door, the colonel vanished for a moment. When he returned, he'd removed his coat and vest and rolled up his shirtsleeves. He held a basin of warm water and a cloth. He dipped the cloth, and then, standing before me, proceeded to wipe away the mud Hannah had lately applied to my face. Once finished, he stood back. "Much better." He took my hand and led me across the room, to one of the blue upholstered settees. We sat, and he kept hold of my hand.

"Well, Sylvie?" he said, his golden eyes searching my face. "What do you want to tell me?"

I hesitated. The colonel had trimmed his hair and beard, and while he still smelled of tobacco and leather, he smelled also of soap. I studied his wide brow, the rose-colored lips framed by his mustache, and as they'd done four months earlier, my instincts spoke up. But on this occasion, they told me it was time to show William Truesdail my hand, so I told the Secret Service chief everything.

I told him about my pregnant, unwed actress mother and my broken, tinkering father. I told him about Silas, my Confederate brother, and his adventures in submarine construction and maintenance. I told him about your aunt Marina, how my sister had metamorphosed into a leviathan. I told him that the Ladies' Aid Society and Nashville's public women were all part of an ancient cult dedicated to the worship of Chaos, and were working together toward a golden era of female sovereignty. I told him I'd been tasked with translating the final, lost comedy of Aristophanes and had been working on it daily since I arrived in Nashville, with the help of a dozen Priestesses of Chaos pretending to be prostitutes. I told Truesdail I'd reached a crossroads in my translation of the *Apocrypha* and was unsure how to move forward.

"A crossroads?" he said, seeming to take my remarkable confessions in stride. "What kind of crossroads?"

I rose from the couch and wandered toward a bookcase—not because I couldn't face the colonel, but because something peculiar was happening to me. I'd grown unbearably hot—as though all the water in my body had been collected in a saucepan and set over a flame to boil. Restlessness and agitation surged through me; the skin of my limbs crawled as though overrun by invisible insects. I felt imprisoned by my Aid Society uniform, which was suddenly far too tight.

"The *Apocrypha*'s resolution is nearly clear to me," I said, "but I'm not sure how to handle the love interest."

"Oh?"

I nodded. "When I read the playscript one day, it seems that Apocrypha and Timon—the man who awakens within her the opening strains of love—will live together, contentedly, as man and wife. When I read the script the next day, it seems that Apocrypha will use Timon for her own ends then toss him aside. I've been writing and rewriting the ending for days, weeks, but I cannot seem to determine which is correct."

"What if," said William Truesdail, "both endings are correct?"

Lowering my gaze, I was shocked to see my own bootlaces. The hem of my dress had risen by four inches, as had its sleeves, which now revealed both wrists and a swath of each forearm, the skin of which was developing a curious silvery glow.

"Both endings?" I turned away from the bookcase. "How is that possible, Colonel Truesdail?"

As he rose from the settee and stepped toward me, I felt myself expanding. Changing. A fluttering pulse ran over every inch of my skin, which was painfully alive. I had a keen new awareness of my breasts, of the humid space between my legs. Turning my head, I looked right through a wall, into the office next door. My mouth seemed to be growing wider, larger, bolder, and I wanted to unhook my jaw, to shriek, to howl.

Truesdail was before me, and as I reached for him, my Ladies' Aid Society uniform fell away from my body in two neat halves, followed by my underclothes. I was naked as a newborn, and as I wrapped myself around the colonel—arms and legs both—he lowered me to the floor. Between the two of us, we tore off his trousers, shirt, underthings. I straddled him, and he suckled my breasts like a starving infant. Then I was beside myself, watching two ancient beings who'd spent centuries in darkness slide out, into the light. I was one thing; Truesdail was the opposite; and we fit together like pieces of a puzzle. I sensed a sound moving up from my toes, through my calves and thighs—wrapped tightly around the colonel—into my lungs, throat, esophagus, rolling over my tongue, until it burst through the gates of my teeth. A howl, a keen, a cry of pleasure and pain, joy and sorrow, creation and destruction, beginnings and endings.

"My God, Sylvie," Truesdail said from somewhere within the elemental creature we'd become, once the shattering echoes of my howl subsided, "how is anything possible?"

* * *

The next morning, I woke in my own bed at the Land of the Sirens. I was heavy with exhaustion, as though I'd taken a thousand-year nap. And I knew instantly—before my eyes opened—that I was a different animal than I'd been the night before. My skin looked normal—a healthy pink, no more silver sheen—and my arms and legs were the lengths they'd always been. In the mirror, I saw Sylvie Swift, the same woman who'd journeyed to Nashville eleven months earlier—but I wasn't the same.

I was carrying the two of you.

My uniform—torn asunder the night before, abandoned on the floor of Colonel Truesdail's office—was now miraculously whole, as were my undergarments, and hung neatly in the cupboard. I re-dressed myself, braided my hair, pulled on my bonnet and boots. Made my way downstairs to the Music Room, took my customary place at the writing desk. As the Priestesses alighted behind me, their flapping louder than ever—the whirr of wings large enough to carry a hippopotamus, or a woolly mammoth—I studied Doc's impassive face. He scanned the sheet music before him, but I wanted the man to look at me, to appraise me. *What am I now?* I wanted to shout. *What have I become?*

As he played, the women sang, but on *this* morning, I detected a new thread in their song. A contrapuntal melody that, I quickly realized, had always been there but escaped my attention all these months. This new line was independent but harmonically related to the original, and the polyphonic entwining of the two melodies resulted in a richer, brighter, more vibrant tune than I had yet encountered.

I read my translation of the *Apocrypha* from the beginning, and by the halfway mark, I understood the play's ending. Having written drafts of two versions already, I reworked the correct one—revising, adding a word here, changing a phrase there. Finally, I ordered the pages of the manuscript, tapped their edges to align them. I placed my English translation of Gaia Valentino's French translation of Aristophanes's final comedy—*Apocrypha*—in a neat stack in the middle of the table, and I cleared my throat.

"It seems that I've finished."

A hush descended. Doc stopped playing; the women stopped singing. The pianist stood, and I sensed that to my rear, the Priestesses did the same. Two sets of footfalls sounded behind me, but I couldn't tear my gaze from the manuscript I'd miraculously produced.

"Well-done, Sylvie," Evangeline Price said, stepping in front of the table, using her lace-edged handkerchief to blot her brow, her chest.

"Well-done, indeed," said Sister Sarah, joining Evangeline. I looked from one to the other—Sarah in black bonnet and frock, Evangeline in fuchsia taffeta with matching elbow-length gloves, red hair swept up in a chignon, face painted like a work of art, cheroot between teeth. As my gaze bounced from one to the other, I became convinced that I'd confused the two women. That Evangeline wore Sarah's usual costume, and that Sarah was outfitted as Evangeline.

"And now?" I looked from Sarah to Evangeline. "What do we do now?"

Evangeline shrugged. "Go on about our business."

"Yes," I said, "but what *happens* now?"

"I don't follow."

"Why have I been translating this ancient comedy?" I asked. "What is the point of any of this?"

Evangeline and Sarah smiled. "We don't know," they said in unison.

"You don't know?" Sensations similar to those that had seized me the night before, in William Truesdail's office, resurfaced—a heat, a quickening, an uncanny expansion of my core—and I leapt to my feet. "How can you not know?"

"No one knows the future," said Evangeline, "or even the past. We have only the present, and we must strive to discover what lessons this moment can teach us."

Sister Sarah touched the pages of the *Apocrypha*, and I watched a concentrated beam of light flash up her wrist, vanish into the shadows of her dusky costume. She shut her eyes, and when she opened them again, they smoldered like hot tar slicks. "Centuries of trial and error have brought us here," she said, her voice unnaturally loud, as though she spoke through a megaphone, "and if we've learned anything, it is this: Every answer, explanation, or resolution is a dead end. Only the *questions* we ask have consequence. Questions are life, blood, birth, renewal. Creation requires confusion, and doubt is the last refuge of hope."

I looked from Evangeline to Sister Sarah—whose features, increasingly, seemed identical. "Have I outlived my usefulness," I said, "now that I've finished the translation?"

"Of course not," said Sarah. "Final dress rehearsal of *Orpheus in the Underworld* starts in a couple of hours, and you must be there."

"Hannah," I said, recalling what had taken place at the waterfront warehouses the night before. "Oh, Sarah! Last night Colonel Truesdail arrested Hannah and the others!"

Sarah smiled. "And this morning, he released them."

"He did? Why?"

"Insufficient evidence."

"But Truesdail caught us in the act! Mud on our faces, torches in hand!"

Evangeline circled the table until she stood before me. She placed both hands on my abdomen, sending a joyful shock through me. "It seems," she said with a wink, "that something you did last night made the colonel change his mind."

OUR OWN PIED PIPER

NASHVILLE, TENNESSEE—GENERAL WILLIAM Rosecrans has been camped at Murfreesboro nearly six months, overseeing the construction of fortifications, preparing another attack on General Bragg's Army of the Tennessee, currently based at Tullahoma. Rosy's aim is to keep pushing Bragg southeast and ultimately deliver Chattanooga into the hands of the Union.

Throughout the winter and spring, Rosy received entreaties from President Lincoln and Secretary of War Stanton to resume his fight against Bragg, but Rosy refused. When asked if he was merely loath to deal with icy, muddy winter roads, Rosy responded, "Hell no! These men needed training for the push against Bragg, and we had to resupply. Besides, if I'd let them return to Nashville, I'd have lost three-quarters of my boys to the 'French disease'!"

A recent comic drawing in another Tennessee newspaper posed a novel solution to Nashville's public health crisis, suggesting that we need our own Pied Piper: a musician whose song will lure the prostitutes out of Smokey Row, so he can lead them, dancing, into the muddy depths of the Cumberland.

The final dress rehearsal of *Orpheus in the Underworld* went off without a hitch. No dropped lines, no missed cues or entrances. After a full run-through, Sister Sarah gave the cast notes, then we broke for the night. Once I'd doffed the diaphanous costume that made me a Spirit of the Underworld and donned my Ladies' Aid Society uniform, I searched for Hannah—to apologize—but she was nowhere to be found. I was walking back toward the Land of the Sirens alone—under the same harvest moon that had lit up the railroad bridge the night before—picturing sheets of water falling from the monstrous body of your aunt Marina, thinking of the creature I myself had become while fornicating with the chief of the Secret Service with the Army of the Cumberland, when I sensed someone walking beside me. Without turning my head, I knew it was Truesdail.

"Thank you," I said, "for letting Hannah and the others go."

"When you hear what I've come to say," he said, "you may no longer wish to offer me thanks."

We stopped walking. Faced one another.

"Well?" I said.

"Tomorrow at dawn," he said, "the provost guard is planning to round up every public woman they can find in Smokey Row, load them onto a riverboat, and ship them to Louisville, Kentucky."

"What?"

"A brigadier general named Granger has ordered the provost marshal to *rid the city of diseased prostitutes infesting it*. And this is the solution

Lieutenant Colonel Spalding has settled on, to keep the troops out of the brothels. Free of venereal disease. Healthy and ready to fight."

"Exile is their solution?" I asked. "Banishment via riverboat?"

He nodded. "Yes."

"It will never work."

"I agree."

"Can't you do something?" I seized his forearms. "Can't you stop this?"

He shook his head. "The wheels are in motion. The guard is already assembling, preparing for the raid. I've been agonizing over this, but I couldn't let it happen without warning you. Don't go back to the Land of the Sirens tonight. Please, Sylvie. The guard will be there at dawn."

I shook my head. "I have nowhere else to go."

"Yes, you do."

"Where?"

"I can get you a place," he said. "A couple of rooms somewhere. I'd be happy to take care of you, if you'll let me."

I thought of Gaia Valentino, the Venetian *cortigiana* who'd portrayed a free woman brilliantly until it became impossible to deny that she was—and always would be—a piece of property with a womb.

"Would you be happy to marry me?" I asked Truesdail. "To spend the rest of your life with me?"

"I am already married," he said softly. "I have a wife and twelve children in Missouri."

"I see." I pictured Evangeline and her girls, Sister Sarah and Hannah and the members of the Southern Ladies' Aid Society—all blissfully ignorant of the storm headed their way. A maelstrom that would disrupt their lives, their carefully laid plans, the opening of *Orpheus in the Underworld.*

"Or maybe," I said, "disruption is the point."

"Beg pardon?"

"Turmoil," I said, "disorder, confusion. Chaos."

The colonel took my hands. "What on earth are you talking about?"

"I can't explain," I said. "I appreciate the warning, not to mention your offer, but I must return to the Land of the Sirens. I cannot abandon my comrades."

"Comrades?" he said. "But you're no public woman."

I embraced William Truesdail. Pressed my face into his neck and inhaled deeply—tobacco, leather, and a briny, woody scent I would never identify. I pulled away, searched his golden eyes.

"Either we're all public women," I said, "or we all belong to ourselves. I do not know the answer, but I'm fairly certain that's the question."

"I don't follow you."

"Shh." I touched his petal-pink lips. "You cannot follow me, Bill. I'm afraid this is goodbye."

* * *

The following morning, a blast jarred all four stories of the Land of the Sirens just as rose-red dawn perforated night's film. The corridors filled immediately with sleepy-looking women wearing nocturnal weeds—rags binding their heads and cold cream slathering their cheeks. Down in the front hall, a portly captain of the provost guard stood atop the purple remnants of the front door, reading from an unfurled scroll, as guardsmen filed into the foyer, arranged themselves to the rear of the captain, and leveled their 1861 Springfield rifles at Ginny's Sisters, Doc's Priestesses, and me.

"Ladies," said the captain, "you have five minutes to evacuate the premises."

A throat was cleared, and we swiveled to see Evangeline Price gliding down the central staircase. Though she'd just risen, her lips were painted bloodred. She wore a plum-colored wrapper, and her unbound curls streamed behind her. As Evangeline reached our assembly, we parted, and she plowed through to the captain, snatched the scroll from his hand. Once she'd read it, she dropped it on the Biblical Persian rug, where it came to rest on the snake slithering at the feet of Eve—who was busy offering Adam a quince.

"It's legal, girls," she said. "No trouble now. Let's not make this worse than it has to be."

I studied the women around me—women I'd seen tormenting, in a chamber deep beneath the brothel, some of the very guards before us. If Evangeline had given the word, her employees could have gained the upper hand in an instant—of that I was certain. This acquiescence was part of a larger plan.

Though we didn't resist them, the guards swarmed the Great Room and shattered dozens of gilt-framed mirrors. Slashed open divans, tore out stuffing with bare hands. Yanked down drapes, hurled breakables into walls—ashtrays and vases, pitchers and ceramic figures. The guards sliced to ribbons velvet paper, split open casks of spirits, and several men, working in tandem, rocked the wooden bar back and forth until that altar of intemperance toppled. In the kitchens, they smashed crockery and cookware, tore down cabinets and shelving, flung every scrap of food-stores to the varnished oilcloth floor. Inside five minutes, the Land of the Sirens looked more like a battlefield than a brothel.

The guards herded us outside, where the streets of Smokey Row teemed with semiclothed women from Nannie McGinnis's, Puss Pettus's, and other nearby brothels. Many screeched, kicked, and clawed, but ultimately, all were forced to submit. Herded toward the Cumberland and its bustling wharf, to be driven—like cattle—aboard a riverboat named *Idahoe*.

APOCRYPHA

BY ARISTOPHANES OF ATHENS

CIRCA 386 BC

SCENE SEVEN

Before the Ephesian Citadel. The CHORUS OF CRONES *sits on the steps, white heads bobbing. The members of* APOCRYPHA'*s army are positioned stage left, hands bound. The* EPHESIAN GUARDSMEN *are gathered stage right, behind a* MAGISTRATE.

CHORUS OF CRONES

Do our tired eyes, full of cataracts, deceive us? This Apocrypha—standing tall before the magistrate, at the head of her band of masquerading whores—cannot be the same girl we've watched year in and year out, slinking through the crowded streets of Ephesus, nose buried in a book, body and face hidden by robes. This sculpted Warrior whose beauty steals our collective breath!

MAGISTRATE

(Addressing Apocrypha's army) You have been found guilty of sedition. Your emissaries have reached their destinations, and even as we speak, women are attempting to overthrow the guards of city-states all over Greece. For your crimes, you will be set adrift upon the Aegean without food or water. We hope this public punishment deters others from following your example and helps bring the rest of the city-states back into order—so they can continue fighting one another, rather than their own females.

APOCRYPHA

I recruited these women. Ephesians have always believed in justice, but your punishment is unjust. I accept responsibility for the actions taken by my comrades, and I alone should be held responsible.

EUDORA

Do not listen to her! I am responsible.

HARMONIA

No, this was my idea!

IRIS

No, I am responsible!

APOCRYPHA

They are only being noble.

MAGISTRATE

What is your name, my girl?

APOCRYPHA

Apocrypha.

MAGISTRATE

You instigated this rebellion against the leaders of Ephesus?

APOCRYPHA

I did.

MAGISTRATE

Do you regret your actions?

APOCRYPHA

I do not.

MAGISTRATE

If you could go back in time, would you follow the same course? Would you tart yourself up like a streetwalker and attempt to take control of your homeland?

APOCRYPHA

I would.

MAGISTRATE

(Sighing) I cannot guess at your motives. You're clearly all women of privilege. You want for nothing. Your husbands and fathers, brothers and uncles have always protected you, always kept you safe.

APOCRYPHA

I hate to quibble, Your Honor, but men don't keep women safe. If anything, it's the other way around.

A creaking groan sounds, grows louder. The stage shudders.

CHORUS OF CRONES

What in the name of the goddesses twain? Why does the ground beneath the citadel shudder? We've not felt such a sensation in decades, not since the hours that preceded the Great Quake of 414! But is this shaking the work of Poseidon—Lord of Earthquakes—or is it merely a plot point?

MAGISTRATE

Poppycock! Are not the men of Ephesus off fighting and dying on foreign soil, even now, for the express purpose of protecting home and family?

APOCRYPHA

In part. But they are fighting harder to protect their holdings, not to mention their egos.

MAGISTRATE

Outrageous! Who has put such ideas in your head, my girl?

APOCRYPHA

No one.

MAGISTRATE

No one?

APOCRYPHA

I was born with these ideas in my head.

A great crack sounds. The stage starts pitching and shaking so forcefully that the assembled players notice and begin murmuring to one another.

MAGISTRATE

(Pounding gavel for silence) Impossible! Such things cannot occur to women.

APOCRYPHA

You are a learned man, Your Honor, but you do not seem to grasp the fact that a great many things are true, and all at once.

MAGISTRATE

I do not follow.

APOCRYPHA

Allow me to illustrate with a story. I was a babe in arms when my mother became convinced that I was not the daughter she'd birthed but a changeling foisted upon her by some nymph. When I learned to talk, she began interrogating me daily, asking me where I came from, who my real mother was, what had become of her own child. I of course could not understand what she meant; I only knew that my mother refused to pick me up or comfort me, to bathe or soothe or clothe me. These duties fell instead to my father, who tried desperately to hide his wife's unravelling from friends, neighbors, and family members.

My parents argued about me interminably, my father trying to convince his wife that I was, in fact, their child.

She is your mirror image! he would say. *How in the name of the deathless Gods could she belong to anyone else?* Years passed, but rather than weakening, her convictions deepened. I was four years old the first time she tried to kill me. I woke to find my mother standing over my couch with a knife, its curved blade a-glint in the moon's glare. My father broke in and wrested the knife away from her; he then moved into my bedroom and began bolting the door against her at night. Two years later—when I was six—I woke one morning to find his couch empty. I crept out, into the family room, and stood paralyzed, watching my parents struggle over a knife. My father gained control of the blade and plunged it into my mother's breast, weeping. He lowered her body to the floor, closed her eyelids, and kissed them. He then drew the knife's blade across his own throat and fell down beside her. His last act was to take her hand.

MAGISTRATE

(Softly) Poor child.

APOCRYPHA

Suddenly looming over the bodies of my parents was a strange, monstrous creature. As I gazed upon it, a carousel of emotions spun through me: devastation, fury, overwhelming joy. Its body seemed at once shapeless and a dragon-headed barge, a forest of deeply rooted cypress trees and the moon, the world's most ancient and mossy temple. Was the being made of air and shadow, of fog and terror and night? I did not know. I only knew that it seemed to be menacing my parents, and I ran at it, shouting and kicking and flailing my fists.

The thing did not resist my attack. Worn out, I fell to the floor and gazed up at the creature, which I now saw possessed innumerable heads, arms, and legs, and seemed to be cloaked in the night sky. *Oh, Apocrypha*, it said, *you are perfection! Well, you are a hideous monster*, I shouted, *and I will hate you until the day I die!* I was sobbing, and the thing reached for me with a bevy of arms, pulled me into an embrace. I then hung in the midst of a maelstrom.

Winds swirled, lightning slashed, thunder cracked, but I was suspended in a profound calm, bathed in warm light, swathed in a humming purr. It did not occur to me then—though it has occurred to me a hundred thousand times since—that this sensation was everything I'd ever craved from the woman who lay dead at my feet. *Poor Apocrypha*, the thing said, and I swear there were tears in its voice. *That's right, my child. Let it out. You are a first, a future, an answer always already given. I know your pain so well, my sweet, for nothing is harder than being one of a kind.*

I opened my eyes and found myself alone with my parents' corpses. I threw myself atop my blood-soaked father. I yanked his arms around me—into the sad pantomime of an embrace. I did not move until guardsmen broke in the door two days later, and I was sent to live with my father's only sister.

CHORUS OF CRONES

O heartbreak! O tragedy! O family plot! We thought we knew everything about the people of Ephesus, but there was much to Apocrypha's story we never guessed! Perhaps it is best, in the end, for some things to remain behind closed doors? Out of the town square?

MAGISTRATE

That is a heartrending tale, Apocrypha, but it doesn't explain why you broke the law and endangered the lives of your friends. Why you incited a rebellion against Ephesus, your homeland, the city that has raised and fed and clothed you. Why you imagined that women could rule Greece!

APOCRYPHA

Women *already* rule Greece, Your Honor, even as men do! Everything we can imagine is true! My father killed my mother because she wanted me dead, but she was the love of his life, and he couldn't go on without her. His move was logical, if not life-affirming. But logic is the enemy of life. Life is too vast to be fathomed, yet it sparks within a microscopic seed that takes root in a womb. In the chasm that yawns eternal, without which none of this—you, me, the guard, those crones sitting on the steps, Ephesus, Greece—would exist.

A trumpet sounds as a breathless ENVOY *rushes onstage, clutching an armload of scrolls.*

ENVOY

I bring urgent news from Athens and Corinth, from Thebes and Smyrna and Lesbos!

MAGISTRATE

What news? Quick, man!

ENVOY

(Reading from a scroll) "Let it be known that the Women of Athens have risen up and taken over our city-state! We newly established female leaders of Athens encourage women throughout Greece—from Thessaly to Aeolia, from Attica to Ionia, and the isles that lie between—to keep up the good fight, and if needed, know that we will send reinforcements to bolster your efforts!"

MAGISTRATE

(Shaking head) Athens? In the hands of women?

ENVOY

These messages all say the same thing, sir! (Juggling his scrolls) "The Women of Smyrna have risen up," "the Women of Thebes have risen up," "the Women of Corinth have risen up"!

MAGISTRATE

Great Zeus!

The ground shakes so violently that every player on the stage—with the exception of APOCRYPHA—*is thrown to the ground. A shrieking, grinding howl pierces the air and hangs there, suspended, before fading.*

MAGISTRATE

(Struggling to his feet) Guardsmen of Ephesus! Seize these traitorous females and carry out the sentence I have handed down! There's not a moment to waste!

The EPHESIAN GUARDSMEN *gain their feet, but none of them move toward* APOCRYPHA *and her army of women.*

MAGISTRATE

What in the name of Lord Zeus is wrong with you men? That wasn't a request; it was an order! Move!

TIMON

(Stepping forward from among the Guards) My comrades, wait!

MAGISTRATE

Who in blazes are you?

TIMON

Timon of Ephesus.

MAGISTRATE

Timon! The man who foiled Apocrypha's plan!

TIMON

I am that man.

MAGISTRATE

Well? Don't just stand there, Timon of Ephesus! Seize this traitor and her band of false whores! Drag them to the dragon-headed barge that awaits them at the shore! Maroon these rebels upon the mighty Aegean!

TIMON

Why?

MAGISTRATE

Because I am a Magistrate of Ephesus, and I have passed judgement on them!

TIMON

Gaze upon Apocrypha, Your Honor. See how she grows and hardens. See the crown of light that graces her elegant brow. See how her feet no longer touch the ground!

All onstage turn to APOCRYPHA, *who does seem to be levitating and growing. The whore's costume she wears increasingly resembles a suit of armor. A halo of winking lights hovers above her brow.*

TIMON

Can't you *see*, Your Honor? Apocrypha of Ephesus is beyond your power. She's not to be trifled with! (Falling to his knees) She possesses the stamp of the deathless ones, and I beg her forgiveness for deceiving her as I did!

MAGISTRATE

As you like, Timon of Ephesus—you will join Apocrypha in death! (Drawing his sword and brandishing it at the rest if the Guardsmen) Guardsmen! I *command* you to seize Timon as well as these rebellious women! If *any*

among you dares to disobey, I will run you through where
you stand!

The **GUARDSMEN** *move forward, seize* **TIMON, APOCRYPHA,** *and the
rest of the women, and begin herding them offstage.*

SCENE EIGHT

On the beach at Ephesus. A barge with a dragon's head is anchored at the waterline. APOCRYPHA, TIMON, *and the rest of the women disguised as whores stand on the barge, bobbing in the swells. On shore, regarding them, are the* EPHESIAN GUARDSMEN, *the* MAGISTRATE, *and the* CHORUS OF CRONES, *who help each other remain upright, leaning on canes and staffs.*

CHORUS OF CRONES
We have not left the safety of our steps in years, and it took every ounce of our failing strength to haul our brittle bones from the citadel to this spot, on the verge of the mighty Aegean. When the guardsmen seized Apocrypha and her army, however, we had no choice but to follow! We have come this far, and we cannot miss the conclusion of this tale of life force and warfare, of tragic circumstances and primordial processes.

MAGISTRATE
You there! Cut them loose!

A guardsman uses his sword to cut the rope that tethers the barge to the shore. The MAGISTRATE *and the* GUARDSMEN *begin filtering offstage, until none are left observing the barge but the* CHORUS OF CRONES.

TIMON
O Apocrypha. I cannot express the depths of my sorrow. If I could turn back time, I would leave that damned key in your pocket.

APOCRYPHA

I forgive you, Timon. You were only doing what you thought was right.

TIMON

But I didn't think it was right.

APOCRYPHA

No?

TIMON

I *never* thought it was right. From the moment the Oracle at Delphi told me of the part I was to play in this drama, I knew it was wrong. When I kissed you, I became even more convinced. Yet I took the key all the same.

APOCRYPHA

I am glad you took it.

TIMON

Why? If I had not, your deception would have come off as successfully as those of the women of Athens and Lesbos, of Thebes and Smyrna!

APOCRYPHA

Perhaps. But if you hadn't gotten close enough to steal the key, you wouldn't have kissed me. And I would not trade that kiss for anything—including the fearsome power of the deathless ones.

TIMON

Nor would I. In the moment we kissed, Apocrypha, I began to live.

TIMON *and* APOCRYPHA *embrace again.*

EUDORA

Look! Apocrypha! Tear yourself away from that man's face and look!

IRIS

What in the name of the goddesses twain?

KHLOE

My stars!

EUDORA, IRIS, *and* KHLOE *stand pointing off stage left.* ARTEMIS *enters and strides forward, wearing her mural crown, her gentle hands open, accompanied by lion and bull, bear and bees, across the "water." As the deity draws near, the women on the barge fall to their knees and bow their heads.*

APOCRYPHA

Oh Artemis, Mistress of Wild Beasts! You humble us with your presence, as we are the only Grecian women who failed to carry out your grand plan.

ARTEMIS

I am not angry, dear Apocrypha, for the plan you failed to carry out was never mine.

APOCRYPHA

What?

ARTEMIS

I never came to you in your bed. I never instructed you to recruit a battalion of Ephesian women, disguise yourselves as whores, and overthrow the male leaders of Ephesus, not to mention all of Greece. Until this moment, I've never visited you at all.

APOCRYPHA

How can you say such a thing? I *saw* you! I *heard* you speak!

ARTEMIS

I'm afraid not.

APOCRYPHA

(Laughs) So I imagined our encounter? I'm a madwoman after all?

ARTEMIS

Heavens, no! You're no madder than I am, but you *have* been the victim of an elaborate hoax.

APOCRYPHA

Hoax?

ARTEMIS

A masquerade. A deception. A pantomime. A certain deathless being—one far more ancient and powerful than I—took on my guise and visited you.

APOCRYPHA

Why?

ARTEMIS

For the same reason any of us does anything: to gain control of the narrative. To be the prime mover. To drag the center over to where we stand—on the outside, looking in.

APOCRYPHA

So the steps we've taken—Grecian women seizing governance of the city-states, bringing the shadows into the light, ending the civil wars that have so long plagued Greece—are *not* things that you desire?

ARTEMIS

I did not say that! I don't disapprove of the steps you've taken, Apocrypha—in fact, I applaud them. The changes you've wrought will alter the political and social realms of mankind, not to mention the course of human history, for the better. Still, *I* did not provoke them.

TIMON

But the events that have unfolded here were foretold to me
by the Oracle at Delphi!

ARTEMIS

I do not doubt it, Timon of Ephesus; however, that doesn't
alter the fact that they were not instigated by *me*.

APOCRYPHA

Who, then? What deathless being committed this deception?

The **CHORUS OF CRONES***, still on the shore, throw their* **CHAOS** *cloak over
their heads and stride across the "water" until they stand opposite* **ARTEMIS***,
on the other side of the dragon barge (center stage).*

CHAOS

I did!

APOCRYPHA

(Softly) You.

CHAOS

Me.

JACINTA

Appalling!

IRIS

Ghastly!

EUDORA

What hideous, monstrous thing is this?

APOCRYPHA

Our mother.

KHLOE

That's not my mother!

HARMONIA

Nor mine!

JACINTA

Nor mine!

APOCRYPHA

(At the top of her voice) She is the Mother of All!

APOCRYPHA *leaps to her feet and opens her arms. The barge pitches and rolls violently, thunder crashes, and lightning flashes overhead. Two spotlights appear; they illuminate* APOCRYPHA *and* CHAOS.

APOCRYPHA

When you held me that day—as we stood over the bloody bodies of my parents—for the first time in my life, I was not alone. Why did you leave?

CHAOS

I wanted desperately to take you, but I could not.

APOCRYPHA

Why not?

CHAOS

I was afraid.

APOCRYPHA

Of what?

CHAOS

My offspring are all so unhappy. They live tortured, painful lives. If I left you to be raised by mortals, I hoped you'd be more well-balanced than Nyx or Tartarus or Erebus. I hoped you wouldn't live your entire life cloaked in fog, shadow, and night. I hoped you might even manage to be happy.

APOCRYPHA

But *you* are my mother.

CHAOS

Yes.

APOCRYPHA

And you've never been happy.

CHAOS

No.

APOCRYPHA

You know that happiness is a myth. A story for children.

CHAOS

Still, I want it for my offspring.

APOCRYPHA

(Smiles) But Mother, *I* do not want happiness.

CHAOS

Oh Apocrypha! (Voice catching) In the interminable eons I've spent haunting my caverns, none of my children has ever called me *Mother*. I seem to have heartstrings after all.

APOCRYPHA

Do you know what *I* want, Mother?

CHAOS

To self-destruct?

APOCRYPHA

No, Mother. I want to spend time with friends, with comrades. To tell stories and relive memories and make one another feel things—good things and bad things, as long as we feel them. I want to marry the man who stands beside me—Timon of Ephesus—a man in whose arms I never would have found myself if not for your elaborate, quixotic, glorious deception. I want to bear daughters—a host of them, an army of girl-children—and build a house for my family—children and siblings, aunts and uncles and cousins, friends and in-laws, mortal and deathless. A home that includes a special place for you.

CHAOS

Me?

APOCRYPHA

You.

CHAOS

But why?

APOCRYPHA

Because you've brought me back my heart.

CHAOS

Impossible, generous Apocrypha! I take up too much room. I have strange needs. I'm too dark and moody to live among other beings. I would cause rifts and schisms wherever I alighted. There is no order, no logic to my rhythms, my whims. I am haphazard and unpredictable and mercurial. I am, after all, Chaos.

APOCRYPHA

We are *all* Chaos, Mother. Happiness may be a myth, but contentment is not. If we ever hope to know such balance, however, we must first learn to accept the changeable aspects of our own natures.

The spotlights die; the lights come up. APOCRYPHA, TIMON, *and the false whores join hands with* ARTEMIS *and walk forward, across the "water," as* CHAOS *tosses off her cloak to reveal the* CHORUS OF CRONES *once again. The* CRONES *arrange themselves on the lip of the stage, dance a series of happy steps, then turn to the audience.*

CHORUS OF CRONES

Thanks to these events, our backs are no longer sore, our feet no longer swollen. Our heads have ceased their throbbing, not to mention their bobbing. In short, we feel more alive than we have in decades! Greece hovers in the doorframe of a fire-new era—one in which darkness is seen not as the opposite of light but as its complement, in which confusion is seen not as the enemy of understanding but as its partner. An era in which we acknowledge that the void is not—and never has been—empty. Man has been trying to order, organize, and categorize the universe for centuries; let us see what happens when we embrace disorder, when we make peace with disorientation, when we dwell—at least in part—in Chaos.

Perhaps Chaos is the answer we've been searching for all along. Perhaps rather than trying to solve mysteries, we should try holding them sacred, try celebrating questions, puzzles, conundrums, then letting them go. Let's start with this one: If these players hadn't assembled here today, upon this stage, if a certain primordial female presence hadn't dragged herself from her chasm, hadn't inserted herself into this modern context, would any of us have heard the famous name of the changeling known as *Apocrypha*?

END

As you can see, Brigitte and Marina, things ended happily for Apocrypha and her army, the Chorus of Crones, Timon, and even mercurial Chaos. But the fate of Nashville's public women—and your mother—still hung in the balance.

A passenger steamboat named *Idahoe* was pressed by Lieutenant Colonel Spalding into our unwelcome extradition. The *Idahoe* shoved off with nearly three hundred souls aboard, a situation that would over-tax the ship and her crew—a Captain John Newcomb and five sailors. The captain wore his graying hair in braids, and though his right leg was missing below the knee, he stumped around on a peg so nimbly it seemed he'd been born with the apparatus.

"We should reach Louisville," he announced in the *Idahoe*'s grand dining room not long after we'd set sail, "in one week. My crew will make every effort to ensure your well-being and comfort."

"Do not make vows," cried one of my fellow detainees, "you cannot keep!"

Newcomb looked bewildered. "I'm sorry?"

"If the six of you," shouted another woman, "try to comfort us all, you'll be too weak to pilot the ship!"

The women doubled over, and the room rang with their mirth. High above the *Idahoe*, the sun scaled the summer sky, and though it was lined with portholes—which allowed air to penetrate its inte-rior—the ship's dining hall grew increasingly stuffy. The *Idahoe* was designed for pleasure-cruising the waterways of the southern and middle-western United States, for transporting well-to-do passengers.

The dining room walls were paneled in blond wood and trimmed with intricate filigree; the ten-foot ceilings held three cut-glass chandeliers, a-swing over banquet tables draped in white; the floors were densely carpeted, and all sixteen American presidents—from Mr. Washington to the then-incumbent, and very ill-starred, Mr. Lincoln—perused the space solemnly, from oil paintings. A bandstand stood in a corner; it was from this dais that Captain Newcomb, flanked by his crewmen, now addressed us.

"The *Idahoe*," said the captain, "is a brand-new ship, so please treat her with respect."

"We vow," boomed one of my shipmates, "to treat her like our own brothel!"

Laughter surged, swelled, crested. Newcomb plunged on. "This steamer was built," he said, "to hold eighty passengers, but you are four times that number, so six of you will be assigned to each cabin. And things will be decidedly cramped."

"Give us enough liquor," cried another woman, "and we can endure any misery!"

"Lieutenant Colonel Spalding," said Newcomb, "provided rations enough to last until Louisville, but they include no spirits. I'm afraid there isn't a drop aboard."

A low rumble, accented by yelps of outrage and disbelief, rippled through our midst. Some of my compatriots burst into tears as Captain Newcomb and his men began assigning us to cabins. I was placed in one of the *Idahoe*'s lavish staterooms—a space I would share with Evangeline Price, Ginny, Pearl, Veronique, and Lisette. Unlike smaller compartments located in the riverboat's interior, ours featured two portholes, six oil-lit wall sconces, and three berths. By the time we reached our quarters, I felt so nauseated that I collapsed into the lowest bunk.

"What's wrong, Sylvie?" said Ginny.

"My stomach," I said. "I'm unbearably queasy."

Someone opened a porthole, and a breeze whipped in, cooling the cabin. I felt the *Idahoe* taking the swells, heard waves striking her hull, as well as the voices of sailors and indignant women. I then detected another voice—a familiar voice that seemed to underscore the river's babble.

Sylvie. Sylvie. Sylvie.

"Marina?" I whispered.

A chorus of voices filled the stateroom, singing sweetly. I listened closely, and my nausea began to evaporate, as did my discomfort. Our cabin was full of women—some of whom I'd never seen. In a matter of moments, I was able to sit up. My illness had evaporated in spite of the *Idahoe*'s pitching and the Cumberland's roiling.

"Oh, bless you," I said.

"What now?" asked Lisette.

"We wait," said Evangeline, blotting her face with a handkerchief.

"For what?" I asked.

Evangeline shrugged. "What comes."

* * *

After veering onto the Ohio River at Smithland, Kentucky, the *Idahoe* reached Louisville eight days later. But the city's authorities would not permit us to disembark. They wouldn't even allow the riverboat to dock. Instead they sent word, through a party of men dispatched in a dinghy, that the Kentucky municipality had no interest in sheltering Nashville's wanton exiles, and that the *Idahoe* should continue upriver another three days, to Cincinnati, Ohio.

But Cincinnati also turned away the *Idahoe*. So Captain Newcomb was forced to moor the steamer on the opposite side of the river, at Covington, Kentucky. Two of his crew rowed ashore to confer with Covington's officials, but that town also flatly denied us entry, as did the neighboring town of Newport.

By now, we'd been eleven days on the water. The captain started cutting down our rations on day seven, but even so, the *Idahoe*'s food stores were sorely depleted. None of us had been able to change our clothes, and the only activity available was a stroll on one of the ship's semicircular decks. We were prisoners—incarcerated on a floating cell—and we all began to wonder if we would ever again touch dry land.

Not that I, for one, would much have minded. The nausea that gripped me when we first boarded the *Idahoe* dissipated in two days, and the rocking of the river began to give me strange comfort. I wanted always to see the water, to smell it, to feel it splashing my skin. I spent all my time on the decks, which teemed with women—some conversing with empty air, some who, sick of their soiled weeds, had stripped themselves naked.

We were a mob, a throng, a multitude, a horde, and the more time I spent among my shipmates, the more curious I grew. Where had they all come from? What events had led them to this situation, this river, this steamboat? My interest must have been written on my face, for my fellows began approaching, one by one, and telling me their stories. This is how I learned about Lisette's older sister Michelle, who at age fifteen delivered a stillborn daughter.

"Michelle would not let go of the body," said Lisette. "No matter how hard we pleaded. She kept cradling the dead child for two days.

"*We must have the baby, Michelle*, we kept saying.

"*She's mine.*

"*The baby is dead. We must bury her.*

"*No.*

"*We must!*

"*I won't let you.*

"*Why not, Michelle? Why can't we bury your child?*

"Michelle looked at us, her eyes pleading. *Don't put her in the ground*, she said. *You cannot put her down there, where it's dark and cold and dirty. Where she'll be all alone!*

"*She won't know the difference, Michelle. She is dead!*

"But Michelle wouldn't budge. On the morning of the third day, we entered my sister's room to find her out of bed, combing her hair before the mirror. When we asked what had become of her child, Michelle said, *What child? I have no child.* We searched the house—high and low—but there was no sign of the body.

"Five years later, Michelle was struck by a carriage in the street and killed instantly. When they brought home her possessions, we opened her handbag, sifted through the contents, and discovered 270 infantile bones. My father tasked me with arranging them into a tiny human shape—with piecing together the puzzle of my sister's lost child."

It was in this manner that I learned the story of Georgia, a redhead whose father killed himself when their tobacco farm went bust, leaving his five daughters penniless. And Alejandra, petite and dark, a promising ballerina impregnated by her teacher, who was also her grandfather. And Nancy, the youngest of three girls, a tall blonde whose parents sold her to a grocer four times her age—a man who forced her to sleep thereafter in a locked cage at the foot of his bed.

* * *

Acting as a repository for my shipmates' stories made me begin to see my own life as a narrative—one that began before my birth and would continue after my death. I was a character, I realized, one of many: Ellen and Benjamin, Horatio and Silas, Brigitte and Marina, Evangeline and Sarah, Doc and Apollo, Hannah and Truesdail. For the first time, I wondered what percentage of our stories—our lives—are a result of our actions, desires, and decisions, and what part can be attributed to happenstance, coincidence, or fate.

More than once, I considered what might have happened if I'd accepted William Truesdail's offer to save me from my Sisters' fate. I felt things for the colonel—genuinely enjoyed his company, his nature, his *way*—and I tried to imagine being his concubine. I pictured the two of us wearing stylish, elegant evening clothes, occupying a box at the theater, sipping champagne, after which I inevitably envisioned the wife and children he'd left in Missouri. I then saw Truesdail growing weary of me, casting me aside.

Far more often—hourly, if I am honest—my thoughts turned to Hannah. I wondered where she was, if she was worried about me, if she missed me. Was the Ladies' Aid Society continuing their work? Were they rehearsing *Orpheus in the Underworld*? When I shut my eyes, the image of our embrace in the Adelphi's costume shop materialized on the backs of my lids, and a novel sensation—affection, but more profound—surged through me, a thrill I soon recognized as attraction.

I knew women fell in love with women—I'd read about it, and a handful of the women I'd met in Nashville felt that way—but I was startled to find such impulses in myself. While stranded aboard the *Idahoe*, however, daydreaming about keeping house with Hannah— planting grape vines and rosemary bushes and cherry trees with her, preparing meals together, sharing a single bed—aided me, above all else, in clinging to my sanity.

* * *

Two weeks after we boarded the *Idahoe*, I started sleeping up above, as our overcrowded stateroom made me feel wildly claustrophobic. I liked to sit on the deck's edge, my feet a-dangle. I imagined what it might be like to live permanently in whatever world existed beneath the Ohio. To be forever cradled by a force contradictory enough to sustain my life one moment and end it the next.

"Marina," I whispered to the waves. "Silas. Marina. Silas."

My siblings were both down there. Your uncle Silas turning hand cranks, laboring in dim concert with his comrades. Your aunt Marina swimming around with a child whose twin was on dry land. The longer we spent aboard the *Idahoe*—enduring that steamy, static existence—the more I longed to join my siblings. I could only imagine what I would find at the bottom of the river, affixed in silt and mud. Boat hulls, lost treasures, the bones of murdered women—corpses whose clothes were weighted with stones. Women whose lives were too easily erased from the reality we all agree, with every breath, to believe in.

A great splash sounded off the *Idahoe*'s starboard bow one morning, jolting me awake. Looking up, I spied the bobbing head of a woman I didn't recognize and was filled with envy. A whistle pierced my eardrums as Captain Newcomb and one of his crewmen hurried in my direction, toting a red-and-white life preserver.

"Here," cried the captain, tossing the preserver overboard, "grab hold of this."

The flotation device landed near the woman, but she didn't touch it.

"Do you want to drown?" called Newcomb.

"No." The tatters of her once-white nightdress billowed around her as she treaded water. "I want to go home."

"Do you think you can swim there?"

She shook her dark head. "I imagine I can swim to shore, then make my way."

"The currents here are quite fierce," cried the captain. "I fear you will not reach the bank."

"Since I cannot survive," she said, "another day aboard your blasted boat, it looks like I will have to try."

Ignoring the red-and-white preserver, she struck out for Covington, which could be seen in the distance. I watched her progress with breath stilled and fists clenched, apprehension churning my stomach. Halfway between steamer and shore, the woman faltered. She turned once, blinked at those of us gathered on the decks. A moment later, she went down, resurfaced, and swam a few more strokes. When her dark head next ducked beneath the swells, I knew she would not rise again.

* * *

More than once, as I sat sweating on the deck's edge, kicking my feet in the river's wet darkness, I spied strange, monstrous forms coiling and twisting beneath the *Idahoe*. Fish weighing more than one hundred pounds have been pulled from the Ohio, and though I knew these large, gliding shapes were most likely giant carp or catfish, or perhaps paddlefish, I couldn't shake the sense that whatever was down there was also watching me.

I was thus engaged one evening when Evangeline Price appeared beside me. Like the rest of us, Miss Price had come undone. Wild red hair encircled her face like a lion's mane; dirt streaked her skin like the stripes of a tiger; her plum-colored wrapper hung in ragged shreds.

"Little sister," she said, taking one of my hands, "how's your stomach?"

"Better up here," I said. "Better near the water."

She nodded. "It's where we all begin," she said, "and some of us end."

"What about you?" I studied Evangeline's formidable profile. "Where did you begin?"

"Would you believe," she said, "that I was born of the original deity, the primal being known as Chaos? That I was spawned in a cavern miles beneath the earth's surface, long before recorded time? That I've been traveling from city to city, nation to nation in various guises ever since, ensuring that humankind doesn't eradicate the quiet, dark cavities where Chaos can swirl, thrive, and proliferate? Pointing out that Order—which lines soldiers up and loads their rifles, which sets us against those who don't look, worship, and think exactly as we do—is the *real* threat to humankind?"

"No." I smiled. "I don't think I'd believe any of that."

"Good girl." Evangeline reached out, tapped the gold pendant dangling from my neck. "I met Doc in the Artemision. This was in 263 BC, when Ptolemy III invaded Asia Minor. The most decorated captain in the Egyptian navy, Doc was one of Pharoah's favorites. His was the first dragon-headed ship to land at Ephesus, and when I laid eyes on him—standing tall before the figure of Mother Artemis, muscles rippling, dark bronze skin aglow, gazing at the Mistress of Wild Beasts in reverent wonder—I mistook him for a deathless god. But as he exited Artemis's Temple, a Seleucid warrior leapt from the shadows and, with a high-pitched scream, attacked Doc with a flail.

"The weapon's spiked head caught Doc's left cheek, then the bloodthirsty warrior wound the chain round Doc's neck, squeezed until he thought Doc was dead. Once the Seleucid soldier fled, I approached and found Doc breathing, but barely. At the time, I was playing a Priestess of Artemis, so I carried him inside the temple to my berth, dressed his wounds, nursed him back to health. When he woke, Doc told me he'd been dreaming of my face since he was a small boy. That over his parents' protestations, he'd pledged not to marry until he found me. We took our vows that day, and we've been together ever since."

"My stars," I said. "What a marvelous story."

"His given name," she said, "is *Dakarai*. It means *rejoice*."

"Dakarai," I repeated.

"Tell me something, Sylvie." Evangeline examined me closely. "Do you regret coming?"

"On this pleasure cruise? Or to Nashville?"

She nodded. "Yes."

I cast my gaze around us. Surveyed swarms of women overflowing the deck, clumping into various configurations of support and comfort, then breaking apart, only to reunite with a new cluster. I squinted, and a troop of my fellow detainees on the far side of the steamship became one enormous being—one gorgeous, treacherous monster with a hundred arms, a hundred legs, fifty heads.

"No," I said. "I needed to see this."

"See what, exactly?"

"Myself in each of them," I said, touching my abdomen. "Myself in all of them."

CHANGELING: THE STORY OF GAIA VALENTINO
by G. S. Valentino

By age thirty-five, Gaia Valentino had given birth to six children, two of whom died in infancy. The maintenance of her household—children, servants, tutors—was astronomically expensive. Though she would not begin to see its ruinous effects for several years, it's believed that Gaia contracted syphilis—an occupational hazard for the *cortigiana onesta*—around age thirty-six.

During this period, Gaia began vanishing from her bustling household and the literary salons of Venice for weeks at a stretch. Unbeknownst to her family members, employees, or clients, she began disguising herself, once again, as a male gondolier. Sneaking away from her responsibilities to ferry people through the canals of her native city. It was while roaming thusly that Gaia met Modesta di Pozzo di Zorzi—better known as Moderata Fonte—a writer twelve years her junior.

Like Gaia, Moderata had been a child prodigy and spoke several languages. Unlike Gaia, Moderata had made a successful marriage with a man who so esteemed her that he returned her dowry two years after their union, so that his wife—as a property owner—was allowed to participate in city governance. Moderata Fonte wrote epic and religious poems, as well as musicals, one of which was performed before Venice's chief magistrate, the doge, in 1581.

When Gaia met Moderata, the latter was at work on her best-known book, *The Worth of Women: Wherein Is Clearly Revealed Their Nobility and Their Superiority to Men.* A dialogue between seven female characters, *The Worth of Women* wouldn't be published until 1600—eight years after Moderata's death. Set in a secluded garden, the book features seven women imagining a world in which men have been silenced, and women are free to reorganize the Venetian Republic as they see fit.

"I've met someone," Gaia told her brother Franco the day after she met Moderata, "whom I believe, with every fiber of my being, to be my soulmate. Is this feeling real? Can my heart contain it indefinitely, or will it soon rupture?"

Gaia and Moderata met each day for a month on the edge of the Grand Canal. They spent hours reading aloud from Christine de Pizan's *The Book of the City of Ladies* and steering Gaia's gondola through the canals, shouting at those in earshot about the inferiority of men, Gaia assuming Moderata could see through her masculine disguise, Moderata believing that Gaia Valentino was a man.

* * *

One month after she met Moderata Fonte, Gaia Valentino wrote her poem "In the Land of the Sirens":

Why cannot we learn a lesson until it is
Too late to apply
Find an answer until it is
No longer valid
See a truth until we have been
Struck blind

The proper companion for man is man
For woman is woman
Like things fit together better than unlike things
Not as puzzle pieces, but as celestial rings that touch
one another at every point
Unceasingly
Not penetration but harmony
If we had not wombs, would we be put to death
Or would we finally be left alone
In the Land of the Sirens
Among those who understand us, or at the very least
Are willing to try

When Gaia presented the poem to Moderata, and Moderata understood at last that Gaia was, in fact, a woman wearing men's clothing, she fled the *cortigiana onesta*'s presence. Gaia camped outside Moderata's home for three days and nights, but Moderata refused to show herself at a window even once.

"So much for your theory," Gaia is said to have screamed repeatedly from the street, "that *amicitia*—true friendship— is a purely female phenomenon!"

As she steered her gondola along a canal not long after, the lagoon began to heave and bubble. Gaia later confided in her brother Tommaso that the same gigantic creature she'd first encountered two decades earlier—six eyes gazing deeply into hers, tentacles waving gently, water cascading in sheets from her silvery body—arose from the water.

"My child," said the monster, "why do you weep?"

"The one I love," said Gaia, "does not love me."

"Do you think," said the creature, "that you might love another?"

Gaia shook her head. "No."

The monster swam alongside Gaia for a time. "Have you ever thought," she finally said, "that you might enjoy taking a new shape?"

"New shape?"

The leviathan's heads nodded. "Fitting yourself into a new frame," she said, "can really do wonders."

* * *

Not long after Moderata Fonte rejected Gaia Valentino, the Plague descended on Venice, and many of Gaia's longtime patrons, including Antonio Pesci, succumbed to the disease. Then two different men whose advances she'd publicly rejected accused Gaia of practicing witchcraft. The *cortigiana onesta* was brought before the Inquisition and forced to stand trial. In the end, she was jailed for two years, during which time her home was overtaken by vagrants and all her possessions stolen.

Upon her release, Gaia found that her children had been absorbed by Venice's feral orphans. Increasingly debilitated by venereal disease, Gaia moved to the Republic's red-light district—a haven for ill and destitute public women.

* * *

Nothing is known of the final years of Gaia Valentino's life. According to census records, one year she was renting a single room in Venice's red-light district; the next year there was no record of the *cortigiana onesta* living in the republic.

Gaia's brother Franco hired a retired Roman constable to search for his missing sister. This man combed every seedy corner of Venice, but he found no trace of Gaia. Here is the final letter he wrote Franco, in its entirety:

During the fifth week of my search, I returned to the Grand Canal and walked up and down, holding a hand-lettered sign that read: *I am in search of Gaia Valentino.* I was surrounded by a pack of filthy children who pulled and poked at me, talking all at once. I quieted them, and one asked how much it was worth to me—finding Gaia Valentino. I offered them ten gold sovereigns to share what they knew, and their eyes grew large.

Taking my hand, they yanked me to a nearby gondola, and we hired it to take us to the southern edge of the lagoon. The tide had sunk to its lowest point, exposing a half dozen hidden caves that dot the sea wall. The urchins kept pointing to the largest of these caves and murmuring, *Gaia, Gaia.* We drew closer, and I heard a sound—a low, guttural cry, the most tragic sound I've ever heard. I began immediately to weep.

What was that? I asked.

Gaia, the children chanted. *Gaia.*

The sun was falling, and from the cavemouth emerged a creature with two heads; a long, spiked tail; and countless tentacles that ended in terrifying talons. The monster slid from the mouth of the cave—as though being born—and splashed into the lagoon. I then spied it shooting around beneath us in the aquamarine water, like a beast at play.

Children, I said, my voice trembling, *did that monster eat Gaia Valentino?*

They shook their heads. *That monster* is *Gaia Valentino!* they said as one—a small, filthy chorus.

I spotted a white object afloat upon the water. It was a single lily—the bloom the poetess always wore in her auburn hair. As night fell and the temperature dropped, I ordered the gondolier back to Santa Croce, paid the feral youngsters their sovereigns, and returned to my rooms. As I pen this missive, though I sit before a roaring fire wrapped in two wool blankets, I am shaking still.

My best guess, Mr. Vito, is this: Suffering physically and mentally from the damaging effects of syphilis—as well as the delusional idea that she could reunite with her long-dead twin, Gianni—your sister Gaia threw herself into the Venetian lagoon, and she drowned.

August 21, 1863
Charleston, SC

Dear Sylvie Swift,

It is with a heavy heart, and immense regret, that I write to inform you that on August 13 of this year, Silas Horatio Swift perished during a test run of the Confederate torpedo boat *Hunley*.

Having worked with your brother for more than a year, I can say that Silas was one of the brightest, most hardworking, and most dedicated men I've had the good fortune to know. In addition, his ability to adapt to any set of circumstances was unparalleled. Silas worked tirelessly on behalf of our submersible projects, and he will not soon be forgotten.

Permit me to add, Miss Swift, that your brother spoke of you often, with love and admiration. I am certain that you were in his thoughts at the end. Mr. Swift's effects are enclosed here, along with a posthumous Silver Star for bravery, bestowed upon him by the Confederate States of America.

Please know that you have my deepest sympathies.

Sincerely Yours,
Horace Lawson Hunley

In the following days, seven additional women sank beneath the squally surface of the Ohio. Under cover of night, men began rowing out to the steamer from Cincinnati and Covington and Newport to avail themselves of the vessel Ohio and Kentucky newspapers christened the "floating whorehouse," and since Captain Newcomb and his crew refused to fraternize with their human cargo, many of my shipmates welcomed this distraction from the riverboat's doldrums.

We'd been anchored outside Covington six nights when I woke from a dream in which the Confederate torpedo boat *Hunley*'s solitary candle sputtered and went out. Silas and his crewmates were unable to reach the surface in time to replenish their oxygen. With his final breath, my brother called my name.

Sylvie! Sylvie! Sylvie!

I sat on the deck of the *Idahoe* and wept as I hadn't wept since your aunt Marina left home, surrendering your uncle Silas and me to life with Papa and his abiding sorrow. Blinded, soaked with tears, no longer able to resist the river's call, I let my body slide from the deck. Slip without ceremony beneath the water. An iridescent glow illumed the world beneath the swells, and as I sank, I wondered if it was always so lovely or only when one is about to die. My downward drift was arrested by an appendage—a tentacle winding gently round my waist—and I was once again confronted by the chaotic shape of Marina Swift.

Above the water, your aunt resembled a monster, but beneath the surface, she was the most dazzling creature I've ever seen. I couldn't stop staring, and weeping, until I saw her child—the daughter she'd called

Artemis—who was even lovelier than her mother. My niece wrapped smaller tentacles round me, then Marina and Artemis took me on an indescribable journey.

We went everywhere. Oceans, rivers, canals, lakes, rivulets, streams. No body of water was out of reach. Marina was the size of a schooner, but in the ocean's depths, we swam into the mouths of whales who dwarfed her and out again. We explored three sunken galleons, laden with Venetian treasures. We swam through schools of glittering fish so thick they blotted out any trace of light, yet agile enough to avoid brushing my body. We encountered a colony of merpeople with webbed hands and translucent skin, through which I saw their internal organs. We played hide-and-seek with an octopus as big as a stagecoach. We found the Confederate torpedo boat *Hunley*—disabled on the floor of the harbor at Charleston, South Carolina. Marina opened the fish boat like a tin can and gently removed our brother. We wept and cradled Silas, then we took him down, down, and laid him to rest on the seafloor. When I'd run out of tears, we moved on, swimming freely through water that was hot and cold, fresh and salty, stimulating and relaxing, deathly quiet and alive.

"Marina," I said, speaking with no problem underwater, "Silas and I never got your letters."

We halted, and I was surrounded by your aunt's telescoping heads, her tentacled limbs. "I hate to hear that," she said. "I hoped Horatio could forgive me."

"Will you share what you wrote?" I asked.

"I wrote that Chaos is the fundamental state of nature, that chance is the most primeval of processes. Most animals accept this without fuss, have learned to tilt and sway with the whims of fortune; humans alone lack the ability to perceive or comprehend Chaos, and are ever in search of its opposite, which we call "order." But Chaos can mimic its antithesis—present itself as order—and lull men into believing that they perceive the world's functions and can exert dominion over them. The mistaken impression that they're on par with Chaos.

"Unlike men, women are able to thrive in Chaos. From the inception of human society, the Cult of Chaos has acted as a counterbalance, a stabilizer, a pendulum. Behind the scenes, we've been making adjustments, righting wrongs, preventing catastrophes for millennia."

"And now?"

"We believe the moment has come," said Marina, "to push the pendulum in a new direction."

"But what does all this have to do with translation?" I asked.

"There are myriad forms," she said, "of translation. We translate one language into another. We convert the food we eat into energy. We transform our thoughts into words. We interpret one event as *cause* and another as *effect*, and from there, we build a narrative. We convert a structure that shelters us from the weather into a home. Even this," Marina said, stretching her tentacled limbs in five different directions, so that I lost sight of their ends, "is a kind of translation."

"How did you learn?" I asked. "Did someone teach you?"

My sister laughed. "No need," she said. "It's astonishingly easy. Once you've made up your mind to take control of your own shape—your own story—you'll know exactly what to do."

"What determines one's new shape?"

"Only the limits of imagination."

"Marina," I said, "why did you bring Artemis but leave Apollo behind?"

"This sort of translation," she said, "is only available to women."

"Why?"

"Creation," she said, "is an automatic act of rebellion. The overthrowing of one generation, the uprising of the next. Women are born revolutionaries, dissenters, and agitators, Sylvie. To generate life, we must embrace the wanton, the bestial, the deadly aspects of our natures, and our strength is beyond imagination, beyond invention." She wound several tentacles softly round my midsection and said, "*When brother slays brother over affairs of state, and Chaos has birthed a pair of identical daughters, the Cult of Chaos will rise to prominence and pull the human race back into alignment with the earth, its Mother.*"

"My stars," I said. "I guess that explains my significance."

My sister's heads nodded.

"Marina," I said, "will I see you again?"

Your aunt exerted gentle pressure on my abdomen, and I felt you, Brigitte, and you, Marina, swimming inside me—two seed-sized embryos. "You can be certain," she said, "that we will meet again."

The next instant we were shooting upward at a fantastic rate of speed. We broke the river's surface, and before us was the steamship *Idahoe*, her decks carpeted with kneeling figures. Each of her passengers—not to mention Captain Newcomb and his sailors, and a handful of men who'd swum out to the boat for a little fun—was down on one knee, head bowed in reverence. Marina lowered me, deposited me on the deck, and as I faced her, I gasped.

Beyond your aunt were dozens of creatures like her. We held this tableau—Evangeline Price and Ginny and Lisette; Captain Newcomb; my sister and my niece and their chaotic comrades; the two of you, my infinitesimal passengers. Then Marina emitted a mournful cry, and her unruly compatriots came alive. They surrounded the *Idahoe*, released her anchor from the riverbed, and we began moving downstream, in the direction from which we'd come. As the sun set, we reached Nashville's wharf. My sister's helpers dissipated; she cried out once more, then sank beneath the Cumberland.

"Goodbye, Marina," I said. "Farewell."

Once she'd gone, those kneeling on the decks stood. Altogether our company had been twenty-eight days upon the water. Our rations had run dry while we loitered at Covington, and we'd had nothing to eat until the captain sent his men ashore to replenish the boat's stores from his own pocket. Twelve of our number had perished; nineteen more were restrained belowdecks, raving nonsensically; and we were all filthy, sunburned, and dehydrated.

But the sight of Nashville revived us. Pulled us back from our wits' end. A cheer arose from us spontaneously and hung in the evening air. Then Captain Newcomb and his men were dropping anchor and lowering the gangplanks, and we lined up to cross the boards, our feet eager for the feel of dry land.

The Daily Evening Star
August 23, 1863

LICENSING OF PUBLIC WOMEN IN NASHVILLE

WASHINGTON D.C.—NASHVILLE, TENNESSEE, has made American history. Three days ago, that city's provost marshal declared the world's oldest profession—prostitution—legal within Nashville's city limits.

This unprecedented step—taken after Lieutenant Colonel George Spalding's attempt to banish Nashville's public women was, unsurprisingly, unsuccessful—was first proposed by Dr. Abraham Armstrong, a surgeon with the Cumberland Army. It is also the most commonsense measure this reporter, in two decades of covering politics, has seen handed down by any government official. Whether other states will follow Tennessee's lead remains to be seen. Here is the Order in its entirety:

> *Be it known that for five dollars, any woman in the city of Nashville can obtain a Public Woman's License, and, for a weekly fifty-cent fee, be routinely examined by a Union-approved physician. Any public woman found to have a venereal infection will be sent to a hospital set up for that purpose, and any woman caught selling herself without a license will be incarcerated for a period of not less than thirty days.*
>
> *—Decreed by LTC George Spalding on this twentieth day of August, 1863*

As we docked at Nashville on an August evening, I was seized by a sense of déjà vu. Awaiting us were three dozen members of the Southern Ladies' Aid Society, rattling tambourines and singing. It didn't occur to me to wonder how Sister Sarah could have known we would arrive on that day, at that hour. After our grueling journey, all I wanted—for the first time in memory—was to stop moving.

To be still.

After disembarking, I found Hannah, threw my arms around her, and kissed her deeply. Pregnancy unleashes pent-up emotions, it's true, but these actions weren't the result of a hormonal surge. The instant I saw my dear Hannah's face, I understood that a series of queer dreams I'd had aboard the *Idahoe*—two luminous, ethereal rings floating in the cosmos, coming together to touch one another at every possible point—were about us.

"Sylvie," Hannah said, "I've been sick with worry."

"You thought of me?"

She smiled. Caressed my cheek. "You filled my thoughts."

They herded us back to the Aid Society Office, where our Sisters wrapped us in wool blankets and brought us steaming mugs of tea, coffee, and beef and potato stew. Told us any of the women who'd been unjustly imprisoned aboard the *Idahoe* were welcome to stay there—in the Ladies' Aid Society office—for as long as we needed to get back on our feet. Rows of cots had been set up around the space, and many of my exhausted shipmates dropped into them.

Doc was waiting for us, as was Apollo, who clung to me for an hour. My nephew presented me with another charcoal and pastel drawing, depicting a wagon filled to the brim with household goods—chairs, bookcases, paintings, mirrors, a mannequin dress form, and many crates. Two figures sat on the wagon's box—one of whom had an enormous belly—and were driving into one of the most breathtaking sunsets I have, to this day, ever seen.

Considering what I'd recently learned about Doc and Evangeline Price, I wondered if Dakarai would sweep his immortal wife—a genuine Daughter of Chaos—off her filthy feet, crush her to him, kiss every inch of her sweat-streaked face. But even in these circumstances, the couple betrayed their ancient relationship with only the briefest entwining of fingers—a move noticed by no one but me.

Doc broke the news that the Land of the Sirens, along with every other Smokey Row fancy house, had been overrun by interlopers—gangs of women who'd moved in to fill the void left by the evacuation of Nashville's public women. Apparently the provost guard didn't care who populated the brothels and serviced the federal troops—so long as they were licensed per Lieutenant Colonel Spalding's Proclamation—and had no plans to restore the properties to their rightful owners.

I thought this news might evoke some emotion from Evangeline—perhaps a tear or two—but Miss Price didn't bat an eye. Puffing on a fresh cheroot, she twisted her copper-colored hair into its customary chignon, leapt on a table, and announced that she would be back in her beloved brothel inside a month.

"Do not be downhearted, girls!" she cried, blotting her decolletage with a lace-edged handkerchief. "I built that house from the ground up, by gum, and no one's going to take it unless I decide to let it go!"

"But the guards destroyed the place," said Veronique. "It's a ruin."

"I don't think we'll have much trouble," said Evangeline, "convincing our clients to help us rebuild."

Picturing the activities I'd witnessed in the Land of the Sirens' subterranean chambers, I had to agree. Sister Sarah then announced that the opening of *Orpheus in the Underworld* had been postponed until the following month, so those of us who'd been trapped aboard the *Idahoe* could participate. But the Southern Ladies' Aid Society would mount their light operetta without Hannah and me, as within three weeks, we were history.

California was Hannah's idea. We wanted a location far from the war that had so viciously fractured our nation. A place where we didn't know a soul—where we could start afresh. I also hoped to be near a large body of water, to facilitate future visits with your aunt Marina and her daughter, Artemis.

"You're sure about this?" I said to Hannah as we loaded our belongings into a wagon parked outside her boardinghouse. While I was on the *Idahoe*, Hannah had retrieved my possessions from the Land of the Sirens. Everything I'd brought to Nashville—three dresses, one pair of boots, the wrapped pages of Gaia Valentino's *Apocrypha* and my French-English dictionary, Papa's tattered sketch of your grandmother Brigitte, and a half dozen volumes of drama, verse, and prose—were still in my care. In addition, Hannah had retrieved *Changeling: The Story of Gaia Valentino*, Apollo's drawings, my correspondence with your uncle Silas, all the newspaper clippings I'd saved, and a copy of my English translation of the *Apocrypha*.

"Sure about what?" Hannah asked.

"Leaving Nashville," I said. "Abandoning the Cult of Chaos. Giving up the fight."

She laughed. "We're not giving up the fight."

"No?"

"This *is* the fight. Wherever we go, no matter how far from where we started, no matter what we may become, the fight comes with us. As long as we live," Hannah said, touching my chest and hers simultaneously, "there will be no escaping this fight."

* * *

The night the *Idahoe* returned to Nashville, I needed desperately to talk— to tell my story—and wanted Hannah alone to hear it. I told her all about Silas and his Confederate submersibles, about your grandparents and Whitley Courthouse. I described our riverboat voyage in intimate detail, including my numinous underwater meeting with your aunt Marina. And finally—reluctantly—I told Hannah about the night I spent with William Truesdail, and the Secret Service chief's offer to make me his mistress.

"Did you have a hard time," Hannah asked, "saying no?"

I shook my head. "Not at all."

She seized my hands, pressed them to her cheeks, her graceful neck. As she kissed my fingertips, I realized that for the first time since I'd met the pillar of strength seated beside me, tears were streaming from Hannah's dark eyes.

"I was so scared," she gasped, "that I would lose you."

"Are you telling me," I said, "that you knew about me and Truesdail?"

"We all did," she said. "But Sylvie, I never expected to fall in love with you."

I smiled.

"Will you miss him?" she asked softly. "Bill, I mean?"

I shook my head. "He's not all bad. But once I met you, the man didn't stand a chance."

* * *

On our last night in Nashville, I couldn't sleep. I finally rose from my pallet on Hannah's floor, pulled on a diaphanous wrapper, and let myself out into the heat of the night. I wandered to the riverfront and stood studying the dark waters of the Cumberland.

I couldn't stop reliving my month-long imprisonment aboard the *Idahoe*—an ordeal that, to this day, remains one of the most harrowing I've known. The only bright spot I saw, at the time, was learning that your aunt Marina was alive, if transformed—or as she would prefer, translated. I knew Nashville's licensing system would improve the lives of the city's public women, and though I wanted to believe that a win for one woman was a win for all women, I couldn't stop thinking about my shipmates who'd gone mad, those who'd drowned in the river. What was the point of their sacrifices? When would we seize power? How did we plan to disrupt men's bloodlust?

I'd asked Hannah these questions, and she'd said I was thinking of things upside down. "Making a plan of action," she said, "is easy, Sylvie. Anyone can do it. What's difficult is making a plan of *inaction*."

As I stood there, trying to picture how one might use passivity to combat violence, I felt a hot, misty gust on the back of my neck. I whirled and found myself face-to-face with a large, dark horse—a blood bay.

"My stars," I said, stroking her forehead—emblazoned with a white stamp that looked a bit like a question mark. "Where in the world did you come from?"

I gazed into the creature's boundless eyes. She nickered softly, and I detected the faint sound of multiple voices, lifted in song. This tone seemed to emanate from the Cumberland, and when I turned back toward the river, I gasped.

A spectral figure was rising from the water. As she came into view—shoulders, torso, legs—I recognized dark hair, and the tatters of a once-white nightdress. My former shipmate, the woman who'd chosen drowning over imprisonment aboard the *Idahoe*. I watched, awestruck, as additional figures joined her—all those who'd perished during our ill-fated voyage. Eight who'd drowned, and four who'd stopped eating and drinking. Clothed in the same grimy, bedraggled weeds they'd worn on the riverboat, they were still dirt-streaked and hollow-eyed, but they were smiling, and I knew they were at peace.

As the singing figures glided toward the riverbank, others ascended from the depths to replace them, figures whose faces I did not know, but whose fates weren't hard to discern—a woman clad in the remains of an elegant wedding gown, lashed to a block of limestone. Another wearing a fitted, multicolored, ornately embroidered silk robe, a dagger handle jutting from her breast. A woman garbed in the flimsy tunic of an ancient Near Eastern slave, her arms and waist chained to an oar she carried. Each of these lost souls—each lost story—wafted across the water to where I stood onshore, and as she drew near—and passed through—me, I was deluged with a sense of strength, resilience, and hope.

I thought of your uncle Silas and the people he'd seen inside fires. My brother had once imagined his phantoms were happy to burn, but now I wondered if he'd been mistaken about the source of their joy. If their happiness hadn't been about starting over at all, but about my twin brother. About the fact that Silas could see them—that someone was able, and willing, to note their existence.

"Looks like I've learned," I told the horse, "to see ghosts."

I observed the parade of forgotten women until the sky began to pink, listened to the phantasmic figures sing a melody I'd first identified in Whitley Courthouse, from the safety of your aunt Marina's lap.

On this occasion, however, I understood the lyrics, which depicted two distinct paths to victory: winning, and living to fight again.

*　*　*

Hannah and I departed Nashville on a still August morning. I tried not to look back, to point my gaze forward, but I failed. As we pulled away, figures thronged the streets behind us: soldiers and streetwalkers, urchins and ragamuffins—Apollo, I am certain, among them. A song of farewell—breathtaking and bittersweet—rose from the throats of Doc's Priestesses, and *my* Sisters. I didn't face front again until their waving shapes were swallowed by the distance, but their song followed Hannah and me for hours, days, weeks.

If I listen hard enough, I hear it even now.

It took us three months to reach California—a setting stocked with forty-niners and fugitives; gamblers and whores; mavericks and madmen; outlaws and deserters, both Union and Confederate. When we arrived in November of 1863, California had been a state only thirteen years, and its sun-drenched environs felt like a foreign land. An uncharted, untamed territory. We settled in Monterey—less than two miles from the customhouse—where the 1862 federal Homestead Act allowed us to lay claim to a villa built in the 1830s by Spanish missionaries, along with twenty acres, after its prior claim was rejected by the California Board of Land Commissioners, under the California Land Act of 1851. Monterey was in the process of becoming a haven for artists of all sorts, boasting the state's first printing press and theater, its first library and public school.

By the time we arrived, I was immensely pregnant with the two of you—so large I could no longer lift myself from a chair. I can still see the astonishment written on the face of the doctor—a septuagenarian drunkard named Vasquez—when he first laid eyes on me.

"How far along?" he said.

"Not yet six months," said Hannah.

He shook his head. "Impossible! I've never seen such girth! You must have gotten in trouble a bit earlier, *mi querido*."

"No," I said. "That is also impossible."

Dr. Vasquez didn't believe me, but he came to our villa once a week to check on me all the same. I couldn't rise for the last three months of the pregnancy, and during this time, Hannah tended to my every need. If not for her, none of us would be here today.

During those long days and nights, I thought unendingly of you. Of being your mother, playing with you, nursing you, dressing you, tending to your hurts. Teaching you. But even as I allowed myself to indulge in fantasies of motherhood, some part of me knew they would not come to pass. One morning in my eighth month, I was awakened by a sound—soft at first, then louder—both familiar and unknown.

A song. A melody sung by two angelic voices.

You did not belong to me, you said. You were *of* me, you would carry parts of me with you throughout your lives, but you were not *mine*. You belonged to the world. In order to reach your full potential, you needed to be given away.

To be set free.

Dr. Vasquez introduced us to the Parkers, who owned a successful cattle ranch and desperately wanted children, and the rest needs no explanation. Hannah and I were both devastated, but we accepted it. She held my hand and mopped my skin during the birth, which, considering my size and how long I'd been bedridden, was absurdly easy. I wondered if you would resemble monsters, but you were of a normal size and perfectly formed. Dr. Vasquez laid you against my chest for ten minutes, and that brief interlude—during which you clung with tiny hands to one of my fingers—made up for all that is surrendered.

All that is lost.

Tuesday, June 26, 1877
Monterey, CA

Yesterday I woke before dawn. I sat up and saw Hannah seated on the stone bench before the Southern Ladies' Aid Society's storefront office, saw her stand as I crossed to her, saw the black dress she held unfurl. I saw everything so sharply; I even smelled the streets of Nashville—boiled peanuts and hoecakes; horses and sweating humans; the musty, sulfuric scent of gunpowder.

"My stars."

Outside, I gathered a basketful of black-eyed Susans and coneflowers—blooms Hannah had planted as a tribute to your grandmother Brigitte and tended with such care. As I headed for the apricot tree, and her grave, following the stream's dips and curves, I heard a small sound—a bleat, or a cry—to my right. I parted the underbrush, stepped forward, and discovered the grizzly bear I'd encountered a month earlier, on the day I began assembling these pages—constructing this narrative. She lay supine on the ground, unmoving. Her cubs tugged at her, burying their faces in her fur, but she gazed sightlessly into the celestial sphere, and I knew she would not rise again.

Kneeling, I plucked a handful of purple and yellow blooms from my basket and laid them on the beast's chest. Her children watched me quizzically, and I smiled. I told them that though not ideal, it *is* possible to grow up without a mother—that it's even possible to find some measure of contentment.

But I do not think they believed me.

At Hannah's grave, I arranged the flowers, then sat back on my knees. "It's done, Hannah. I wrote it all down. But I don't know if I can give it to Marina and Brigitte. The story is my burden, not theirs."

On the way home, I heard a twig snap twice, turned, and saw nothing. The third time, I caught sight of one of the bear cubs. The young grizzlies followed me back to the villa. From the veranda, I watched them chase each other through Hannah's vegetable garden. Frolic in her wildflowers.

* * *

The year I spent in Nashville, Tennessee, had an indelible impact on my life. I met my dear Hannah there, and I learned the true fates of my mother and sister—the women whose names you bear. I taught myself to translate in Nashville, to deconstruct and reconstruct language. I learned to act there, to beguile, to spy. I uncovered the story of an Ephesian maid named Apocrypha in Nashville, as well as a Venetian poet named Gaia Valentino.

And most importantly, the two of you began in that divided, war-torn city.

I've been considering these events and characters for fourteen years, but it wasn't until I gathered together these fragments—until I rebuilt this unruly record—that I understood what I have to give you.

From where we stand in time—the present—we're all people moving through the world, making a living, tending to our families, eating, sleeping, fighting, getting married, making love. But once our time has gone—once we're as dead as Ovid and Aristophanes, as the magistrates of ancient Ephesus and the *cortigiane oneste* of Renaissance Venice, as Aldus Manutius the Younger and Christine de Pizan, as Abraham Lincoln and John Wilkes Booth, as 360,222 Unionists and 258,000 Confederates—we become mere shades, following the fixed arcs imposed upon us by our histories.

Do not let your lives—your stories—be written by a third party, my daughters. Women are patient, crafty, and strong, but few comprehend how strong. Your strength, Brigitte and Marina, Marina and Brigitte, is beyond imagination, beyond invention, and if you take nothing else from the motley pages your mother has assembled for you, take this:

Your lives are yours for the telling.

* * *

This morning, when I returned from Hannah's grave, I found the grizzly cubs curled together, asleep on the veranda. Swallowing against a lump in my throat, I gathered handfuls of stones from Hannah's garden, filled my pockets.

Inside the villa, I took up this manuscript and considered placing it on the fire grate. Striking a match, touching it off, watching every scrap of my remembrance turn to ash. In deference to your long-lost uncle Silas, however, I renounced that fiery course. I decided, instead, to ferry my tumultuous pastiche with me to whatever comes next. To clasp it to my chest as I departed the villa I shared with Hannah for a decade and a half. As I moved through this summer day—full of wildflowers and wayward scents—past the red roof and balconies of the customhouse and into the salty, wet arms of the sea.

Before I could do any of that, however, a fist fell against the front door.

Or rather, two fists.

I crossed the room, opened the door to reveal you both—Marina and Brigitte, Brigitte and Marina—standing outside.

"Miss Sylvie Swift?"

I nodded.

"You're the translator of *Une Femme Déchaînée* and *Justine dans la Ville*?"

"That's right."

"My name is Brigitte Parker."

"And I'm Marina Parker. We live about a mile from here."

I nodded. "I've seen you both. How do you do?"

"Very well, thank you."

You looked at each other, then back at me. It was all I could do not to lunge forward, throw thirty-six arms around you, smother you against my chaotic breast. I longed to release an inhuman cry that would shake the heavens, not to mention the earth. I longed to unhinge my jaw and swallow you, to bury you in my primordial cavity, to imprison you forever. Instead, I gripped the golden icon dangling from my neck—and all her foremothers—for dear life.

"Sorry to barge in unannounced, Miss Swift."

"Oh, I do not mind."

"We're wondering if you . . . well . . . if you might be willing to teach us?"

"Teach you?"

"French. And the art of translation. We're interested in languages—the ways they're alike and the ways they differ. To what extent the shape of a vessel defines its content."

"I see," I said, and in that moment, I finally did. I understood why Evangeline Price had sent me Gaia's translation of the *Apocrypha* at the start of the War Between the States. Fifteen years earlier, when I'd completed my English version, I'd expected some immediate, large-scale revelation. Profound questions answered, specific instructions for bringing about a female-centered world made crystal clear.

But translating the *Apocrypha* hadn't been about answers—it had been about me. My education, my enlightenment. Just as, three hundred years earlier, Gaia Valentino's work on the playscript had been about hers. My predecessor, however, hadn't given birth to you, and you.

I had.

"We'll gladly pay you for your time," you said. "Or our parents will. Have you met them? Richard and Elizabeth Parker?"

"I believe I did once," I said, "a long time ago."

Gazing into your identical golden eyes, I felt an almighty current moving among us. "I would be happy to teach you, Marina, and you, Brigitte. I would be honored to share everything I know."

"Wonderful!"

"You won't regret it, Miss Swift."

"I regret nothing." Before ushering you inside, Daughters of Chaos, before emptying the stones from my pockets and making you honey sandwiches and hibiscus tea, before introducing you to two recently orphaned bear cubs, before teaching you to wield all available weapons—how to arm and shield yourselves for the battle I know you'll spend your lives waging—I extended my monstrous hands, eager for you, and you, to complete our human circle.

"I will hold you sacred," I said, "then I will let you go."

Author's Note

This book was sparked in 2014, while I was researching another book. The instant I read an online *Smithsonian Magazine* article titled "The Curious Case of Nashville's Frail Sisterhood" (July 8, 2013), I knew I would try to fictionalize its subject.

That subject: In July of 1863, authorities in Nashville, Tennessee—Union headquarters of the Civil War's western theater—rounded up the city's prostitutes, packed them onto a riverboat, and attempted to banish them.

This exile failed fantastically; as a result, prostitution was legalized in Nashville, which offered "public women" licenses and required them to be treated for venereal disease before plying their wares.

Reading more deeply into these events, I found no record of the women's experiences. I found period news reports, modern academic analyses, mentions in Civil War chronicles, a 2007 master's thesis. But the specifics of what happened to Nashville's prostitutes—blamed for the spread of STDs that sidelined huge numbers of Union troops—is lost to history.

Characters and settings began taking shape in my mind: a red-haired madam chewing on a cheroot; a flamboyant four-story brothel; a small boy wearing clothes crafted from gaudy, cast-off finery. A river of women—of all shapes, tones, temperaments—began flowing through me, and I was seized by a wild thought.

Who better to comb through the extant record—through the stories selected and arranged by those in power—and breathe life into these lost circumstances than a writer of fiction?

I wrote three drafts of a book that, quite frankly, was never working, then set the idea aside. It wasn't until I read *another* text—Aristophanes's radical comedy *Lysistrata*—that I saw a new approach to my story of "Nashville's Frail Sisterhood." Employing a few of my favorite things—mythology and monsters, theater, and the epistolary form—I overhauled the book.

The result was far better, but still lacking. So I turned to yet *another* text—the *Encyclopaedia Britannica* (1860, eighth edition), a set of reference books possessed by my novel's narrator. There, I discovered excerpts that fit beautifully into my book—fragments that act not only as ligaments, but as agents of enlightenment.

While *Daughters of Chaos* is a work of fiction, I like to think of it as a braided alternate history that owes its existence to the many texts that inspired, informed, contextualized, and strengthened it.

Not unlike its author.

Acknowledgments ·

This novel's road to publication has been long and winding, and I am so grateful to those who supported me along the way. Friends who granted me shelter while I worked on various drafts include Brittney Scott, Christine Harris, and Elizabeth Spencer, with whom I took refuge repeatedly in Nashville. Early readers include Sarah Anne Strickley, Heather Newton, Kevin Brockmeier, Clare Beams, Elizabeth Gonzalez James, Gwen E. Kirby, and Megan Giddings. I must also thank those who helped me get *Daughters of Chaos* out into the world, primarily the great and powerful Tina Pohlman, as well as Mark Gottlieb, Regan Mies, Jamison Stoltz, and everyone at The Overlook Press and ABRAMS.

Much of this book is based in historical reality (such as it is). The events of the American Civil War recounted herein—including the failed exile of Nashville's prostitutes and the evolution of the Confederate Navy's submarine engineering program—are recounted as faithfully as possible.

This will necessarily be an incomplete list, but I'd like to acknowledge some of the texts that inspired *Daughters of Chaos*: Margaret Atwood's *The Blind Assassin*, *True Grit* by Charles Portis, *Housekeeping* by Marilynne Robinson, *Lysistrata* and *Frogs* by Aristophanes, Angela Carter's *Wise Children*, *Jitterbug Perfume* by Tom Robbins, *The Mountain Lion* by Jean Stafford, Virginia Woolf's *Orlando*, *Ragtime* by E. L. Doctorow, *Lincoln in the Bardo* by George Saunders, *The Scarlet Letter* by Nathaniel Hawthorne, *Drum-Taps* by Walt Whitman, and Ethan Rutherford's "The Peripatetic Coffin." Louis Malle's *Pretty Baby*, *The Civil War* by Ken Burns, *North and South* (1985 TV miniseries), *Das Boot* by Wolfgang

Peterson, Victor Fleming's *Gone with the Wind*, *Dangerous Beauty* by Marshall Herskovitz, *Summertime* by David Lean, and John Ford's *The Horse Soldiers*, *Fort Apache*, and *The Searchers*. Catherine Clinton's *Stepdaughters of History: Southern Women and the American Civil War*, *Wild Rose* by Ann Blackman, *All the Daring of the Soldier* by Elizabeth D. Leonard, *Women's War: Fighting and Surviving the American Civil War* by Stephanie McCurry, and Margaret Rosenthal's *The Honest Courtesan*.

I must also thank my mother, Julie, and my sister, Anna—two genuine Daughters of Chaos—as well as my husband, Bill, and our (cat) children, Tessio and Clemenza.

About the Author

JEN FAWKES is the author of *Mannequin and Wife*, a Shirley Jackson Award nominee and Foreword INDIES gold medalist, and *Tales the Devil Told Me*, a World Fantasy Award finalist and Largehearted Boy Favorite Story Collection of 2021. Her fiction won the 2021 Porter Fund Literary Prize and has appeared in *One Story*, *Lit Hub*, the *Iowa Review*, and others. A two-time finalist for the Calvino Prize in fabulist fiction, Jen lives in Little Rock, Arkansas.